THE WAY WE DIE NOW

MICHAEL Z. LEWIN

Also available in Perennial Library by Michael Z. Lewin:

ASK THE RIGHT QUESTION

MISSING WOMAN

THE WAY WE DIE NOW

MICHAEL Z. LEWIN

PERENNIAL LIBRARY
Harper & Row, Publishers
New York, Cambridge, Philadelphia, San Francisco
London, Mexico City, São Paulo, Sydney

A hardcover edition of this book was published by G. P. Putnam's Sons. It is here reprinted by arrangement with the author.

First PERENNIAL LIBRARY edition published 1984.

Library of Congress Cataloging in Publication Data

Lewin, Michael Z.
The way we die now.
Reprint. Originally published: New York : Putnam, 1973.
I. Title.
PS3562.E929W3 1984 813'.54 83-48956
ISBN 0-06-080710-5 (pbk.)

---

84 85 86 87 88 10 9 8 7 6 5 4 3 2 1

To

MAZ AND BEAU,

MAGGIE SIMMONS ZINN,

and the memory of Sergeant Dwight H. Johnson,
winner of the Congressional Medal of Honor

THE WAY WE DIE NOW

1

It was a busy morning. I got a phone call. Since I believe in miracles, I answered it. "Albert Samson."

"Samson," said a very loud voice, a lady's voice. "Here it is. What I wanted to know was your rates. How much you charge for investigating on a case."

"That depends on what sort of case and who I am working for."

"My name is Mrs. Jerome." She emphasized the "Mrs." so that she would be sure to qualify for my married lady's discount. "And I don't appreciate being fenced with. You must have a basic working rate you figure from."

"Thirty-five dollars per eight-hour day plus expenses."

"I see," she said. "And the eight-hour day, how do you count that? Is it what you actually spend working? Or do you include the time you take getting to and from places? And does it include payment for a lunch hour?"

With or without burp? "I never take an hour for lunch, Mrs. Jerome."

"No need to be flippant. And references? Do you have references?"

"Should I agree to take your case and you require them, I can provide references." I write them myself.

"I see. Thank you, Mr. Samson. I have twelve more agencies to call, and when I have gotten their particulars, I shall make my decision."

"I just hope it's not a matter of life and death, Mrs. Jerome."

For the first time she hesitated. My right ear appreciated the rest. Then she said, "In one sense it is a matter of life and death. But my daughter is not a wealthy woman, and I have to do the best for her that I can."

I finished talking to Mrs. Jerome at ten minutes past eleven. I tried to estimate how long it would take her to find out that I am the cheapest private detective among the thirty odd of us listed in the Indianapolis Yellow Pages. Unless some new threadbare has opened up in the last couple of months. Long enough, what with busy signals and misconnections, for me to close up shop and spend the rest of the morning on physical therapy.

I did take other variables into consideration. The building elevator was out of order, and it had been a long time since a client walked up three flights of stairs to consult me. Also, it was a lovely day. And I do have an answering service.

So I walked down to the car and drove over to West Lockfield Gardens. At thirty-eight one may be past one's basketball prime, but with concentration there are ways to compensate for the physical deterioration. Craft. Finesse. Overview.

By two o'clock I was working my way back up the stairs—taking them one at a time—and I was burned. On such a lovely day, too. Why the hell are people the way they are? Especially young ones.

When I got to my floor, I went straight to the office suite next to mine. Through some quirk of plumbing history it is equipped with a rather comfortable bathtub, while my office has only a cramped shower stall. For the three-odd years the suite has been untenanted I've been using the facilities. I find baths much more suitable places to cool down. When I am burned.

Just as I was slipping into the murky brine, I heard the phone ring on the other side of the wall. Four rings, and then it was taken by the service. So there would be a message when I got back. Having an answering service is just like getting extra mail deliveries.

I presumed it was Mrs. Jerome. I wondered if she was calling to ask whether I'd go to thirty-two dollars and fifty cents per nine-hour day with seventeen minutes for lunch. Probably I would.

I soaked until I was wrinkly, till the steamy warmth had soothed my aching legs and back. Basketball is a game of legs and back. They are the parts which wither first when you don't play for a while.

I'd been missing this left-handed reverse lay-up off a trot when I'd noticed a kid watching me. Young, maybe ten. About five feet even. It wasn't that I was an intrinsically fascinating spectacle, but at midday on a mid-May Monday I was the only available spectacle.

"OK if I shoot with you, mister?"

"Sure."

"Hey, you want to play a game, mister? One on one? We can play for money."

Every star needs game action to bring out his best. "I'll play," I'd said, "but save your lunch money, kid."

I wrapped myself in the bath mat for the trek home, having neglected, in my passion, the foresight which provides a towel.

Back in the back room I dried off and then called the service about the call I'd heard them take. "It was a wrong number, I'm afraid, Mr. Samson." Dorrie, the girl on the service, is upset when I check in and she hasn't taken a call for me. If you can't inspire loyalty in the people you employ, I suppose pity is better than nothing.

Damn smart-aleck kid.

I made some lunch and spent the rest of the rest of the afternoon contemplating. I am trying to find some sideline, something that I can make or do in my spare time around the office to bring in a little extra money. But it has to be something which can be left for days at a time when I have a case.

At five twenty the phone rang again. It was Mrs. Jerome. "Mr. Samson, I'm glad to have caught you still at the office. Working late on a case, no doubt."

"No doubt. What can I do for you?"

"I've found out that you are the lowest-price detective in Indianapolis. Does that reflect on the quality of the investigative service you give?"

"I'm a bargain, Mrs. Jerome. As long as you understand that I am a one-man show and as long as your job is suitable for a one-man show."

"I'd like to have a look at you," she said.

"OK."

"I would like to talk to you about the problem. Actually it is my daughter's problem, but after all, she is *my* daughter, so that makes me concerned."

"No doubt. Shall I come to you or will you come to me?"

"I, that is, we live at 1634 Wolfe Street. It's the seventh house on the left, north of Sixteenth Street"

"I'll find it. When would you like me to come?"

"Tonight, please. At eight. My daughter and I will be waiting."

I would have offered to bring those references, but two and a half hours is pretty short notice.

2

I didn't have a lot of idea what to expect. The west is my weakest side of town, but from her ease in giving orders I had expected to find Mrs. Jerome reasonably well-to-do.

I was surprised when I pulled up in front of a small frame house which was at least as decayed as the rest of the neighborhood. There is a style: narrow, covered wooden porch running the width of the house in front of the door and the two single windows which flank it. Swing hanging on one end of the porch. Half a dozen plank steps up to the porch from ground level. It's the sort of house you find in small Indiana towns. They're not that common anymore in the big city.

Not that it couldn't have been a perfectly pleasant place. It just wasn't. The swing was down and resting askew. A mud track led around the house at the right, presumably to the garage. The expanse of long grass at the front was interrupted by muddy depressions. It was as though someone had been digging in the yard for treasure, long ago. The paint blisters on the house were visible in the streetlights.

I sat in the car for a few minutes. Not that it is really my business to try to prejudge people and circumstances. But following a little unasked-for but sympathetic publicity I'd had over the winter, I had been getting more offers of work from private parties than I had had in all my previous eight years in business. Most I'd had to turn down. The same case that got me the publicity had put me in hospital for three months, and until the last few weeks I hadn't been up to even routine work. Now that I felt better my fame had faded, but at least I'd had a chance to look at the sort of people who hire private detectives. And what I was sitting and thinking about was the contradiction between this house and that sort of people.

I got out of the car no wiser. I had to walk from grassy island to grassy island because there was no formal path to the porch.

I rapped on the glass pane in the front door. There were lights on, but heavy lacy curtains obscured images.

"Who is it?" I was asked from inside.

"Albert Samson."

The door was opened by a short woman. Maybe five feet. And heavy. "Why are you late?" she asked. I recognized the voice from its sheer volume.

"No good reason," I said. I watched her trying to penetrate me with a pair of dark bright eyes. It could have been the moment for a smile, but instead she made a suffering sound and waved me in. It was as if I had added yet another to the roll of petty annoyances she'd been born to endure.

There was no entrance hall. A step put me in the living room.

"Rosetta! He's here," she called.

The living room had three closed doors. The one farthest away opened, and Rosetta entered determinedly. She was taller than her mother, but thin. Languid, like, and she wore a lavender print dress. She stooped as she walked, but not from physical need. When she came to a stop behind her mother—just out of my handshaking range—she straightened up sharply.

"This is Rosetta Tomanek, my daughter. Mr. Samson. *Mrs.* Rosetta Tomanek."

"How do you do, Mrs. Tomanek?"

"Fine."

"Call her Rosetta," said her mother loudly. The

neighbors would all be calling her Rosetta. "Come on. Sit down, both of you. No point in wasting any more of Mr. Samson's valuable time."

It seemed only a matter of valuable time before I would begin talking back to Mrs. Jerome, but for the moment I obeyed as abjectly as Rosetta. I sat down in a red armchair whose volume belied the shakiness I felt under my weight. Rosetta and her mother shared the matching couch. Rosetta was forced to sit at the end closer to me.

"Now," said the redoubtable Mrs. Jerome, "tell the man what you want."

Rosetta looked at her mother, glanced at me, and then tried to begin telling her tale to the laminated end table between us.

"I," she said, and cleared her throat.

"Look at the man. After all, you're hiring him."

"All *right*, Mother!" Daughter pushed mother's urging hand away.

"I . . . I am married. My husband who is Ralph, Ralph Tomanek, he's in trouble. I want you to find out, well, some way to help him." She stopped and looked at her mother as if to say, "There, I did it!" I applauded, mentally. I awaited the encore, the turn in which I finally began to get a notion of what was going on, apart from a filial struggle for survival. Mrs. Jerome was leaning back on her side of the couch. Silent. Rosetta had spurned her aid; now Rosetta would pay for it. So I decided to help Rosetta as well as I could. The poor kid was nervous, I gathered.

"What sort of trouble is he in?"

"The police have him," she said. Her voice was high and spookily musical because it was faint and clear. "They say he killed somebody, I mean, he *did* kill somebody, but they say he did it on purpose. I mean, that it was his fault."

"What are they charging him with?"

"Manslaughter. They say he didn't control himself." Which was progress. It was his fault, but he didn't do it on purpose.

"And what does Ralph say?"

It almost stumped her, but finally she said, "He says the

other man got him real worried." Ah, well, I could find out the police story easily enough.

"When did all this happen, Rosetta?"

"About a month ago."

"On Friday the twenty-eighth of April," said Mrs. Jerome. She could not maintain control in the face of such flagrant disregard for the truth.

"Which makes it three weeks and three days ago," I said, it being May 22. I began to realize that to get a decent conversation out of Rosetta, I'd have to get her mother out of the way. Maybe find her a lover. "Then you want me to investigate Ralph's side of the story because you think the police aren't going to do it thoroughly enough?"

"That's right," said Rosetta. "They aren't doing anything."

"Does Ralph have a lawyer?"

"Yes. The court appointed one."

"Was that because Ralph couldn't afford to choose a lawyer himself?"

Mrs. Jerome's attention was regained. "My son-in-law couldn't afford to take a bus home from jail."

"Oh, Mother!" said Rosetta. She dropped her head to her lap and looked like she was going to cry. Only she didn't.

Mrs. Jerome continued. She had let the guest stars carry on long enough; it was time to remind us whose show it really was. "But you needn't worry about your money, Mr. Samson. Rosetta works, and after paying me for rent and food, she's saved up lots of money. Oh, a fortune." It didn't take a detective to recognize sarcasm.

Rosetta's head came back up like it was hollow in the sea. "Ralph had a job. A real good job."

"And after four weeks look where it got him." Mrs. Jerome let the shiv sink in, and then after a histrionic pause she twisted it. "In jail, that's where!" Not subtle, Mrs. Jerome.

It was me now near tears. "Much as I hate to interrupt, I do have a few more questions." They came to order immediately. It occurred to me that they were unused to having a man around the house. "First, if I am to be employed, may I have it clear who it is that is employing me? Is it both of you, or is it just you, Mrs. Tomanek?"

"Well, I'm not involved," said Mrs. Jerome.

"I want to hire you," said Mrs. Tomanek. "I can't think of anything else to do."

"If you would be so kind as to give me a dollar, you may consider me formally hired."

She hesitated on the couch, as if surprised that progress now depended on action on her part. She came through like a trooper. She jumped up and scurried back to the room from which she had originally come. I occupied myself with studiously writing a receipt and avoiding an exchange of glances with Mother Jerome. Never has a receipt been more exactingly crafted. Rosetta accepted her copy like a ticket to freedom and handed me four quarters.

"Now," I said, "what is the lawyer's name?"

"Sidney Lubart."

I rose. "All right. I'll check with the police and with Ralph's lawyer. By tomorrow or the next day I should know whether it's likely that I can be of any use to you. I'll get in touch with you then."

Rosetta accompanied me to the door. "I. . . . All I have saved up is about, well, two hundred and thirty-seven dollars. But I'm working regular."

"Please don't worry about money now," I said kindly. "You must realize that I will be working on other jobs at the same time. I'll only charge you for the time that I work for you. It shouldn't cost much before we know whether I'm going to be able to help or not."

"Thank you," she said. For the first time I began to think it possible that this creature was really somebody's wife and not just a voodoo pincushion for the stout little mother lady who still sat on the couch. I would have said good-bye to Mrs. Jerome, but she had her back turned to me.

Instead of driving straight home, I took a sentimental side trip around Victory Field. It was the only amenity in the neighborhood that I could see. Victory Field is where the Indianapolis Indians play baseball, and have played baseball for as long as I can remember. I drove all the way around it. They've changed the name, call it Bush Stadium, but it's still Victory Field to me. I spent a lot of hours there as a kid. Mrs. Jerome and her daughter had probably never been inside. But that's the way it is. I've never been to the Indianapolis 500.

On the way home I realized how cunning I'd been with that bit about my other clients. This way, if somebody called, I'd have already arranged free time to take his case too.

Or time to go and play some more basketball. To play basketball alone. It was not being rubbed into the asphalt by a runty ten-year-old that had burned me. At least that's not all. It was his lack of sympathy when I explained that it was my first time playing this year. That I had been in the hospital for three months over the winter. That my legs were not strong. That I still couldn't lift my right arm all the way up. That I was thirty-eight but felt ninety-one and that my back hurt.

The score stood at 48 to 6 in a 50 game by twos, and the kid had looked up at me and said, "Shit, man, if you sick, you should be in bed."

Am I to be despised because I hate ten-year-olds who play the game better than I did when I was eighteen?

Or am I to despise a kid because on recollection I hate myself for not having the maturity to lose like a man?

Yes! A thousand times yes! And damn him. If I'd met any real little mother the whole day, it was that kid.

3

I negotiated the fine weather's continuation into Tuesday. As a concession I woke up a few minutes after nine. Early for me the last few months. The internal weather was not so good, though. My legs ached. My body had not cleared the bronchial constrictions I get when I run more than I'm fit for. You can't win them all.

The back was weak, but the mind was strong. I rolled

over. Then I rolled over again and fell on the floor. I sleep in a double bed. I sleep on the inside, close to the wall so no one would have to climb over me to find herself a comfortable place. I am ever the optimist.

Lying on the floor, trussed in blankets, seemed like a nice thing to do. Didn't get in the way of thinking about my prospects for the day. The possibilities were numerous and equally lacking in appeal. Not that they disappealed, but as ignorant as I was of who, what, where, and why about my employer and her husband, I could hardly choose efficiently between visiting the police, the lawyer, and the detainee. Or going and having another chat with Rosetta Tomanek herself.

What the hell was it the lady wanted me to do, anyway? I stretched out. I appropriated my shirt and underwear from the delicate pile at bed's head and balled them into a pillow. It was likely to be a long stay. One can hardly move on in life until one has a goal to move toward. So what *was* it that Mrs. Tomanek hoped I would do?

I got the feeling that I had taken that fine one-dollar retainer in response to Mrs. Jerome's repressive personality as much as anything else. Get the husband out of jail? Prove Ralph Tomanek had done it, killed a man, for no better or worse reason than to get away from his mother-in-law? You win a few, and you lose a few. And some weeks you lose more than your share.

It wasn't much more than an hour before I got restless on the floor. At which time I got up and put on my pillow. Plus a few accouterments for my lower, and today definitely not better, half. I took my notebook and went out. The elevator was still out of order. That made six calendar days. I kicked its door, but it was as tender as a ten-year-old basketball player. I limped slowly down the stairs at the end of the hall. I refused to use the handrail.

One of the virtues of living in the inner city is that when one is flush, there are a variety of places close at hand in which one may help to reflate the economy. I picked the nearest, a diner across Alabama Street from my building. I bought breakfast. Bought . . . after all, I was employed, was I not? I was class stuff. A gent. I shot the whole dollar.

By eleven I was back on the streets. It was to be a fact-gathering day. Once I had the facts, ma'am, I would be able to ask an appropriate question or two, solve an appropriate insoluble puzzle or two. Collect all the available cash and some IOU's for thousands more.

I found a phone booth and dropped a dime. In hardly more time than it took me to find another booth and come up with another dime I was speaking to Sidney Lubart, Att'y.

"Hello, Lubart here," he said.

Fair enough. I explained what I understood of my relationship to his client Ralph Tomanek and asked for an appointment.

He paused. "Oh, well, I can give you about ten minutes if you can be here at one. I'm booked absolutely solid the rest of the day. I'm going to have to plead a couple of clients guilty as it stands." A rather serious joke.

I promised to be there at one. I crossed my heart and hoped to die.

I blew another dime and picked up a *Star*. And I dropped in at police headquarters for a social call.

The police live in the City-County Building. A multistory construction plum which houses a lot of the modern services provided by the city. If you're on the right kind of case, you can spend the morning being rehearsed by the district attorney and the afternoon being cross-examined in court without exposing yourself to the light of day. It's a giant step for mankind.

Their elevator was working, so I went up to the fourth floor and appeared at Homicide and Robbery. The desk officer was very civil and told me that the acting lieutenant I sought was out but was expected any minute. Would I care to have a seat? If I'd been a wisecracking private detective, I would have told her that they didn't match my decorating scheme. But being humble and hardworking, I sat down and read the paper.

Acting Lieutenant Jerry Miller did, in fact, appear within fifteen minutes. Well before I was forced from sports section and comics to sections of the *Star* which I find less congenial. When I want bad news, I dust the inside of my filing cabinet.

He came to where I was sitting, rattled my paper, and said, "Mr. Samson, I presume." After a rather close association centered on a case for which I was a witness and he was arresting officer, we hadn't seen each other for several weeks. Sharing important business changes a relationship with a friend. When the business is over, you've got to do a little rebuilding so you get to laughing as much as you used to.

We laid some skin on each other.

"I've got something to show you," he said. He took me past a nod from the reception desk through a brief maze to the violence room. On the end of a row of cubbyholes a paunchy man in overalls was putting up tissue paper to make a new cubbyhole. He was in his fifties and bald. He made me start. I am a little paranoid about bald pentagenarians. Among other reasons because I am old enough and thin enough up top to see that I shall be one not too long from now. Miller was oblivious to my paranoia. In fact, he seemed positively to revel in the activities of the gentleman.

"There it is," he said proudly.

"They sure keep acting lieutenants in style around here."

Fulfilled ambition radiated from his face. "It shouldn't be 'acting' too long. The mayor's got me on his desk now." In Indianapolis the mayor keeps a greasy thumbprint on police promotions at the rank of lieutenant and above. Delicate times require delicate racial, political, religious, ethnic, cultural, educational, and sexual balance. You also can't have too many lieutenants with the same favorite flower; it makes the public nervous. Life is very complex.

"Come on," said Miller. "Let's sit in it while you tell me what's on your mind." He tried to lead me into the middle of the construction zone. Paunchy Pate wasn't having any.

"Hey, buster, go the fuck somewhere else. I'm working here." I guess he didn't know who he was talking to. I would guess that Miller blushed, inside. A kid who got his fingers slapped for fooling around with the wrappings on his Christmas present before the sacred day. It was good to see Miller happy about his promotion, though. All the years he waited had enhanced it, and now it was enhancing him. I bet he was getting on better than usual with his wife.

"All I want is an introduction to another of the pretty faces around here," I said. I urged him to retreat from the dormer of his content. We moved away slowly. "I'm on a case," I said. "I need a little information."

He finally turned his mind and his face back to me. "You're feeling better then?"

"Quite a bit."

"It's good," he said. "Now, what can I do for you?"

We sat down on a couple of empty chairs against a wall next to a vacant desk.

"I need some background information on a case one of you guys must be handling. I've been hired by the wife of someone you've got locked up. A Ralph Tomanek."

"You're kidding." Then he laughed, a quiet little chortle. Not the kind of response I liked best, in the circumstances. "I can help you on that one, all right. Come on, that's Malmberg's case."

His turn to lead, we passed by all the cubbyholes and arrived in front of a desk. Behind it sat a ten-year-old kid.

"This is Sergeant Malmberg," said Miller. "Malmberg, this is Al Samson. He'd like a little information on one of your cases. I'd appreciate it if you'd help him however you can."

Malmberg jumped up. "Yes sir, Lieutenant Miller. I'll be glad to help him however I can."

"Thanks, son," said Miller. He patted me on the back and left with the kind of twinkle in his eyes that gave me a sinking feeling in my stomach. Like being top lobster in the pot and knowing that before you can get that second claw over the lip, you'll be pulled right back down where you started. That's the way lobsters, among others, seem to help each other.

"Which case can I help you with, Mr. Samson?" Malmberg asked me earnestly. I sat down and dug in. I thought about asking him how old he was, but I figured I knew. Twenty-three, twenty-four. And without asking I knew why Miller had left me mirthful. They don't assign cases to fresh kids like Malmberg until they're already in the bag. I had the feeling that I might be back to premature retirement all too soon. Which was a shame because I was, at last, feeling better. Stronger. More alive. I also regretted spending the whole dollar on breakfast.

Malmberg waited for me to answer him, but before I got around to it—one is less polite to young men at my age than to one's chronological peers—he said, "Excuse me for asking, Mr. Samson, but haven't I seen you around the division pretty recently?"

An observant kid, too. "I was involved in the Crystal business," I said, "but the case I need information on is Ralph Tomanek."

He nodded sagely. "A very interesting case. Very interesting."

Nails in my coffin. "I'd like to see the file," I said. "Would you get it for me or do you have it here?"

I could have gone the question and answer route. I knew, I mean, I *knew* that he knew by heart everything that I wanted to know. But it amuses wheelchair cases to test youngsters.

He said, "I. . . ."

I could see his thoughts flash in bold lights like the news in Times Square. Showing me the file was against regulations, but Miller had asked him to help me. He said, "I . . ." again, and then said, "I'll get it for you."

The kid could play ball. He'd go far. Probably the kind who put down "I want to be a policeman" in his kindergarten yearbook. And then majored in criminology with a minor in forensic medicine. And took a law degree in night school.

In ten years he'd be giving Miller orders. I wondered if Miller realized that. I wondered if the kid knew that.

He came back with a homicide file. I knew it was homicide because it had a red crayon stripe around it. "Here you are, Mr. Samson."

"What's your first name, Sergeant?"

"Joseph, sir. Joe." I'd be able to say I knew him when.

"Joe, is there a place I can sit for a while and study this?"

"Um, I, I was just about to go out for lunch. If you don't mind, you could use my desk."

"Would you mind?"

"No, sir. I'd be pleased to be a help to you."

"Your desk will do just fine. Thank you."

"If you'll just let me. . . ." As I stood by him, he gathered up three folders, including one with a red stripe, and carried them carefully off to his lunch hour.

It was two minutes before twelve. I settled in for a half hour's read.

4

By twelve thirty-five I was back on the streets, walking to see Sidney Lubart. I was not very happy.

I am not a man of violence, and I am especially not a fan of violent death. It's too random as it is practiced in the modern world. Too equally likely to happen to me as to anyone else, and for no good reason.

There was another reason I wasn't happy. The case looked like a loser all the way. A lieutenant called Graniela had taken the case for the first two days. That's all the time he needed to put it on Malmberg's level.

Ralph Tomanek had been an armed guard for an outfit called Easby Guards in a high-rent complex on the east side called Newton Towers. On the evening of April 28 he had used his weapon, a shotgun, and killed a man who had been waiting outside one of the tenant's apartments.

Why? One might well ask. Graniela, who'd been on the scene within minutes, did. Tomanek told him he had thought the guy was going for a gun.

The late lamented had indeed carried a gun, but the lab's report on the mortal remains stated it had been in its holster on the guy's right hip, whereas the right arm had been reaching under the left side of the jacket.

Did Tomanek see the gun or anything that looked metallic? "No," said Tomanek.

The killing had happened in front of a witness, one Edward Ephray, in front of whose door the victim had been waiting. Did Ephray see anything remotely metallic? "No."

Mr. Tomanek, if you didn't see anything, why did you think the man was reaching for a gun? "The man," Tomanek had said, meaning Ephray. "He told me to shoot."

Graniela noted from the beginning that Tomanek was somewhat less than helpful, but not, apparently, because he was unwilling to talk in the usual sense. "It was like his mind was elsewhere," was Graniela's observation, "if he has a mind."

Intensive questioning produced Tomanek's version of the story: that Ephray had been telling him all week that he owed money and was afraid someone was out to collect it.

Mr. Ephray, did you tell Tomanek that you owed someone money, someone who might get violent? "Hell, no! I don't even have a mortgage."

Tomanek also claimed that on the night in question Ephray had come into the building in a particularly nervous state and had insisted that Tomanek accompany him to his apartment door. That on seeing the man at the apartment door, Ephray had started shouting and saying that the man was going to kill him. That the man had given a funny smile and had reached under his overcoat. Ephray had shouted to shoot. Tomanek had shot. "I didn't know what else to do," said Tomanek.

Mr. Ephray, did you in any way suggest the victim might be a threat to you? "Certainly not." Or suggest that Tomanek should use his weapon? "That's fucking ridiculous. He caught me completely with my pants down, and I was afraid there for a minute that he was going to shoot me too." Did you know the victim? Had you ever seen him before? "No."

Lieutenant Graniela noted that Tomanek seemed upset when told that Ephray didn't confirm his story, but that he couldn't get Tomanek to come up with another version. In fact, as time went on, Graniela had difficulties getting Tomanek to say anything.

At the end of his first full day on the case Graniela had come up with a report on Ephray. Real estate agent and auctioneer, quite well to do, and in good financial condition thanks to a beneficent mother-in-law. No known connection with any of society's negative elements. No previous convictions. Only a couple of speeding tickets.

The net effect of the first day's work had been to leave Graniela uneasy about Tomanek. "He seems to act crazier and crazier" was Graniela's note.

So the second day on the case Graniela found out that Tomanek was crazy.

Army records on Ralph Tomanek: born May 3, 1947. Drafted July 21, 1966, after graduation from Arsenal Technical High School, Indianapolis. A draft board notation stated that Tomanek had been married in June, 1966, and had applied for a deferment because he was married, apparently unaware that marriage deferments had been ended in August, 1965. By November, 1966, Tomanek was in Vietnam, and in January, 1967, he saw his first action. Hospitalized near Saigon in May, 1967, but no award of the Purple Heart. Reactivated in June, 1967. Rehospitalized in July. Sent back to the United States—a San Diego hospital—in November. Shuffled between three California hospitals through June, 1968, and then, simultaneous with a medical discharge, he was placed "by arrangement" in a "Benjamin Johnson Hospital" just outside Crawfordsville, Indiana.

Graniela's next-to-last act on the case was to call the Benjamin Johnson Hospital. Tomanek had been discharged on November 19, 1970.

Before that phone call the major question had been whether the charge would be a manslaughter or second-degree murder. Subsequent to the call to the hospital, Graniela had apparently been convinced that it was likely that Tomanek would be declared unfit to stand trial for anything. His last act on the case had been to turn it over to Joe Malmberg with instructions to arrange for psychiatric evaluations and for liaison on the case with the city prosecutors. There was no rush.

I had stopped reading when the report had been taken up again by Malmberg. I had already found out more about the case than I was happy to know.

There was one final reason that I was unhappy as I approached the offices of Sidney Lubart. It had to do with a little coincidence concerning the deceased. The dead man had been Oscar Lennox, of Selwood, Indiana. He was fifty-nine when he died, and in his lifetime he had been a private detective.

5

Sidney Lubart was late. Two minutes late. I was standing outside his door, and I watched him come down the hall. On looks I never once considered that the gangly black man marching toward me was he for whom I waited. Until he said, "Samson?"

I said, "Lubart?" He unlocked the door, waved me in and to a chair, while he went to one of the dozen filing cabinets lined up around two of his tiny office's walls. He extracted a file folder and sat down across his desk from me. The desk was bare; the cabinet tops were bare. There are lawyers' offices which reek of garlic, and there are lawyers' offices which reek of organization. Personally I prefer garlic.

"You want to know about Tomanek," he said. "Can I see your license, please?"

I showed him my plastic ID card. The actual license is on a wall at home "in a conspicuous place" as required by law. "I have most of the background," I said. "What I am looking for is some reason to believe that there is anything I can do."

"My guess is not much besides take their money. A psychiatrist has been appointed for evaluation. They'll find that he is incompetent, or at least that he was. They'll sock him away."

"And your defense?"

"No defense. He has a better chance of being released from a hospital than he would from jail. The prosecution agrees." He spoke coldly, mechanically.

I had not been enamored with the prospects of the case on my way over, but in the face of this write-off from Tomanek's advocate my internal pendulum was starting its inevitable swing back.

"How did you get the case?" I asked. Although I knew from Rosetta Tomanek.

"I was assigned. The day he was charged."

"And how much time have you put in on it?"

Lubart sat back and cleared his throat. "Look, what you want to know is where I stand, right? OK. I'm thirty-five years old. I've come the night school route to a specialty in criminal law. I'm too old to make my fortune by starting at the bottom in the sort of two-bit law firm that would take me. So what I do is take all the court-appointed cases I can get. Out of a given batch I pick the two or three I figure I have the best chance with, and I work like hell on them, and I win them. That scores me points. With my other cases I bargain to get the best deal I can, but I don't waste my time or the court's time. If they're guilty, the faster they get into jail, the faster they get out. So I get points there, too. Tomanek is a losing case as far as I am concerned. I've talked to him, and his story is not sensible. He has a mental history. Probably he should never have been given a job where he carried weapons, but he was, and this is the result. Now he'll be hospitalized within a month."

"And you'll have another step up for being sensible and businesslike."

"Right, a step closer to the kind of job I deserve and my first million. Don't get me wrong; if in the course of your investigations you come up with legally important circumstances or, well, whatever, I will be only too glad to see them."

"Because if you can pull one off which looks like it is out

in left field, then you get that many more bonus points."
"Something like that. I'm not a bad lawyer, you know."
"Just a trifle too ambitious."
"I don't mind being called ambitious," he said. In fact, he seemed to quite like it. "But I've come a long way in three years, Samson. I started a lot farther down on the totem pole than even your Tomanek did."
"You're not going to let your unhappy childhood put my man in jail when he doesn't deserve it, are you?" Which must have been a hypothetical question at best.
Lubart was too thoroughly a lawyer to let the sarcastic form of the question put him off the content of it. "No," he said. "I don't deny that help for Tomanek *might* exist; I just don't think it likely."
"I'll want to talk to him."
"No problem."
"Probably I won't get to see him until tomorrow. Would you tell him that I am coming?"
"You're pushing again, Mr. Samson. I won't see him until the prosecutor calls me about the psychiatric evaluation. Whenever that happens. But let me give you a form that says you are working on his case for me. That'll give you free access to him while he's in jail."
"As a court appointee do you hire enough private detectives to have a form authorization?"
"There is money allowed for reasonable investigation. It's necessary to provide a fair defense."
"I'm beginning to see. The cases you think have promise get the investigation money for the ones you write off."
"Something like that. There is an accepted average investigative expense that one can put in for on even relatively hopeless cases."
"As long as you have some operatives who will help you on the paper work."
"Most of them will, I find."
"Did you ever hire Oscar Lennox?"
"No, he didn't have a license anymore, but when he did, he was a divorce specialist and well established. I find I have better results with younger men anyway."
"Who are ambitious like you?"

"I said I don't mind being called ambitious. I'm not going to defend the Tomaneks of this world the rest of my life."

He gave me an investigator authorization, complete with a place for me to sign. A copy for me; a copy for him. Which meant he would turn it in for reimbursement from the city. The money would then be spent on background work to find creditable witnesses to show that Joe Citizen had bought two bottles of wine at seven thirty on December 18 and that he was therefore drunk in an alley at nine thirty and that he therefore could not have been involved in the poker game he had been arrested for participating in at ten.

When I was back on the street, I found that it was nearly one thirty and seventy-two degrees. Nice for a leisurely walk. I was not feeling tired. I began to believe that I would be well and whole again. I tried three times to raise my right arm above eye level, to the amusement of two little girls who passed me on the sidewalk going the other way. I wasn't sure, but I thought I did get the wrist a little higher than my previous all-time record. I didn't think I was bending my elbow. Physical therapy is a great profession for authoritarians. "You're bending that elbow! Straighten it out immediately!" You keep telling them you can't, they tell you you can, and after a while you can.

But how do you straighten the elbows of the mind? "Don't pull that trigger, Ralph!" But he had. It is hard for me to understand a sane man killing another man. Of course, the fact that I can't understand it, feel it in my gut, doesn't mean that it doesn't happen. No one contested that he had pulled that trigger. What kind of help could one possibly find? That he was under duress? That he was mesmerized? That the devil made him do it?

They were premature questions. One can hardly pick the right question to ask before one has a few words with the man one is asking about.

I found myself nearly home. Passing the City Market, which is on the other side of my block. City Market is one of the remaining bastions of "the old" in a city very much dedicated to bringing in "the new." Various plans have been made to raze it for some or other public good, but none, to date, has succeeded. It's a large building with stalls full of vendors always trying to sell you a little more. I usually buy a little more when it comes down to it. I'll be sad when "they" finally get it.

I went in and bought some lunch to take home. Some cheese for the brain.

6

My answering service had taken a message. "Where the hell are you?" it read *in toto*. No name. No name needed. Clearly from my woman, the only person in the world who would care enough to call and ask. My mother cares. She just wouldn't call.

I ate my cheese, and doodled.

> Where the hell are you? the kind lady inquires.
> I sigh; then I scratch. I just wish I knew.
> But before I can give the response she requires
> In my turn I ask, Just where the hell are you?

An essential question for establishing relative location. Einstein taught us that. See, cheese is brain food.

I toyed with sending it by Western Union. Then I reread it. Paper airplane was clearly the optimum vehicle. I made it into one and came very close to the wastebasket. Jolly good try, old bean. Now beans, there's real brain food.

I decided I ought to take a nap. My therapeutic routine called for naps for another two weeks. But the body said no. Plunge on, oh, plumber's friend.

I checked my notes for the name of the place where Rosetta Tomanek worked. I didn't remember it offhand. For good reason. I had apparently neglected to ask. I had a fairly strong sense that I wanted to speak to Rosetta again before talking to her husband. Looking over my notes, I found that I had asked her remarkably little in the way of useful questions in our first contact. It worried me a little. I try to make reasonably good use of the time I have with people. If not necessarily getting information from them, then in getting impressions. I have the egoistic delusion that my impressions are more useful than misleading. But I realized that I had done less than not ask many questions. My visual image of Rosetta Tomanek was not very strong either. I couldn't swear that I would be able to pick her out of a crowd, if I had to. Of course, how many times have I had to pick someone out of a crowd?

But yesterday was yesterday, to coin a phrase. I realized how much sharper my mind felt. Minds grow rusty with disuse. It was good to be working.

I called the number I had for Mrs. Jerome. I got Mrs. Jerome.

"I would like to talk to your daughter, Mrs. Jerome. Would you tell me where she works please?" I was sweet as apple cider.

"She'll be here about six, Mr. Samson. How is your investigation coming?"

"Just fine, Mrs. Jerome. But I want to have a few words with her before this evening." And away from you.

"Perhaps I can help you. I know everything there is to know about Ralph. What is it that you need?"

When did they start calling you "Brick Wall," lady? When you were two months old or three? "I need to talk to your daughter. Are you refusing to tell me where she works?"

"It's not the way you seem to be putting it. It's just that Rosetta has a job of some responsibility, and her employer doesn't really like her private life intruding in work time. Besides, when you're talking about that Ralph of hers, it takes hardly a word before she's fallen to pieces." Especially a word from an expert hatchet jobber. "So you see it's really better for you to see her here at home in more supportive surroundings. Shall I tell her you'll be by tonight?"

"No, I wouldn't tell her that if I were you, Mrs. Jerome."

"Oh."
"Thank you very much for your time and trouble. Bye-bye now."
Which made two consecutive days I'd been burned.
How do you go about finding out where a Rosetta Tomanek works in this city anyway? Neighbors? Or wait down the block for her before her return at six?
I gathered my notebook. I'd have to do something to help Mrs. Jerome someday.

7

I had no trouble getting to see Ralph Tomanek, and the letter from Lubart even got me into a room alone with him. If he was hesitant about seeing someone he'd never met, he didn't show it. But when you're in jail, it takes a special kind of hostility to deny the opportunity for a change in routine. For the few short stays I've had in the less fashionable sections of the Indianapolis jail, I've been more than eager to see anyone. My problem was that no one wanted to see me.
Ralph Tomanek was a thin kid. Maybe six feet and a hundred and forty-five pounds. His hair was extremely light and cut in a shaggy crew. It suggested someone not long out of the Army. Which was OK except that he had been out too long for the stuff not to have grown any longer. Either he had had subsequent crew cuts, or he was a very slow hair grower. He wore black-rimmed glasses, which set themselves off against the very pale background of his general coloring.
A cop led him into the room I was waiting in. Tomanek watched the cop leave. Then he turned to me and gestured with his hand to say, "You wanted to see *me*?" Except for the partition which sealed the room into two parts, we were alone. The kid was young, unresponsive. Undoubtedly the more so for the circumstances he found himself in. The more that people insist on determining your life for you,

the less life you have left for yourself. Here was a kid who had been drafted, hospitalized, and jailed. He was all of twenty-four.

Through the microphone on my side of the glass wall I said, "I'd like to talk to you, if you don't mind."

He sat down. "Oh, I don't mind. They said you work for my lawyer?"

"That's right. I'm also working with your wife. We're trying to help you." I felt I had to simplify relationships and talk slowly for him. Not so much because of his position or condition in the world, but because I had so little concrete notion of what I could conceivably do to help him even if everything went the right way.

"How is she?" he asked, meaning Rosetta.

"I think she's pretty well. I only met her last night. With her mother."

He was silent. What can you say about Mrs. Jerome? I wondered how I could pin it all on her.

I said, "I've only just started working on your problem. I'm going to have to ask you some questions."

His shrug said, "I don't mind."

"How did you come to get the job with Easby Guards?"

"I saw the ad in the paper. I was looking for a job a long time, and I was going for everything. I didn't want to be a guard, but it said that veterans would be given a preference. So I went."

"And you got the job?" Somehow I felt impelled to help him along. Though he didn't need it. There was no actual hesitation in his voice. He didn't stumble over his thoughts.

"They gave me some tests. Then I had an interview with Mr. Holroyd. He said I had the job."

I know a little about security companies. I worked for one in the mid-fifties for three years. "Did they assign you straight to Newton Towers?"

"He put me on the salary right away but didn't place me anywhere for two weeks. Then he said to go to Newton Towers."

"No training or orientation?"

"Oh, yes. Mr. Holroyd went through what I was supposed to do with me. I talked to him a lot."

It struck me as unusual, but who was I to say? Maybe Holroyd felt it more important to know his men personally than the outfit I had worked for. Easby Guards had not been in business in my day. Maybe it was small.

"I have to ask you about April twenty-eighth," I said.

"OK."

"What time did you go on duty?"

"Nine o'clock. At night."

"What time did Ephray come in?"

"Mr. Ephray? About eleven fifteen as near as I can remember."

"Did you know him?"

"He was a tenant for about a week."

"And what did he say to you that night?"

"He said he owed a lot of money, and he was afraid there was a man after him, that there was a man going to kill him." For the first time in our interview Ralph Tomanek seemed to begin to show some emotion.

"What did you think about that?" He looked at me queerly, cocked his head. I said, "Did I ask you something wrong?"

"Are you really a detective working for my lawyer?" A question a little too exacting for my liking.

But I said, "Yes. Why?"

"Because last week there was this psychiatrist in here asking me all that sort of thing like you just did."

"Like what?"

"Like what did I think about this set of spots and that picture and about killing a man. He asked me that for a long time."

I smiled. So that's all you have to do to make thirty-five dollars an hour instead of thirty-five a day. I showed him my ID through the glass. He studied it pretty hard. "I couldn't help asking," I said. "It's the sort of thing I need to know. How you think about things. But I am not a psychiatrist, and I am a detective, and I am working to help you."

Without returning my smile he said, "OK. I believe you."

"While we're on the subject, how do you feel now about killing that man?"

He was sweaty. "I don't feel nothing. I killed him. I thought he was going to kill Mr. Ephray. I told Mr. Holroyd that I didn't want to carry a gun around as a guard, but he said that I had to. Mr. Ephray told me to shoot because he was going to kill him. He said, 'Shoot him. He's going to kill me.' I couldn't let him do that. It was my duty."

"Do you know that Ephray says that he didn't say he was afraid?"

Tomanek looked down at his microphone, then back at me. But he didn't avoid the question. "That's what the policemen told me. They tried to get me to say that I was just, well, kind of nervous and that I tried to make it look better after I did it by saying Mr. Ephray said he was scared."

"Did you?"

"No." If one gets truth points for looking into another person's eyes while saying something, Tomanek got them. He went on. "They said I was crazy. They said that Mr. Ephray said he didn't do that."

"Why would he say he didn't if he did?"

"I don't know why. I guess I'm crazy."

"Why do you say that?"

"Well, I used to be crazy, so maybe I still am. I didn't want a job with guns, and I took it anyway. That's crazy, isn't it? And now I killed a man. That's crazy, isn't it? Maybe I just am, but this time I don't know it."

"I don't know about all that, Ralph. But have you told me what really happened?"

"I told you the way I remember it, but the policemen said I was making it all up because I wasn't man enough to face up to what I'd done and take my medicine."

"Policemen?"

"There were three of them."

"Did they hit you?" I have an old-fashioned mind.

"Oh, no. They were very nice. They even got me a glass of water after I told them my story enough times for them to understand it right."

"I see," I said. At least vaguely I did see more than I had. "I'll be going now. But I will probably be back from time to time." It's not that I had run out of things to ask, but if you have a source of information which is readily available, you tap it at the rate at which you can best digest the information. I already had enough to make a chewable cud.

He knew the score, too. "I won't be going anywhere," he said.

"If you had your own choice, where would you go? What would you do?"

"Shucks," he said, "I never really think about that. I think I like that hospital I was in in San Diego the best. Better than the one in Crawfordsville."

"That's not a lot of ambition for a man your age."

"I just haven't had a lot of time to really make plans," he said. He was un-self-pitying, factual. "You can answer a question for me."

"My pleasure."

"If I get sent to jail or to a hospital for a long time, can Rosetta divorce me?"

"I think she can."

"Oh," he said. "Would you tell her to? Like you were talking, I don't think I have a lot of future for her, and she should divorce me and go do better for herself." He said it as coldly and calmly as a butcher who has decided a pork roast would sell better as chops.

Then he said, "I love her."

As far as I could tell, the divorce she needed most was from Mrs. Jerome. "I'll tell her that. Can you tell me where she works?"

The question surprised him. "She still works?"

"She said she did."

He said, "Oh," and settled down again. "She used to work. Before I came to jail. It was at the Green Stamp place in Speedway."

"I'll try it," I said. And I signaled the guard that our conversation was ended.

8

When I hit the pavement outside the jail it was about four twenty-five. I liked the timing. If I went straight home without sniffing in any doorways or passing over any fire hydrants, I could drive to Speedway just in time to catch Rosetta Tomanek leaving her Green Stamp Redemptioneria at five. I could drive her home, and we could have a little talkie-poo all by our selvsies. I could find out, once and for all, whether away from her mother she was a woman or a mouse. Already it was the busiest day I'd had in months. It still felt good. I was well again. Well!

My car has its own personal parking lot. There is a narrow alley behind my building, and the builders, in 1923, created a bay by indenting the back wall. It gives space for about a car and a half. I grant that they had in mind space for trash barrels, which apparently they needed. But when I moved in in '63, downtown Indianapolis had long begun moving to the suburbs. At that point, the landlord was so pleased to have me that he offered the space no longer needed for trash to park my car. Rent-free. It's the best deal I ever got from him. I enjoy it while I can. The original lease was for ten years.

Traffic was on the heavy side, but I found the redemption center and planted myself in front of it by five on the button. It was in the Speedway Mall, a flesh-and-concrete example of the sort of suburban expansion which got me my parking space. Everything was surprisingly crowded. That is, it surprised me until I remembered that everything in Speedway is busy this time of year. Everything except Green Stamp redemption centers.

The door was locked. No amount of screaming "I want to trade my three books for a can of gooseberry dumplings" would free them. Not only that, the lights were out. Not only that, there was a sign, bold as brass, saying, "CLOSED Hours 9-12 1-4:30 daily. 5:30 Saturdays." What the hell right did they have to close on a day I was feeling good?

More than that, I'd been taken. I'd taken at face value Mrs. Jerome's casual statement that Rosetta would be home at six. Never trust a Mrs. Jerome. Why should I believe that she would give me the time Rosetta set foot through the decrepit doorway as opposed to the time at which Mrs. Jerome would be willing to have me come? I went back and sat in my car in the parking lot. I could always come back in the morning to see Rosetta. Make a firm time to have a chat. Or I could drop by at six and try to wrench her away. Didn't Mrs. Jerome have any outside interests, hobbies? Didn't she belong to a witch-dunking club or something?

When I burn, I burn bright. The flames don't usually last that long, but then I smolder. At five fifteen I got out of the car again and walked two stores to the north to a drugstore. I went to the phone booth in the back. While I was on business, I looked up the addresses of Easby Guards and Edward Ephray. Then I called my woman. She wasn't there. Anyone with any sense would have known that. But Lucy was there. Her daughter. I invited myself for dinner. She accepted.

While I was about it, I did some shopping. Aspirins, shampoo, a book called *Law and the Home Business*, and a Clark bar. When I was nine or ten and had a paper route, I ate five Clark bars a day. I don't like them much now, or candy bars in general. But I was feeling kind of childish.

I was second in line at the cashier when I looked out the window. A stooped female figure walked briskly past. Even though the window was crowded with reversed writing, I recognized Rosetta Tomanek.

I didn't know what to do. The woman being served in front of me was paying with a twenty. The cashier called out for change from the manager. I placed my four near purchases on a box of baseball bubble gum and I walked, then ran, out of the drugstore. They may have shouted after me, or it might have been the wind rushing past my ears.

I shouted, "Rosetta! Mrs. Tomanek!" She was at the end

of the line of stores, about to turn left around a bank branch and mailbox. She heard me. Paused as if she couldn't believe someone was calling her. I shouted again, and she turned around. By which time I had caught up. Panting.

"Why, Mr. Samson," she said. She was pleased to see me.

My voice was funny from the running. About the same as it had been the day before while explaining my infirmities to my basketball-playing juvenile acquaintance.

"I need some sort of exercise to get into shape," I said to Mrs. Tomanek breathily, senselessly. "But not basketball." She was fascinated, but quiet. "I'd like to talk to you for a few minutes. I'll drive you home."

She thought, and said, "All right."

We walked in silence to the car. My lungs responded gratefully to the respite. I held the door for her.

"I mustn't stay too long," she said when we were settled inside my charger. "Mother watches for me, and tonight we're going to see Ralph."

I nodded approvingly. "It's pretty hard to get to talk to you without your mother being there."

"She's always been like that," said Rosetta Tomanek quietly. "You get used to it after a while." I started the car and pulled out into the flow of traffic. The creep of traffic.

She looked quite different to me in her working clothes. Not so frail, not so much like a teen-ager. But part of it was that I now knew her husband was twenty-four. "I've found out quite a lot about your husband's case today. I've seen the police; I had a chat with the lawyer; I talked to Ralph." She looked tentatively hopeful. I said, "I need more idea of what Ralph is like, how he acts with people, and what his problems are. I don't really know if I'm going to be able to help yet, but there are things that might be followed up."

"What things?"

"The difference between Ralph's story and the other man's. The man he was with when the killing happened. Ralph says this Ephray was nervous and said he was in danger and then urged him to pull the trigger. Ephray says he didn't." She nodded in confirmation. "Well, the police don't feel it is worth following up because of Ralph's mental history. They think Ralph is crazy and that he is therefore lying."

She took the straight statement in, but said heatedly, "I don't think Ralph's crazy. And he doesn't lie."

"The question is just how strongly you believe those two things. If either of them is wrong, then you may well be throwing hard-earned money away. But all I can do is to take Ralph's story, whatever it looks like, and assume what he says is true. I have no idea of what is to be found, whether I can find it, or whether it will help him."

She didn't face me head on to say, "That's what I wanted to hire a detective for." Her voice was more ethereal than ever. "But I believe Ralph. I *know* what he tells me is true. You wouldn't believe how much we understand each other. I know just how he feels and what he thinks when he does things. I can't believe that he was really wrong when he did what he did. He just wouldn't do it if it were wrong, so it's not right that he should be locked up."

I considered myself commissioned to the extent of her financial and emotional resources.

"If you do find something, will the police listen?"

"It depends on what it is. If they can explain something in a simple way, then they don't have time to go looking for complicated ways to explain the same thing."

"I see," she said.

We drove the rest of the way home in silence. I was getting tired, and while I would have been interested to listen to a lot of things about her husband, I didn't yet have enough information to be able to ask specific questions. One thing I'd intended to ask was her permission to research Ralph's mental history. But now I felt that permission was obvious. A few blocks before the turn off Sixteenth Street to her home, she said, "I have my money at home for you. Mother got it out of the bank today for me."

"I trust you, Mrs. Tomanek."

"Why should you?" she snapped, and the irritation caught me quite unawares.

"I don't know."

"I love Ralph, but I don't see why that means you should trust me for your money."

"I am happy to be paid if you want to pay me." Then just before I turned down Wolfe Street, I realized what had been going on. I said, "You have to work yourself up to go home each day, don't you?"

I struck some sort of chord. I felt she liked me for the first time. There was some depth to Rosetta Tomanek. Her potential for withdrawal could be reversed. "I do," she said. "That I do."

"Why do you live with her?"

"I, we, never had a chance to do anything else."

"Can I phone you at the redemption center?"

"No. I can phone you in the lunch hour, or you can meet me after work like today."

"On the door it says you close at four thirty."

"I get out at five thirty. We have to tally, reorder, clean up. It's sort of like a bank."

"OK. And in a pinch I'll call you at home."

"Try not to." I could guess why. Momma really gets mad when she's not on top. It occurred to me that the big reason I wanted to burn Mrs. Jerome today was that she hadn't told me the truth about when Rosetta would be coming home, and it had been the truth, after all. A standoff. There might be a time to talk to Mrs. J. To find out her first name.

"What's your mother's first name?"

"Martha."

I turned into Wolfe Street. Martha was waiting on the sidewalk. I pulled up in front of her. In the driver's seat of my high old Plymouth my face was almost on line with short Martha's. I smiled and said, "Hello."

Rosetta stepped quickly out of the car, but before closing the door, she said, "If you'll wait, I'll get you the money." I waited. She walked around the front of the car.

"I saw the bus go by," said Mrs. Jerome to her daughter. Rosetta passed on into the house, leaving the two of us.

Mrs. Jerome looked at me and scowled.

"Do you come from Indianapolis originally, Mrs.

Jerome?" I asked pleasantly. I thought it was pleasantly. She didn't answer pleasantly. She didn't answer.

Rosetta returned bearing an envelope. "It's two hundred and thirty-seven dollars," she said, stepping around her mother to hand it to me.

"Get a receipt," said her mother.

"Oh, Mother, please!" said her child. I wrote out the receipt.

"Well, are you going to get Ralph off scot-free, Mr. Detective?" Mrs. Jerome wasn't showing herself in her best light.

But I answered as seriously as I could. "I'll do what I can." I thanked Rosetta for her time and attention and left.

9

The evening I idled away making papier-mâché masks and fighting gas pains. Lucy cooks a mean meal, but it doesn't take into account that a thirty-eight-year-old stomach can't handle spicy food the way it did when it was, say, thirty-seven.

Business was preying on my mind. I made a mask looking like my memory of Ralph Tomanek. That extreme fairness, stopping short only of albinism, and the double target eyeglasses. Lucy thought it was a ghost; her mother scolded me for making a corpse. I'm not very arty. In the end, I satisfied them both by painting it green. Agreement, a Martian. Coat hanger antennae. Poor Ralph.

I got home a little after 1 A.M. Very tired. The clothes hit the floor in a matter of seconds, and I was abed. I pitched only two World Series innings before I was asleep. In the winter I shoot key jump shots to get to sleep, but this was May, after all. That's why I had a bad time with that little kid. Proper people play baseball in May, not basketball. I would try to improve myself.

I woke up at eight and again every half hour until ten

thirty. It was a sweet, dozy time: waking up and drifting back, oblivious to the urgencies of life. It was not that I had nothing to do. I was just at peace enough to know that I didn't have to get going compulsively. I was at peace enough to be satisfied that whatever the result or effect, I was at work again, whole of mind and body. I *was* a World Series pitcher.

My harmonies were interrupted, finally, by my landlord. He burst in, then knocked.

"Samson! Hey, Samson, are you awake?"

He's called Andrew Kapp. He's a bastard, and his delight is in following the fortunes of people named Kapp in more public lives, though he's related to none of them. That's all I know about him because that's all he's ever told me. Did you know that in 1963 there was a mayor of some Montana village called Minkus Kapp?

"All right. Lie there if you damn well want to, but I just want to tell you that I've rented the office next to yours, and you're going to have to get your stuff out of the bathroom. Today, understand?" He clumped out and left the door open. The open door, that was the killer. Not that I am modest about being seen sprawled in bed late in the morning by anyone who was renting the joint next to mine. To rent in my building one has to be tolerant of squalor. It was the knowledge that there was a chance, however slight, that a would-be client might walk in the door. About clients I am modest.

I rose and closed the door. Just what constitutes a landlord's right to reasonable access? He'd be sorry when I left. To get married, say. And go into the mask business. I could export Martian masks to Hong Kong.

Still, it had been a pleasant morning on net. It rated clean underwear and a clean shirt. Done.

When I put on my pants, they seemed unduly heavy. I searched my pockets and found a bag of money. A pleasant morning on net. I went out for breakfast.

The spare time I gained through not having to scramble my own eggs I spent analyzing, trying to analyze, the relation of my client to various people. I was struck on remembrance by the marked difference between the Rosetta

Tomanek I met *cum* mama on Monday night and the Rosetta Tomanek I'd driven home from work on Tuesday. She wasn't dumb, and she wasn't really shy. Excellent attributes in a client.

The time between finishing my second cup of coffee and receiving my third I spent making plans. I had lots of questions to answer: What was Lennox doing there? Who was Edward Ephray? What was the kind of problem Ralph had been hospitalized for?

All lovely stuff. I finished my coffee and took a little walk.

But when I called upstairs at Police House I was told that Wednesday was Malmberg's day off. A Sergeant Owen Stone was covering his cases if I wanted to speak to him. I figured five to one against Owen Stone coming through for me without intervention. I didn't feel like bothering Miller again on something less than specific. I would wait for Malmberg. Thanks, honey.

It was fairly warm but cloudy. The sort of conditions in which seaweed gets slimy: humidity going up, rain soon likely to be coming down.

10

Easby Guards was a bigger operation than I'd thought it would be. It had a whole houseful of guards and an enormous busnified red brick house to keep them in. On Mount Street, just south of Washington out east. I know the neighborhood. They have an ice-cream cafeteria out there. You pick up a tray and a dish and build your own ice-cream fantasia. Twelve flavors later. . . .

There was no cherry topping Easby Guards. The receptionist was forty and plodgy. She looked, well, secure. "What can I do for you, sir?" she asked.

"Is Mr. Holroyd available?" The man who'd hired Ralph Tomanek. "My name is Albert Samson. I'm a detective working on the case of a former employee of yours, Ralph Tomanek."

She sat down and carefully selected a button on a large intercom unit.

A voice crackled a "Yes?" It sounded like it was coming from California.

"Mr. Holroyd, there's a detective here who wants to talk to you about Ralph Tomanek."

There was no reply.

But within a few seconds there were footsteps coming closer. A door behind the reception desk burst open, and a short, portly man strode forward. He had the air of an unstoppable force. His features were unremarkable, but he was such a figure of energy that his sudden presence was startling.

"Where is he?" Holroyd said to no one in particular. I was the only new boy in town, so it didn't take him long to find me. "Ah, glad to meet you," he said. "A pleasure to meet you." His handshake was robust. "Why don't you step back to my office? We'll have a good talk. Marie, tell Alice to bring me down the Tomanek file. And no calls."

He led me whence he'd come. We passed steep stairs and walked down a hallway toward a pair of doors. The stairs and the hallway were extremely well lit, by long fluorescent bulbs. The walls were papered gray.

"Right back here, detective. A terrible business, terrible." His comment could be taken more generally than he meant it, but I went where he beckoned. The pair of offices bore the names Easby and Holroyd. We went into Holroyd's office. Fair enough.

"Have a seat. Do you smoke cigars? They're very good. No? Not on duty, heh? Here, let me open the window for a little air circulation while I have one." He took a cigar, opened the window, and sat down across his desk from me. No shelves in his office, but walls eye-high with metal drawers.

"Yes," he continued, "we were most upset to hear the news about Ralph Tomanek. I liked him; I really liked him. Must have been some sort of momentary lapse, some misunderstanding. I can't see him just off and shooting the man." He puffed furiously, then set the cigar down on the edge of his desk and leaned back in his swivel chair. "Can you?" For the first time the mouth was occupied with nonlingual functions, and he was all ears. His ears were large.

"I don't really know, Mr. Holroyd. I don't know Ralph Tomanek very well. I was hoping to learn a little about him from you."

He nodded sagely. "Well, Easby Guards stands completely behind him. We'll give Ralph our full support, for whatever it's worth."

"He'll be glad to know that. Considering this sort of incident can't be very good for business."

He half smiled. "It doesn't help our public relations. And the police don't much like it." He flashed what could only be called a knowing smile. "But business? I can't say that it hurts business. You have to understand that the people who hire guards in this world have property they feel needs protecting. People like that. . . ." He looked contemplative. "They are apt to see something like this as an indication that Easby Guards are trained to live up to their commitment to protect. I don't say that I take their viewpoint as my own, but I do understand it. And I can't really say that Ralph's action, unfortunate as it was, has hurt business."

How about saying that it helped business?

Of course, one knows the people he was talking about. As long as it doesn't happen in their building, one innocent man more or less helps deter other would-be building deflowerers. I had yet to find out, to be sure, just how innocent a man Oscar Lennox was.

But another question. "Is it usual for your guards to carry loaded shotguns on the job?"

"Wal." He drawled and drew hard on his cigar. "Wal, you see this is explained by the times. With the world the way it is, there's a lot more need for security operations than there used to be. That's the first point."

He paused for breath and to give me a lookover. "Now the second point is that because of the need there is a lot of competition for the work. So small companies, like this one was when my father-in-law took it over in 1961, they need some kind of edge to survive."

I began to comprehend. "So to beat out the established companies, you gave your guards shotguns as a promotional gimmick."

"That's it. That's it exactly." He was pleased. Mighty pleased. "We never really expected that they would be used, certainly not often. In fact this is only the third time a shotgun has been fired on company time and only the first death. But I mean, my boy, you can see the appeal! They aren't really much of a danger, yet they allow us all sorts of advantages."

Which I could see. I worked in security for three years and never got very high up in the business. But even in the late fifties I'd found a lot of employers who felt they'd been cheated when I showed up without a gun. If you're going to be armed, there are advantages to being conspicuously armed.

Holroyd carried on, probably seeing that I had some grasp of the concepts he seemed eager to confide. "You see, the essential function of a businessman, the real entrepreneur, is to find the economical niches in society. The situations where there is still some consumer need which you then fill. That's what I do in this business. I may not like the conditions that make my business necessary, but everything is good for something. I don't have to work for a living, you know."

"No, I didn't know."

"My father-in-law left me and my wife quite comfortably off. But I enjoy working. Dealing with people, understanding how to make them work. And I like the idea that decisions I make can make me money. It's the times. Violent times. When they've got the street violence licked, Easby Guards won't need their shotguns. And probably people won't need Easby Guards." He leaned back, and he puffed the way some people laugh or applaud or eat.

Everything is good for something. I wondered what Ralph Tomanek was good for now.

Holroyd was positively garrulous. I was in no hurry. "But mark my words," he said, "it'll get worse before it gets better. Take it from an expert, there's going to be a lot more need for security before there's a lot less. Here, let me tell you a little brainstorm I had today. You tell me what you think of it, OK? My idea is that before long it's going to be the same here as it is in Chicago and New York. Not safe to be on the streets, if you look halfway prosperous. It's almost that way now. My idea is this. A combination of a guard service and taxicabs. Do you see it? Every cab has a guard riding."

"Like riding shotgun?"

"Yes! That's it exactly. Maximum security cabs with a driver and an Easby shotgun guard. The guard picks you up, escorts you to the cab. Then delivers you to the door wherever you're going. Safe and sound. You could use the same cabs we already have, just put the guard in the front seat and adjust the prices."

Like tripling them. There was a knock at the door. "Yes!" Holroyd bellowed. The door opened, and a very dolly young lady wafted in on a cloud of dreams and handed a manila file to her boss. Very nice. A fine contrast with the man himself.

"Thank you, Alice," he boomed after her, and he grinned at me, the kind of grin that older men can trade. "Nice, eh? But we were talking about my cabs. I figure to put a little doohickey up on the roof, paint them Army green, and call them Turret Cabs or Tank Cabs."

"Or Sherman Shotguns."

"Something like that. There's time. I don't think the city is ready for it yet, but I don't think it'll be more than ten years coming. What do you think the boys down at headquarters would think about something like that? Should be some sympathy for it, wouldn't you say?"

"Could be. I really don't know."

"But they are generally, well, upset with the tenor of the times. The way things are so dangerous now. They couldn't have much to object to in a service that took a little of the danger out of life, could they?"

"I don't really know. You'd probably do well to ask someone there."

He frowned. "Damn it, don't play cozy. That's what I am doing, isn't it?"

And we had a look at each other. The effusive businessman turned cagey before my eyes. I just sat. It was a comfortable chair. You can't ask more than that for sitting. It's not as if I'd done much talking or had refused to admire the plans or peons that he'd offered for admiration. Or as if I'd found anything out, for that matter.

"A cop," he said. "You're not a cop."

"I never said I was."

He squinted, trying to remember. He remembered. He was as cool and collected in the reconstruction as he could be. "Marie," he said. "She said you were a detective. I suppose that makes you a *private* detective?"

"I suppose it does." I felt a little apologetic in spite of myself.

"Some people never learn what details are important to me."

"Is it that important? You haven't given away any family secrets, have you?"

He looked at me, a little smile showing in his eyes. His manner had changed from verbose ebullience to studious evaluation in a dramatic, almost schizoid way. Even his accent changed. His whole being seemed to invert, and what surprised me was that the calm followed a mixup which, if anything, would have upset an ordinary man.

"A private detective," he repeated. He shook his head. "I suppose you're working for Tomanek's lawyer."

I nodded. "I guess this would mean that the police haven't been here to talk to you yet."

"Good guess," he said. He took the Tomanek file and put it in his desk's top drawer. That got me worried.

"I'd like to know how you came to hire Ralph Tomanek," I said.

He put out his cigar and stood up. "You'll have to go now," he said so quietly I could hardly hear him. I didn't want to hear him. "I hope you won't take this personally, but I make it a rule never to talk to private detectives."

The whole thing, the change of play in the middle of an

act, annoyed me. "What's the matter, you jealous of our carefree lives or something?"

His vocal volume went up only slightly. "That's all there is to it. I won't talk about Ralph Tomanek with you. If Ralph's lawyer wants to ask me some questions, fine. But I do not converse with private detectives."

"But if what you said about supporting Tomanek was true, then surely you understand that his lawyer must have help."

He didn't answer. He just walked out of the room.

I didn't know what to do. He seemed very certain of his wishes. I began to feel fear of the man. I stood there for three or four seconds, long enough to daydream about him going to a shotgun cabinet for the instrument of death with my name on it. I decided to leave.

I peeked out just as the receptionist, Marie, came through the door at the end of the hall. Perhaps she was mined and would explode on contact. I stepped out to share the hall with her. I took the offensive. "What's wrong with him?" I asked.

"He told me to come back here and get you out. I guess he doesn't want to talk to you anymore."

"I don't understand," I said. Damn it, I'd said all my pleases and thank-yous.

"I don't understand it," said Marie. "The last couple weeks he's been on top of the world."

I didn't push it. I let myself be led quietly out. Down the steps. Marie closed the door gently behind me. I don't think I would have minded if it had been slammed. I crossed the street slowly to the car and stood outside, at the driver's door. Then I turned around to look at the Easby Guards building. I wondered just how far Holroyd's aversion to private detectives would go. Maybe I fancied I would see him brandishing his shotgun at a window.

What I saw instead was Alice. On the second floor, distorting venetian blinds to watch me. It made me feel important, but evil. The way a virus must feel as it looks back up the microscope at the eye of the man who isolates it.

I waved. Alice stepped back. The blinds vibrated. I

waited. Alice reappeared. They can't resist me. Holroyd must have gone upstairs to get Alice to watch me leave. Different jobs in this world have different duties. WANTED: pretty gal/guy to watch private detectives leave offices.

Why a gal/guy? Well, it's against the law now to advertise for a woman when a man can fill the job equally well. So just make it pretty, sweetie.

11

Instead of going to do whatever I should have gone and done, I went to Willard Park for a sit-down. I found a bench. I thought.

About the peculiar experience I'd just been through. Holroyd, a man who apparently had two personalities he could turn on and off like faucets, cigar-smoking, lecherous man of business for dealing with fuzz and a more measured, hostile gentleman when misdirection had been righted. Yet both his faces had had an extreme quality. My very expulsion was a contradiction because there aren't many kinds of work closer to private guarding than private eyeing.

A lively day. My only regret was that in the moment I had passed alone in his office I hadn't had the presence of mind to go to his desk and acquire the Tomanek employment file. A private eye with panache would have done it and walked out of the place with the file under his arm.

I had to admit, whipping the file had occurred to me at the time. I didn't do it because I was afraid. Afraid of . . . well, indeterminate fear is more paralyzing than a specific fear.

Holroyd must have been surprised that the police hadn't been around before. It's only reasonable to expect them to come calling when you've put a shotgun in a man's hand and he's killed with it. The police are not inclined to over-solve. They had come up with one passable explanation. *Ergo*, they work on something else they have no solutions for.

Still, arming a man with a mental record. The question being just what kind of mental problems Ralph Tomanek had suffered. I wanted a look at that file which I had, through cowardice, missed my chance at.

Break and enter, right?

Wrong. Even less fearful private eyes know better than trying to break into a security company's offices. Still . . . they would hardly expect it. And if they were just a guard service, then it might not be so bad, not so bad as a company which transported money and cared for valuables. Of course, that's guards too, isn't it? So it would depend on just what kind of work the company went in for.

It began to rain. I got up and went to sit in my car. Internal-combustion umbrella. I wondered if I was hungry.

It wasn't as if Easby Guards was likely to have any information in its files that I couldn't get myself. And probably better, having not only the horse itself to go to the mouth of, but the horse's wife, and, yes, the horse's mother-in-law, the horse police, and a few other equines.

In a pinch I might even be able to get Lubart to go talk to Holroyd. Or better yet, Malmberg to go and take the employment file as evidence.

The more I thought about it, the more negligent it seemed to me that it hadn't been done already. I could see that the initial investigator, Graniela, wouldn't have done it, but in three weeks Malmberg should have. I'd have to speak to the lad about that. Now see here, son, you want to be police chief when you grow up?

I drove all the way back to town before eating. In part because I felt a need to start again, symbolically to recommence. Also because there's a nice eaterie I hadn't been to for a while. John's Famous Stews. On the corner of South Street and East Street, a corner of the square-mile wheel surrounding Indianapolis' hub and spokes.

There was a big crowd when I got there. Not that John draws them in from miles around. The place is next to the Farmer's Market, not to be confused with City Market, and it was a market day. Fresh edibles. I have a bit of a penchant for markets.

I found a parking place on Ogden Street and a sitting place in John's.

What did I need information on most? On the horse himself. Preferably impartial information. A notion of what I'd do next popped up, and while the sun did not burst through the clouds as an augury, the rain did slacken a little. And then the fat man behind the counter undercharged me marginally.

12

It was getting on to one thirty when I hit the stretch of countryside between Indianapolis and Crawfordsville. I spent the time worrying whether I was old-fashioned to use a notebook for my notes. Not that I've had any complaints with its service. I used to misplace it, but since my first year in business it is virtually screwed to my left hand when I go out the door. I treat it with the respect it deserves, too. I never doodle in it. Well, hardly ever. But I was thinking about a portable recorder, like a cassette jobby that I could record tones of voice with and which would free my hands for pinching things.

Bottoms?

Employment files?

Holroyd would approve of my switching to cassettes. That was reason enough for not doing it. I would wait till the technology of the things reduced them to shirt-pocket size with batteries which recharge from body heat.

It was definitely not my normal rustic-drive train of thought.

Of course, the place I was visiting wasn't exactly normal either. The Benjamin Johnson Hospital.

Quiet and pretty, striking even on a lightless day. Lots of

grass, trees. And a cluster of small buildings, both frame and brick. Not at all what I had expected.

I followed signs along the winding drive to an "Administration Building." I had the choice of a dozen empty parking spots marked "Visitors."

As I was going up the steps to Administration, the door opened before me. A man came out on the porch and carefully closed the door behind him. He wore a white smock over white shirt and trousers; a small white cap, white shoes and socks. A white surgical mask dangled below his chin. I didn't have the faintest idea of what he did for a living until I noticed a stethoscope banging on his chest.

He came toward me with his hand extended for shaking. I shook it.

"Gut afternoon," he said, smiling, in a fairly heavy German accent. "I am Dr. Vurst. Vat can I do for you?"

I began to explain who I was, but he interrupted, saying, "You don't mind if ve valk, do you? It's not raining hard. I vas chust coming out for a breather. I don't get much chance, you zee, mit all the vork I haf to do."

So we walked slowly around the grounds. I was a bit afraid he would refuse to talk to me at all, so I explained carefully what I was doing and showed him the letter from Lubart. It worked wonders. All reluctance appeared to be blown away. "I think I may be able to help you," he said. "Ordinarily there is a matter of doctor-patient prifilege, you understand, vere the doctor doesn't tell other people vat he knows about the patient. But in zis case, mit police und everything, I think it vould be of more help to the patient if I let you know vat I know, don't you zink?"

I thought. Positively, emphatically.

"Tomanek, you zay the man's name is? A dark-haired man?"

"No, very fair. He was here from May, 1967 to November, 1970."

"Released, huh? November. Let me zink. A young man, vas he?"

"Yes, very young. He was sent here from Vietnam via a number of other hospitals."

"Ahh, dat var," he said. "It can do terrible zings. Terrible."

"Do you know which doctor handled his case? I would very much like to talk to him."

Dr. Vurst stopped abruptly and frowned at me. He didn't speak for fully five seconds, but then he smiled and said, "But of course. You vouldn't know, vould you? I am the doctor vich handled his case. We are not zo big as to have more than one doctor for zis. I handle all the psychiatric azpects of all the cases. Und I have four assistants who handle the medical azpects. Medical normality is very important in mental normality, you know. Und den we have qvite a few well-trained nurses and orderlies too, you know. Qvite a tight little ship we run here." He chuckled, once. "You don't get the choke? We have a lot of Navy men here, from Vietnam und places. So it's a choke ven ve talk about having a tight little ship, you zee?"

"I see," I said. For all his ostensible cooperativeness the good doctor was not exactly straining my supply of notebook pages. But you have to be tolerant of foreigners. I chuckled once too and said, "Quite good. But I need some information about Ralph Tomanek."

"Ahh, yes. Tomanek. Ralph. Yes. I remember the case. Some oedipal broblems, not helped by the var. Yes, I remember."

"What I need to know is more detail about how stable his situation was and how it related to weapons, to put it concisely."

"Concisely put, ya. Vell, I can tell you zis, he vasn't crazy, if zat's vat you vant to know. We dun't really deal mit crazy people here. Only, you know, zoldiers and zailors who haf broblems."

I was beginning to have "broblems" myself. "You see, this man, Ralph Tomanek, came back to his wife and his mother-in-law and had trouble finding work. He seemed to have a considerable aversion, I understand, to handling weapons. Then, when he was offered—"

I was interrupted by a female voice behind us. About two hundred yards away, at the bottom of the steps to the porch of the building next to Administration, stood a female nurse in a tidy blue uniform. "Doctor!" she called. "Dr. Vurst!"

My garrulous colleague turned abruptly to look at her. He grabbed my hand and pumped it twice. "Nice ta meet-cha," he said, and holding his stethoscope in one hand and the skirt of his smock in the other, he loped across the grassy lawn which separated us from his siren. I just stood as I watched her take him by the hand and lead him into the building she must have come from. I just stood there. I wondered if perhaps I hadn't found myself a home. Dr. Vurst. My impulse, insofar as I had one, was to go away and lie down and start the day over again. Maybe I should lie down where I was. Ya, dat vood be gut, ya? Except for its being wet. It was the low point in my day. In my life. A slight break in the clouds showered me with the day's only sunlight. I spat.

But few things are really soul-destructive. As one gets older, one learns how to tolerate humiliation. Practice makes perfect.

I walked slowly back toward my car, toward the Administration Building. To try again to do what I had allotted one afternoon of my life to try to do.

By the time I was mounting the Administration steps, as I should have done half an hour earlier, I was loaded for bear. Keep your damn information, I can get it elsewhere. But while I'm here. . . .

The little secretary in the Administration office was quite sweet. "I need some information about one of your former patients who's gotten himself into trouble. I'm working for his lawyer, and I want to see whoever's in charge." Got that, sister?

She said, "Would you like some Chiclets? I'll see if Mr. Grue is free." I was a tough guy. I refused the Chiclets. Even though I like Chiclets and they were peppermint.

I waited ten minutes. For once in my life I was glad, rather than even tolerant, to wait. I calmed down some. I unloaded; if bear came my way, I could load up fast enough. No need to walk around just waiting to discharge.

The secretary returned in the company of a man. "Come in," he said. He smiled. He pointed to a door on which was written "Michael Grue, Director." I followed him through it.

"I understand you are inquiring about a former patient." He was a dapper, rather tall man, intermediate age, but with a shock of red hair teetering over his eyebrows. Already I could see he smiled a lot. Perhaps needing to keep a sense of humor in his surroundings.

I handed him my ID and the letter from Lubart and sat down. "It's important for us to get some idea of the nature of his problems. Can you help?"

He glanced at the documents and handed them back to me. "I'm not a doctor. I never treated Tomanek, though I met him several times. I must say I didn't remember him at first, but about three weeks ago the Indianapolis police called me, and I got out his files. Quite interesting. A little sad. I offered to put them in touch with the man I'll introduce you to, but they weren't that interested."

"Lieutenant Graniela," I said. His eyebrows raised in question configuration. "The policeman who called you." He nodded.

"My brother, Dr. Herman Grue, he's the psychiatrist here, and he should be able to help you some on Tomanek."

"Your brother?"

"It does seem a bit nepotistic, doesn't it? But it's not that easy to get people to work here. It's a bit isolated, and it is Indiana, after all."

"Some people would consider that an advantage."

"Oh, it's pleasant enough. Especially if you can make it something of a haven for people you get along well with. Our cousin works here too. She's a nurse in Recket House. And her brother-in-law and his stepsister."

"Cozy."

"Yes, rather. But it's good for a family to work together."

"You aren't related to a Dr. Vurst, are you?"

"Ah, you met Dr. Vurst, did you?" He laughed. I laughed inside. Ha. "He's our worst doctor if I do say so myself."

"You wouldn't catch me saying it."

"Oh, I might, I might. Poor old Vurst, or Dick Sims as he was known to the outside world, when he was known to the outside world. He killed his sergeant in Korea. He's been here ever since. He does a marvelous German accent, doesn't he? Considering he's never heard one except on television."

I nodded. He got up. I got up.

"Let's go see Herman. He's the man who can help you."

I followed him to the reception room. The secretary offered us Chiclets. I refused. Mr. Grue accepted. "I'll have one and a half, thank you," he said. She poured out two and cut the second in half with a letter opener. We walked out the front, Grue chewing happily, me looking back to see what she did with the other half Chiclet. I saw. She put it back in the box.

"What relation is she?" I asked.

"Mistress," he said. "Is this your car?"

"Yes."

"Fifty-eight was a good year for Plymouths. Would you mind if we drove to see my brother?"

We drove to see his brother. Around the parking lot twice, and into a visitor's space at the end of the parking row opposite from the one we had set out from. A total distance of twelve car widths. We'd taken the scenic route.

"Nice year for Plymouths," he said. "But it's not tuned as well as it might be."

"I know," I said.

"Oh," he said.

Dr. Grue was with a patient, so we sat down and waited. It wasn't long. A door slammed. Then another door opened, the door we were waiting for. A craggy man in a blue sweater peered out. The elder brother. He said, "What's up, Mike? Your appointment isn't until five, is it? Who's that?"

I rather expected my Mr. Grue to come up with something cute and coy, but he just said, "This is Mr. Samson. He'd like to ask you some questions."

Herman Grue shrugged and retreated into his office.

Mike Grue turned without adieu in the other direction. I followed Herman into his inner sanctum.

"Well," he said. "Questions. Do you want the five-dollar version of our good works at Benjamin Johnson Hospital. Or the twenty-five-dollar saga? Or will you take this week's special, the fifty-dollar epic marked down to forty-nine ninety-five?"

I just stared at him. I was getting tired.

"Or perhaps," he continued unabashed, "you would like to know if we are all like this?"

"That would be interesting."

"Well, we are and we aren't. We don't get a lot of visitors, and the humor gets a little ingrown."

"Could I cultivate the answer to a question or two?"

"A serious man on a serious mission?" He sounded apologetic. A welcome sound.

"You might say so. And I did have a little warmup with a Dr. Vurst."

"Ahhhh. I suppose he led you away for a little chat."

"Yeah."

"All right. Let's start over. Query away."

"I need to know about Ralph Tomanek."

"Tomanek? Now if I remember correctly, my brother mentioned that we had a police inquiry about Ralph a few weeks ago. So who does that make you?"

I went through the routine again. I began to see myself applying for permanent quarters at the hospital, intent on spending the rest of my life accosting people and identifying myself.

"And he actually killed a man?" said Dr. Grue.

"He's charged with manslaughter at the moment. From the description of the remains I've read I think the charge was taken literally."

"But actually with a gun!"

It's a very popular technique. "It was while he was on his job. As an armed building guard."

"That, that is preposterous. Monstrous."

"What exactly was his problem, Doctor?"

He smiled, but professionally rather than gamesily.

"Your question asks for a more precise answer than I can give you."

I staged a sigh. "You know what I want to know. Perhaps you would frame the question for me in such a way that you will be willing to answer it."

He leaned back in his chair and for the first time took his eyes off my eyes. It was a pressure relieved. "I don't know how much you know about Ralph's history. . . ." I made a gesture to indicate I knew some, but he didn't see it. "But when he graduated from high school and got married, he never in the world suspected that he was going to get drafted."

"Why not? Every kid in this country is a draft lawyer these days."

"How can I explain? Ralph was not exactly a passive boy, but he was what you might call a good boy. In the kind of neighborhood he grew up in, around Brookside Park. In Indianapolis, do you know it?"

"I grew up in Indianapolis, too," I said.

"We don't have a lot of facts," he said. "By the time he got here Ralph was already very quiet about things that mattered to him."

"I don't need the case proved backwards and forwards. I desperately need to know your opinion of Ralph's problems or problem or whatever."

"Yes. All right. But you see, Ralph grew up without a father, and he was never what you could call physical. And I do know that he seemed to have a lot more friends among girls while he was growing up than he did among boys. Not determinate details, but for whatever reasons, Ralph grew up with nothing of the manipulator about him. He has never grasped the way that people or rules or the law operate in such a way as to allow him to use them for his own purposes. So without exactly being unaware of his draft liabilities he never once anticipated, before he was drafted, what being in the Army might actually entail."

"What, did he run when he first got shot at or something like that?"

"Without going through everything we've been able to reconstruct of his life in the Army, it led through the natural processes to his posting in Vietnam and to his seeing action there. He apparently did everything that was asked of him for several weeks. But the critical incident grew out of the kind of situation he'd been experiencing daily, and his reaction was quite the opposite to cowardice."

"And the incident?"

"Ralph's platoon was on patrol. They were walking in pairs, so each could defend the other's back. They were ambushed. Three men were hit on the first volley, and Ralph's partner was one of them. Part of his head was taken off. Ralph doesn't really remember it, but other members of the platoon say that when Ralph saw this guy at his feet, he sort of cracked up. He picked up the guy's rifle and ran straight at the VC fire. You've heard how ephemeral those ambushes are, how they evaporate under counterattack and you hardly ever see the enemy, much less get a good shot at him. Well, about an hour later they found Ralph four miles away. He was sitting on the ground hugging his knees, with not one, but two dead VC piled on top of each other at his feet. Both of Ralph's rifles were empty, and so was his handgun. It didn't take a medical expert to figure out where most of their contents had gone. That's the story."

And the good doctor had been telling it as if he'd been there.

"He wouldn't talk when they found him. He was hospitalized, and they tried to rehabilitate him for more active service. The Army apparently considered giving him a major decoration for his heroism, but when he stayed broken down, they couldn't. In the end they sent him back to this country, gave him a medical discharge, and made a special arrangement to have him sent here."

"And he stayed the same? Or got better?"

"I think we did pretty well by him. He was younger than most of the men we get here. He had a wife who cared, and though he stayed semipassive, he was certainly a far cry from the way his platoon found him that day."

"So he was well when you released him?"

"Well? We could never remove his sense of what he had

done. His guilt at being alive while the man protecting him was dead. His dismay that the Army lionized him for things he'd done the one time in his life he'd lost control. But the essential things that we helped him understand were that he was young and had a life ahead of him, that whatever was in store for him there was certainly no chance that in civilian life he'd be put in a circumstance which would bring out what he feared."

"But being an armed building guard was not the sort of job that he should have had."

"Definitely not. I'm sure he understood that. He knew he'd be all right in civilian life as long as he didn't go looking for trouble. His wife was really a great help, you know. It gave him someone to value, for the interim, while he couldn't value himself."

"Would a prospective employer be likely to find out about his mental situation?"

"I should think so. Veterans register with a placement bureau when they get back, and the bureau has a standardized evaluation form. Prospective employers have been getting rather knowledgeable about this sort of thing in the last few years, you know. Ralph's case—particularly as it contributes to his being unable to fulfill his civilian promise—is unfortunate. But it is by no means unique. Most men go through a period of depression and hopelessness when they get back. And quite a few have a hell of a lot of trouble."

"I know he was having a real hard time getting a job."

"It's a crime, of course. The one thing that would have brought Ralph back into the everyday world quickly was a reasonably good job that he could put his energy into. That he could focus on, say, to support his wife with. But the very unresponsiveness that a job would cure is what keeps him from getting the job in the first place. And employers are cagey about veterans. Most employers, given an application on behalf of a man like Tomanek, would smell trouble and ask for further details."

"Which they'd get?"

"Which they'd get."

* * *

After getting a promise of testimony for Ralph if it would be useful, I left Dr. Grue to the flaky humor of his daily life. He'd provided me with the first mitigating evidence I'd found for my man, though it was not for me to decide how and if it would be used.

I walked slowly to my car. I thought about my day. I hoped I would not be accosted by a Dr. Vurst. I was tired. I'd been through a lot for a sick man. I figured that if Vurst did come to meet me, I would kill him and fry him with an egg. That was the kind of mood I was in. An irrationally depressed hopelessness. Extended conversation about killing upsets my equilibrium. It makes me violent.

But instead of Vurst, the Administration door opened, and the little secretary bounced out to meet me. She wasn't entirely little. And she bore blandishments. For a second I was afraid she was going to run me down. She stopped closer to me than most strangers stop. But she didn't run me down. She extended hands full.

"Mr. Grue told me to give you these. This set of spark plugs. He says they're cleaned and set for a fifty-eight Plymouth. It's his hobby, you see." She dropped the lot in my hands. I caught a glimpse of two packets of Chiclets warming in her cleavage. Hot Chiclets, forsooth! An madhouse!

I drove very fast down the driveway out of the hospital grounds.

13

The sky was lighter as I headed back to town, but my net mood had darkened. The exertions of the day, the stoppings and startings of a life too structureless to provide smooth regular completions of its appointed rounds. I am not satisfied with myself when I am tired. I drove more slowly than I otherwise might have.

As I left Crawfordsville, I came face to face with a vision. A girl, auburn-haired and wearing lederhosen, was hitchhiking by the side of the road. Her thumb was insolent on the end of an arm held straight and high. You can't hold an arm like that very long. It was as if she was challenging the world to leave her there long enough for her arm to start hurting.

I took up the world's banner and its responsibilities. I stopped for her. Overshot her a bit and backed up. She was a personal vision. She reminded me of the first time I met my ex-wife, who also had beautiful auburn hair.

I rolled down the window. The hitchhiker stuck her unsmiling face in and said, "You going to Indianapolis?" Her accent was Eastern American College. I was disappointed. With the lederhosen I hoped for naturalized Austrian, at least.

She picked up her knapsack with one hand and then waited for me to open the door for her. I hesitated; she had a free hand, and I was a sick man. "For Christ's sake," she said. "I never been anyplace where they had so many hicks." Had I not borne the world's colors, I would have left her. But I opened the door, a last final gesture of respect for the mother of my only natural child.

This girl heaved the knapsack into the back and plopped herself in the passenger's seat next to me. She bounced up and down on it. "Nice comfortable seat," she said sarcastically. "They don't make them like they used to." I concentrated on getting back into traffic.

She said, "I don't know why I hitchhike. I really don't. I was coming up from Champaign—I know this swimmer there—and I get this guy, and I'm just getting comfortable, and he wants to put me out. I mean in the middle of the country, and it looks like rain. Christ!"

There was a break in front of a big truck which was laboring to get its speed up again after slowing down through town. I pulled out in the break and settled my impatient horsepower in line. The truck passed me. She said, "Christ!" Then she said, "What part of Indianapolis are you going to? Not some 'nice' little residential development on the outskirts somewhere filled with dowdy wives and little hick kiddies?"

"I live downtown," I said.

"Well, that's something!"

"My wife," I said, "she's gone crazy and she's in an asylum back in the town I just came from. She's a Chiclet fetishist."

"Christ! I get all the lulus!"

I concentrated on the behind of the truck that was gradually pulling out of sight ahead of me. I was tired of the world's mantle. I spoke no more with my hitchhiker. Any illusion of similarity between her and the woman I once loved had long since vanished. My ex-wife may have become a dragon when things didn't go so well for me, but I'd a lot rather be married to a dragon than a viper. At least with a dragon you always know where she is. What with the clumping around and the belching of fire.

I dropped the asp on Monument Circle. You can't get any closer to the middle of town than that. I even got her knapsack out for her. It's smart to keep on the good side of an asp. She left without a thank-you or a cheerio.

I was tired. I wanted to get home. I didn't know whether I had done a decent day's work or not, but I didn't much care. I was feeling residual fatigue. The excitement of being back to work was wearing off. The work of being back to work was coming on.

If it is possible to speed between Monument Circle and the corner of Ohio and Alabama in a '58 Plymouth, I sped. Got home about six.

About ten o'clock I woke up for a while. So she has a Chiclet fetish. Does that alone make her crazy? I didn't think so. Craziness isn't something different from what you find everyday. It's just a difference in proportion. If you walk around a mental hospital, the worst you will see is exaggeration of things you could walk around a hotel and see.

And Ralph Tomanek? Is he crazy? He got upset when he killed people and when he saw people he knew getting killed. He didn't forget it. He didn't like it. You can't really fault a guy for that.

I realized that the Easby Guards job must have been a nightmare for Tomanek. Hell revisited. The fact that he'd been able to bring himself to take it at all, to hold a gun in his hands, must have been, for him, a remarkable demonstration of his self-control. Of his reclamation from the salt brine of the submerged.

Under that assumption, his "mental history" spoke against the likelihood of losing control, of his finger itching. Mightn't a man in that position be more inclined just to let himself be shot than to go through the experience which had given him his personal nightmares, the sort of experience which had robbed him of his youth? Guilt in those lucky enough to survive a war is a well-documented cause of civilian suicide.

Just what would it have taken to make Ralph Tomanek enter again into a situation of death and counterdeath? To make him adequately self-controlled to kill someone?

I could hardly believe that he had not believed his life was in danger. His life? No, not necessarily that, but perhaps the life of the man he was charged with protecting. Ephray.

Perhaps the pressure of not having been able to find work between November and April, of erosion in the home by his mother-in-law after so much erosion before he got home, perhaps he had taken the job and decided to make the best of it. Perhaps the defense of Ephray had represented all his progress, all his freedom.

Not inconceivable. If he was determined that Ephray's life was indeed threatened.

I resolved to have a chat with Ephray.

And I spent a good long time thinking about whether I should get up and check my notes on Tomanek's version of what Ephray had said and done. Was I too tired to get up? I had almost decided when the phone rang. I fell asleep to its rhythmic ting-a-lings.

14

I had trouble buying a house that Thursday—from the man himself at any rate. Not that the office wasn't open. Not that two middle-aged and very plain ladies didn't offer, in unison, to let me speak to "our Mr. Robertson."

"I'm sorry," I said, "but my mother was very explicit. She will buy me a house only if I get it from Mr. Ephray himself."

"Oh," they said in unison. Then they looked at each other. One of them was slightly taller than the other. She deferred to the shorter, who said, "Well, Thursday is auction day. If I was you, I'd go to the auction gallery because by the time you got to the other real estate office, if you left now, he might have already left for the auction gallery, where you would be sure to catch him before the auction began if you left here now."

The taller colleague smiled beneficently.

"Well," I said, "Mother didn't say anything about auction galleries. Where is it?"

The taller one handed me a sheet of paper with a full headdress of titles, activities, and addresses around the name of Edward Ephray. It sufficed to get me to the auction gallery, which was on the north side, about two blocks from where the Booth Tarkington Civic Theater used to be.

It was not as old a joint as most auction palaces are. It looked as if it had been cleaned out and remodeled in the last ten years, either after a long and profitable lifetime or in an attempt to put some new life into it. I was increasingly curious about what Ephray had found to do in the Newton Towers at eleven fifteen on April 28.

Ephray Gallery was humming with people. Upstairs and down, two large rooms were filled with potential bargains. "Every Thursday, Modern and Antique Furnishings." One hopes not to get a modern antique.

I took a quick stroll around, to get the feel of the place. Pots and pans, motorless electric devices, china bric-a-brac, children's toys, living-room furniture. Just the sort of things for a private detective. The only thing I saw that I really fancied was a large, finely finished wooden pulpit. It was high, had lots of flat space on top for eating on, and had wheels to accommodate he who likes to rearrange what furniture he has. It turned out to be the auctioneer's lectern.

At the back of the first floor I found the office. There was a service window through which I saw two women and a man sitting stonily around a desk drinking coffee. No one seemed eager to serve.

I coughed. A rather stylishly dressed woman of about forty noticed me. So did the man. Simultaneously each poked an arm of the other lady and pointed to me. She got up and came to the window.

"What can I do for you? You can have a catalogue for a nickel. We do them in the order of their lot numbers, and we do a hundred an hour, hundred an hour. Got that?"

"Yes," I said, "but I want to see Mr. Ephray. I was told that I could see him here this morning."

"What's that?" she said. From a sweater pocket she pulled out the business end of a hearing aid. The end in her ear looked like part of a chain to keep her glasses on. I hadn't noticed it. I began to repeat my speech when the other woman got up and came to me. I stopped talking as she approached, and the first lady, having lost the dulcet sound of my voice, pushed the aid's microphone perilously close. The stylish woman shook her gently by the arm, which was adequate cue to rewrap the aid in the wire she'd unraveled, kitelike, to listen to me with. I felt kind of sorry for her as she went back to the table and took up her cup.

The woman who now confronted me had never been pretty but was in a phase of life where clothes and style were beginning to carry the day. She reveled in it.

"What do you want to see Mr. Ephray for?" she said.

"My mother is considering selling some of the things her grandmother left her. She'd like to have an idea of what they might bring at auction."

"What sort of things?"

"Mostly small, but very old. Some needlework, a hair wreath, some Civil War medals, two old clocks, some plates. There are about twenty things altogether, but they all date from before 1870, and they are all from Indiana, Illinois, or Ohio." They are. I was listing things my mother has, things it would be worth my life to get her to part with.

"Why would she want to sell them?"

"I think she thinks she is going to die soon, and she wants to leave my sister and me some money instead of knickknacks." If she only knew my mother. And my sister and brother—who would pick each other clean for the old family things.

"I see," said the lady. "Well, I can have one of our representatives call on your mother to explain our terms and have a look at the items. What day would be convenient?"

"She said that she would only see Mr. Ephray himself."

"Oh?" said the woman. The fur on the back of her neck stood straight out. "And why would that be?"

"She said," I said, "that she has had dealings with him before and that he was very helpful to her." I watched the hackles rise, the respiration rate increase.

"Oh?" she said.

I let her moult her displeasure. Then I said quietly, "If it is of any interest, my mother is seventy-eight years old."

I could see her assessing me. I look maybe forty-five. That would make my mother thirty-three when she had me. That would put her roughly where having a pre-Civil War grandmother would be perfectly possible. The lady began to relax again. My own conclusion was inescapable. The lady was Mrs. Ephray, and the lady was a jealous lady.

"I'll tell Mr. Ephray, and he'll be in touch with you. I'm sure he'll be pleased to know that he has a satisfied customer who insists on dealing only with him." Any but a detective's highly honed sensitivities might have missed the hostility which even now remained in her voice.

I helped her some more. "I don't want to waste his time unnecessarily," I said. "I could bring some of the better items to him, say, this evening. My mother will be happy enough as long as she knows I am talking to him personally. That would save him a trip all the way out to my mother's house."

The vision of her husband alone with my mother in a dark and distant house, no doubt very large and rife with bedrooms, agitated her once again.

"If you could bring them tonight about six, it would be appreciated."

"Fine," I said. She gave me the address, and I left her window for the long walk back through the gallery. I glanced back. She had returned to the table and was puffing on a cigarette *and* drinking her cold coffee. I wondered idly what it would be like to be married to a jealous wife.

In a flash I realized why I saw so many dowdy ladies in the offices of Ephray Enterprises. Mrs. E. was obviously personnel manager.

There would be no Alices in any of the Ephray Group.

Just outside the showroom I passed two men getting out of a gunmetal gray sports car. One was laughing loudly. He was thirtyish and had more clipboards, envelopes, and briefcases *in toto* than he could carry with distinction. The other was about five feet six, jolly-fat, and had a Vandyke beard. He looked about my age, and he dressed with authority. I heard him say, "So he says, 'But how do you know the guy who raped you was an idiot?' 'He had to be,' she says, 'I had to show him everything to do!' " The younger man struggled, either to contain or to maintain his mirth while balancing his chattels.

"Well," said the bearded man, contorting his voice to a mimicky twang, "let's us go sell some o' these here potatoes, hokay?"

By which time they had disappeared from my audio and visual range by passing into Ephray Gallery.

15

I drove back to town basking in accomplishment. I always feel good when I can find out things without leaving a name. I hold it as the rarely attained par of properly aggressive interviewing.

It was eleven o'clock when I rolled back into my parking niche. But I did not homeward turn after locking up. I went to call on the police.

The law of averages, as they say, was with me. Not that there is such a "law," or that if there is, it applies to the specific present rather than the aggregate past. At any accounting when I appeared at homicide not only was Mighty Joe Malmberg there, but my man Miller.

I could see across the room that Miller was not happy. The fact that I could see Miller across the room should have been enough for a deductive mind to figure why Miller was not happy. The office extension which had been the focus of much attention my last visit was now apparently complete. But Miller was sitting at his desk in the main room.

As I approached him, a lieutenant I didn't know walked by his desk and clucked sympathetically. Miller didn't look up. Miller just isn't like that.

I sat down in front of him. He'd been doing his whole month's doodles at once. There were pages—I could see five—in a neat and tidy stack. He was nearly finished with a sixth. The ream of blank paper near his creative site boded ill.

I watched for a minute. He wasn't entirely gone. He looked up. He said, "Hello, Al," as if he had expected me and I was right on time. It was like I had dropped in to console him at a funeral; only I didn't know who was dead.

Always cannily perceptive and tactful, I said, "Who died?"

He tried to smile. "I did."

"Well, that's a break. I was afraid I was going to have to get my tuxedo back from the hock shop." Pause. "What happened?"

He shrugged lightly, not expending much life energy. He tried not to speak, but I was a friend, I had asked, and I really had to be told. "I found out this morning," he said, "that my appointment may well not come through after all."

"I see. I'm sorry."

"Thanks, Al."

"Janie know?"

"Naw. I haven't had the heart to call her. She had my first year's raise spent, as well as half my pension."

From behind me, a voice, none too quiet, said, "Gee, Jerry, I only just heard. That's a tough break, I feel for you, fella."

Miller looked up and said, "Thanks for saying so, Bob." A captain whose back I did not recognize passed the side of the desk.

Miller's eyes followed him briefly and came back to me. "Was there something you wanted me to do for you?"

"You kill my landlord; I'll kill your mayor." It wasn't the world's best humor, I'll admit. "Actually I came in to see Malmberg, but I wanted to ask you first. Is there any special reason why so little work has been done in nearly four weeks on the Tomanek case? I mean, has there been some pressure or anything that isn't the way it seems from the records I read the other day?"

He looked at me warily. "You on to something?"

"Not exactly, but from what I've found out so far—and I'm only just beginning—there seems to be more going on than I would have gusssed."

"You think Tomanek didn't kill that private eye?"

"No, I think he killed him. I just can't write him off as crazy from what I read in that file. Certainly not without finding out who everybody else is and what they were doing."

"You mean Tomanek had some connection with the guy he killed? He did it on purpose?"

I sighed. "I didn't say anything of the sort." But I could

see him sopping it up, the light in his tunnel. "All I want to know is why nothing's happened since the first two days."

He was still suspicious. "There's nothing that's not in the report. Except for you, nobody's mentioned the case in two weeks." He looked at me like I was a big steak and he was trying to decide if he was hungry. "I can get back on the case," he said. "I can get it from Malmberg."

If he'd been in a better mood, I'd have teased him about trying to take Malmberg's lieutenancy away from him. I was in a bad spot. Some cases you work on and you get nothing but your pittance. Others seem to get you some reputation. My last work, the one I got hurt on, had given me some general credit among the local constabulary. Credit I had sorely lacked in the past. But now I was like a Broadway producer with a hot hit under his belt. I couldn't ask, "Who wrote that book?" without everybody wondering whether he could raise the money to buy the rights out from under me.

Some Broadway producers just like to read books. And I didn't want Miller, in his present mood, thinking that I had a superscheme to free Tomanek and pin the rap on the mayor. All I had was some questions. Like what was Lennox doing serving papers at eleven fifteen at night? And where was his witness? Simple questions just to fill in the holes of why everybody was there, what they were doing, where they had come from, where they were going. That sort of thing.

"I can get the case, Al. I can get it back. Just say the word."

"Don't bother, Jerry. I haven't got anything but questions. No hint of an answer."

"But you don't see it the way that it looks in the report, right? You don't see Tomanek as just a psycho with an itchy finger, right?"

"Christ, I'm working for the man. I'm being paid to see everything different."

"But you think it might not be the way it looks? I mean possibly not, right?"

"Well, I guess so. I don't know."

"Right. I'll get in on it. It can't hurt, can it? It'll be something to take my mind off, well, these." He waved doodles at me. "You just tell me what you want to know. Everything. And this afternoon I'll read the file and ease myself in. It can't hurt, and then, if there is anything, you know, that won't hurt either. There'll be some for Malmberg, and there'll be some—" He shrugged innocently, grasping for words.

"For Lieutenant Miller."

"I have to admit, I had gotten used to the sound of it."

"Here lies Jerry Miller," I said, "last of his race to make lieutenant."

The man wanted some questions to answer for me. And questions roll off me like aqua off a quacker. He took up his pen and reached for a fresh sheet of paper.

16

When I emerged from the police station to the cheers of the downtown throngs, it was nearly one o'clock. I felt good. Good enough to consider taking the afternoon off. But self-control was not far behind. All I had to do was remember the time I'd passed detailing nuances to Dr. Vurst. Just how do you bill a client for that? "0.5 hours: explanation of case to nut. $2.19."

Speaking of clients, it had been two days since I'd seen Rosetta Tomanek. I thought about going out to see her. To assure her that if she didn't hear from me for days at a time, it didn't mean that I didn't love her. Private detectives need a bedside manner too, you know. When they're lucky.

I decided to call her instead.

I called her from home. It was just as well because the amount of time which elapsed between someone answering the phone and Rosetta Tomanek's being told about it would have caused an operator to decide the line was dead. Rosetta did finally talk to me. I suppose the holdup was that she was trying to find a well-stamped customer a guacamole serving dish when all they had in stock were dishes for chutney.

"Has something happened to Ralph, Mr. Samson?" She sounded worried. I was sorry I'd called.

"Excuse me, Mrs. Tomanek. It's not an important call. Nothing has happened to Ralph. It just occurred to me that I should make clear that I'm working on the case, but that you shouldn't hope for any real results soon. A lot of the preliminary work on a case always sounds more slight than it really is."

"I'm glad nothing's happened to Ralph," she said. "He's not in very good spirits."

"I'm sorry if I've disturbed you. I just thought it would be better than calling you at home." I wished I had professionaled it out. Strong and silent.

"I appreciate that," she said quietly. "You would have heard from me soon anyway."

"I would?"

"I wrote you a letter."

"You did?"

"I thought about what you said. When you drove me home. About needing to know what sort of man Ralph is. So I wrote you about him. I tried to explain something about Ralph. Not much, I can't explain it all. But I tried. I know what a busy man you are and that you have other cases besides mine, but I hope you will try to find time to read it."

"Of course I will, Mrs. Tomanek."

"Well, thank you. I'm glad you called. But please do excuse me. My employer gets very nervous."

So does your employee, Mrs. T. A letter? At least it would be mail.

While I was on the phone, I called my woman. I was glad of that call. It showed that even when I am working, I still think of her and remember her birthday. We decided I would be allowed to stop over after dinnertime. What better present for a widow lady? Take me, I'm yours, I would say. Knowing full well that she has the better sense about such things.

I went back down to the car. Two things that I definitely had to do were to acquire some Hoosieriana and eat some lunch. The best place I could think of to do both was my mother's.

Bud's Dugout, out Virginia Avenue a ways, past the tracks. The place was half full. Maybe three-fifths. Lunchtime. All four pinball machines were occupied, so I went into the back, which may be the weirdest cross between a parlor and a pantry in existence, but she has it laid out exactly as she wants it. Meat freezer here, tea table there. Loose-leaf notebook of postal chess games on the mantel. Financial records of the church auxiliary group in a file underneath a file of the financial records of the luncheonette underneath a file of the letters she's received in the last seven years or so. And on the filing cabinet, a pie rack.

Something to serve each portion of her life. I relaxed on the chair she keeps for me.

About one forty-five she brought in a bowl of chili and a mug of tea. "That's the shirt I got you for Christmas, isn't it?" she said, and returned to her public.

I took care not to spill chili on the shirt. Not everyone is so deft as I.

I set the empty cup and bowl on the floor and drifted near to sleep.

At what must have been almost three I heard tinklings from the luncheonette. Ma was fixing the bell to the door, so the rush was over. She came back to me before I was roused enough to go out to her.

"Heard from the child?" She sat on her "resting stool"—near enough to the diners, but definitely resting.

"Not recently, no." She was asking after her granddaughter. Not her only grandchild, but her only granddaughter. She despairs the modern trend to small families among ambitious people. Would that the smallness of my family were from ambition.

"Where is she?"

"Switzerland, I think, for the summer. Or if it isn't summer yet, then the Bahamas."

"You might just as well as died, for all the chance you'll get to see her again."

"One of these years, Ma. They work on a two-year schedule. Next year they have the whole spring and half the summer in Connecticut. I'll see her then."

"You bring her out here."

"OK."

"She can stay with me."

"OK." And because it had reminded me, I said, "I'll write her a good long letter." When routine is interrupted, it takes you awhile to work yourself back into all the little obligations of life, even the pleasant ones. I am not normally the sort of man to forget a birthday or to delay writing a letter to my only child and heiress. "I need to borrow some of your things for a day or two," I said.

She knew which things. She knew she didn't want them out of her sight. She knew I knew she didn't want them out of her sight. She knew I wouldn't ask unless I thought it fairly important. So after a deep breath she just said, "Which ones?" I told her. She took another deep breath and got them for me.

I spent a good visit. It had been quite awhile. There was a lot to hear about the work and workings of the vixens and shrews and angels and hypocrites of my mother's acquaintance.

I left just as the four copies of the Indianapolis *News* arrived, about five fifteen. She gets them for her evening clientele. I asked if I could have one. She said, "No." Fair enough. I could pick one up if I was so fascinated.

I wasn't so fascinated. I was more fascinated to get on to my good friend Ephray.

17

Edward Ephray's address—2835 Davis Road—didn't mean anything to me. No sweat, I have a map. Except when I got to the car, I found I didn't have a map. I'd left it in the office, filed under "D.A." Detective Aid. I didn't know whether to be annoyed with myself or not. I wouldn't know until I found out where Davis Road was whether I was taking myself vastly out of my way to go home to find where I should be going.

I eased gently into my parking niche. As I walked past the elevator to the stairs, I was in a vaguely disquieted mood. The flush of the morning had quite escaped me; I couldn't remember what I had been so proud of myself about.

Or maybe my disquiet was something else. Some sense of more immediate anticipation. A sense of somebody. A fear of a surprise.

I walked down the hall slowly. Nothing seemed amiss. Just bad vibes. Can one vibe with one's office? I was afraid, somehow, of what I might find when I went in. Call it a hunch. Of what circumstance in combination with coincidence might be cooking up for me.

I listened outside my door. Nothing.

I took a breath; I turned the handle. It was unlocked. But it is always unlocked. It doesn't lock. Usually I am pleased by that; somehow it befits someone whose business is a service.

I resolved to have a big lock with a six-digit combination slapped on the door in the morning. If I was alive in the morning.

I pushed the door open in front of me. At least it didn't squeak. It used to squeak, but when I was recuperating at home, I fixed all the little things like that.

I peeked through the hinge crack between the open door and the wall. No one behind the door. I glanced around the room. Nowt. That made it my inner room, my living room. The room I daydream in and sometimes call out loud in my sleep in. How dare anyone muck around in *that* room?

I threw caution to the wind. I whipped its door open, jumped in, and threw myself against the wall next to the door.

Nothing. No sound. And then the crash of one hand thunderclapping. A book fell on the floor to my left. I had knocked it from its precarious perch on the edge of a shelf by throwing myself, with violence, against the wall that was the shelf's support.

I just stood, sweat wetting the wall I was now supporting. I watched the book. Waiting for it to jump back to the shelf for another take or for it to hop around. Or anything.

The room was absolutely devoid of human life, save what portion of myself I now classed as human.

Why does the world put men into children's work? No one in his right mind becomes a private detective by choice.

Except me.

Perhaps not an exception to the statement.

The problem is that when a man values his sensitivities, his hunches, he becomes to some extent the servant of them.

I was less embarrassed by my kiddy exercise than perhaps I should have been. I wrote it off as a hazard of the suspiciousness of my so-called profession; I wrote it off to living too much alone.

And if I hadn't been sweating, I might have been able to tell myself that I had never believed there was anyone there. But I was sweating; I am not brave in the face of danger, real or imagined. Not gratuitously brave, anyway.

I found the map, in the office desk drawer. I found Davis Road, mostly east and a little bit south. If they'd only said it was the next one past the Post Road, I would have known. If they'd only said it was on a line with Mitthoeffer Road. . . .

I went back to the car, drove to my neighborhood gas station to fill up with gas and oil for the evening's excursion. And I set off out U.S. 52.

I didn't look at my watch until I'd made the right turn onto Davis Road. I was late. It was about six twenty. I wondered if it would make a difference. It made a little difference to me, I wouldn't be able to drive around the neighborhood, scout it, as I might have done otherwise. What neighborhood there was. Davis Road is not exactly the most densely populated part of town.

2835 was a well-defined property. Bounded by hedges, labeled with big numbers over a drive-through gateway. It was set well back from the road. There seemed to be land to burn.

The house itself was a modern hybrid, sort of Georgian-ranch style, insofar as such could exist. Not totally unfitting for someone who made lots of new money by selling old property and goods.

I pulled up on a large gravel rectangle laid out by the side of the house. I gathered up my mother's memorabilia and stepped into the twilight. I rang at the door. It was answered quickly. My hostess, the well-cared-for lady from the auction office, let me in. She was dressed to the gills. I was worried that maybe I should have gone to the delivery entrance.

"You are late," she said, "and we're very nearly late. We're going to a dinner where Edward has to make a presentation. He can only give you a few minutes."

"I am saving him a trip by coming here, Mrs. Ephray."

"I know. This way, please."

At least she didn't ask me why I'd been late. Chasing shadows is not the kind of excuse everyone will appreciate. She led me down a spacious hallway to a T junction. At which we turned left and walked down a narrower hall to a closed door. I could hear rough noises from inside the appointed rooms. I felt too encumbered to face someone making rough noises, but Mrs. Ephray knocked on the door anyway.

It opened. Mrs. Ephray said, "Have you been kicking furniture again, Edward? What can't you find?"

"A black clip-on to go with this shit-ass suit." The tubby little man with the Vandyke beard I'd seen going into

Ephray Gallery stood before us. The joke teller. He was wearing most of a tuxedo and not looking so jokey.

"Well, I'll look around while you talk to the gentleman."

"Well, hurry the fuck up, will you?" he said to his wife. As she departed, I stood in the doorway holding the cardboard box of my mother's things. "Come in," said Ephray. "Come in. Just a little trouble. I have to make an award at a fucking dinner tonight, and I can't get up in front of people with a tuxedo jacket and a fucking everyday tie."

"No, you can't," I said.

"I mean, suppose I wore this one." He picked up a black tie from the top of a chest of drawers and gave it to me. It was a necktie, but it caught me off guard. On the front was a startlingly realistic picture of a naked lady. "The fellas would like it better, but I would look like a real dumb ass," he said. "Edna said you wanted me to look at some things," he said. "By the way, I'm Eddie Ephray. Glad to meet you."

When in Rome. "Al Samson," I said pumping his hand after putting down his tie. "Glad to meet cha. These are the things, the ones my mother is thinking about selling."

I put the box down where he could look in, and in a manner much more delicate than I would have given him credit for, he examined the articles one by one. "I'm not the real expert," he said, "but they look pretty good. We've been getting pretty good prices for this old Americana stuff lately. I think it's in style."

"Gee, that's good to hear," I said. "Do you have any idea how much they'll bring?"

"I don't really know. I've got a guy called Morton who is my expert, but I'd expect four or five hundred. But you really should bring them in and let old Morton have a look at them."

"Tell you what I'll do, Eddie. I'll have a talk with my mother, and then beginning of next week I'll bring them in."

"Check," he said. "Afternoons Monday or Tuesday is best."

"Righto. Hope you have a real good dinner."

"Ah, fuck it, that tie. Where the hell is that woman?" He kicked the hell out of a dresser drawer leg.

"It's the little things in life that give you trouble," I said, and left the room protecting my mother's precious things.

I met Mrs. Ephray in the hall. Edna. "I'll show you out," she said, but first darted into Eddie's room to give him a tie. Where a clip-on tie had been that wasn't where it was supposed to be I didn't know.

"There we are." Edna Ephray rejoined me, and we walked together back to the wide entrance hall and then back to the front door. But she didn't whisk me out. "Might I look at the things you brought?"

"Sure."

"Let's go in here," she said, and led me through a closed door into what had to be the biggest dining room in town. It looked like a ballroom. Elizabeth Bennet would stand here; Fitzwilliam Darcy thus.

She led me to the long dining-room table, and I put down my box. She examined my mother's items one by one, as carefully as her husband had done. "They're very nice," she said at the end.

"You know a lot about antiques?" Then it struck me that there wasn't an old thing in the whole room.

She smiled politely. "I do my very best to keep knowledgeable about my husband's businesses. I think it helps keep two people together, don't you?"

"Definitely."

We exchanged formal valedictories, and I left.

18

The drive back to town wasn't long enough. I had too many things to do on it. I had to figure out how to celebrate my fair maid's annum. I had to decide what to do with my mother's valuable possessions, whether to continue this little game of selling them. And I had to think about what, if anything, I had gained by successfully entering the Ephray household.

I felt that I understood the lady better than the gentleman. But that was perhaps because she acted much more like a lady than he did like a gentleman.

I could make a decent case for him being out of place. Out of place in a ballroom, out of place in a tuxedo, out of place in such a big, fancy house unless he was doing a lot better than the two offices I'd seen looked.

It was interesting. People out of place are. I couldn't say I was any closer to knowing whether he was capable of lying to the police or, indeed, whether he had lied. Much less to a reason.

I stopped at the Irvington Shopping Center. I did a short tour. Boozery first. Nearly made a mistake there. Nearly bought champagne. If I had, she would have known for sure that I had forgotten it was her birthday. A thirty-ninth is just not a champagne birthday—like a first. I ended up with a bottle of hard cider. Genuine English Somerset Cider.

And flowers.

Then I went to the drugstore, for a trinket. It's always nice to be given a trinket on a birthday.

But I never bought a trinket. While I was there, I picked up a *News*. On the front page it said: "Four Police Promotions." There were pictures. And last, but not least, was the picture of a new police lieutenant: Gerald Arthur Miller. It wasn't a smiling picture, but I knew that wherever he was he was grinning to beat the band.

So I joined him. I smiled, and I dashed straight to the car to be off to my birthday girl.

I forgot to pay for the paper.

19

In the morning I stopped at home to lock my mother's valuables in the closet I use as a darkroom. After changing clothes, I headed for the police station.

It was Friday. I'd put in three full days of work, and I still couldn't say I knew much. Why Ephray was at Newton Towers that night when he had a nice house not far from town. Why Lennox had been there. I've served enough legal papers in my time, but very few at eleven at night. Not to someone like Ephray, who was so available around town.

Not that I even knew for sure that the paper had been for Ephray. It would be interesting if it had been intended for Ralph Tomanek.

My sympathetic feelings for Tomanek had diminished somewhat as I got further from talking to him and thought more about the hard fact of what he had done. Anyone can *not* pull a trigger. It takes very little talent.

Miller was not visible. I asked if he was in. The receptionist said he was. At least on shift for the day, but she didn't know where. Whether he was in the building or out on his first case. Nor did she know trivia like when he would be back. I gave her an insolent message to lay on him, and then I asked after Malmberg. She checked and found he wasn't in either. I asked her for his home address, but she wouldn't give it to me. I asked her for her home address; she wouldn't give me that either. I asked if I could tell her about the case I was working on and solicit her advice. She didn't want to be solicited. I asked her how she came to be a policewoman. She said she drifted into it after she got out of the Army.

I was in a kind of feverish mood. I was annoyed all over again that the police hadn't done a decent job on the case background in the first place. I knew the reasons; I just didn't like them.

I went outside, to the nearest phone booth. I waited several seconds while a teen-age girl giggled and scratched her backside against the door. I went to the next nearest phone booth. My luck was in. It was both empty and had the directories still in it. I looked up Oscar Lennox to get his office address. And for the heck of it I dialed the phone number.

It rang. And rang. And then was answered. A sweet female voice. My favorite. It said, "Hello?"

I asked for Lennox. If I could get in touch with him, it had to be worth something.

She said, "I'm afraid I have some bad news for you."

I said, "Oh? I hope it isn't too bad. I haven't been having a very good day." For the heck of it, right?

"Well, it's not very good," she said haltingly.

"I can take it, I guess. Tell me. He's gone to South America, and I'll never collect the seventeen fifty he owes me."

"I'm afraid he's gone farther than that. He got *murdered!*"

"No!"

"I'm afraid so. Yes." It was a very sweet voice.

"Well, that's too bad."

"Oh, it's awful. I mean I never knew when I got this new phone number that I would be getting the number of a *dead* man."

"That must have been a shock. Do you get a lot of phone calls for him."

"Oh, not recently. You're the first for, I guess, nearly a week. But I've only had the phone number for about three and a half weeks. I must have told, oh, lots of people. And some ladies too."

"I guess everyone was shocked."

She hesitated. "Well, I wouldn't like to say anything against the dead. But I gather he was a detective, you know, a *private* detective, and, well, there were a few people who sounded *happy* when I told them."

"Gee!"

"I think that's kind of sad, don't you?"

"Oh yes."

"To tell the truth, there was only one or two who said anything nice about him at all. I really wonder how a body can go through life and leave so many people that when they call me aren't unhappy to hear of the body's decease, if you know what I mean."

"Oh, I know just what you mean. But you would have thought that most people would have seen about it in the newspaper."

"You know I thought that. I mean *I* saw about it, and I never dreamed for a minute that when I put in for a new phone number, I would be getting that murdered man's phone. I mean there are things that happen on a girl's phone that you just have to have a new number, if you know what I mean. But a number you've read about in the paper, well! I never dreamed. Of course it wasn't a very big article in the paper."

"It wasn't?"

"Oh, no, just little stories. They didn't even say he was a private detective."

A woman banged her umbrella handle on the phone booth door behind me. It was a sunny day. I ignored her.

"I wonder why not. You'd think that would be one of the first things they'd say."

"Well so would I, but I gather"—and her voice hushed—"I gather that he was killed by a maniac and that they didn't want to get people upset. I mean they caught the man and all, but well. . . ."

She paused. I said, "Yes, that makes sense," but I think she had run out. The woman with the umbrella banged again. I didn't like that, but what can you do? I said, "I'm sorry to have taken up so much of your time. Thank you for telling me about Mr. Lennox. I'm very sad to hear it."

"That's OK," she said. "I wasn't doing anything else much. Just washing my hair."

"Bye-bye."

After I hung up, I tried to think of someone else to call but let it ride. I would be replaced by a woman who would bang on the phone with her umbrella.

I opened the door. But the woman, instead of entering wherein I departed, spoke to me. "Are you deaf? I tried to get your attention in time, but it's too late now. Too late." She gestured to a Volvo parked at the meter nearest to the phone booth. A ticket writer was writing a ticket. The meter had expired. Oh horror of horrors. I didn't speak. The woman abhorred a vacuum. "I tried to get your attention when he first spotted it. If you had not been so engrossed with whomever you were speaking to, you could have saved yourself a fine."

I put my hand up to my ear and said, "What's that, lady? What you say? I find it hard to hear you because I've got a banana in my ear."

I walked away quickly.

What the heck.

20

The late Oscar Lennox, private detective, was just like me: He worked out of the same building he lived in. I admit to a few differences, however. Like the fact you could put my whole office-apartment into one of Lennox's downstairs rooms. Like he had a whole two-story house to call his own. Like his income must have averaged twenty times mine over our respective careers.

There were other differences, too. He worked out of Selwood, a little town southeast of Indianapolis proper. That might seem unusual—Selwood ain't a town big enough to support me, much less Lennox—except that it dovetailed with another difference between us. Lennox worked only on divorce work. People who are anxious to maintain strict secrecy regarding their suspicions often feel safer hiring investigators from out of town. Lennox had an Indianapolis phone number and a Selwood address—a most appealing combination to a lady who wants the goods on her lord.

I got to Selwood a little after noon and didn't have any trouble finding the Lennox building. It was on the end of the main road shops. Probably when he bought it, there had been residences between him and town, but the commercial district had grown to meet him. There was a newly built plumbing supplies store on the adjacent land and a café right across the road.

It's not that there was a uniformed guide to take me around the house when I pulled up in front of it. What I knew I'd learned from his ad in the Yellow Pages. And from walking around the outside of his house. I tried the door, for kicks. For kicks it was locked.

It was twelve thirty. I decided to be hungry. I crossed the street to the Travelers' Rest Café.

While I was waiting on the white line in the middle of the road for a snub-nosed blue panel truck to pollute me, I saw a man watching me from the café window. I felt a momentary urge to tap dance. But it subsided as the truck wheezed by. Just as well; I don't know how to tap dance. The kid next door got lessons when he was eight, but I didn't.

As I came toward the door, the man retreated. I found him behind the counter as I walked in. I sat down at one of the dozen available tables. A woman came in through a door behind him; she seemed in a hurry until she saw me. Then she hesitated but came all the way out front and stood with the man. They exchanged guarded looks; I wondered whether they'd been about to close the joint for half an hour for a midday quickie.

Ever tactful, I asked, "Are you open for lunch?"

The woman, middle-aged, middle everything, came around the counter toward my table. "Yes, oh, yes. We're open, ain't we, Paw? What'll you have?"

"Whatever you reckon is special today, with coffee."

"What's special today, Paw?"

"Mighty good roast pork, Maw, unless the stranger is Jewish or something."

"You Jewish or something?"

"If the roast pork is special, I'll have it. And coffee first, if you don't mind. Cream but no sugar."

"No sugar on the coffee, Paw."

"No sugar," said Paw. "Got it." He drew the coffee and brought it to me while Maw retreated to her demesne.

Things didn't seem what one might call congenial, but it had to be done.

"Thanks," I said as he set it down in front of me. "I've been across the street there." Rude or not, I pointed. "You don't know whether the house is for sale, do you, or who I'd go to . . . talk to about it?"

He cocked his head and looked at me. "You thinking of buying it?"

"You got it."

He looked back to the kitchen door. Then back at me. "Wal, it is vacant."

"It sure is."

Simultaneously Maw reappeared from the kitchen, and I heard car tires skidding to a halt. Out front I saw a policeman slam his car door with one hand and loosen his holster flap with the other. He was standing in front of me quicker than Maw could draw Paw out of the line of fire.

Strange policemen with loosened flaps are not my favorite luncheon companions. I kept my hands in sight, on the table. I didn't sip my coffee coolly: My hand would have shaken and spilled it. I hadn't realized it was a crime for someone with a Jewish great-grandfather to order roast pork in Selwood. I'll never do it again, Officer.

Paw spoke first. "It may not be what we thought, Bob. But this is the fella."

The state fuzz looked down over his bay window at me. "We'll see, Mr. Mason. OK, son, let's see your driver's license, if you please."

There were a number of legal niceties which the bay-windowed gentleman was bending. I mean, my driver's license! Surely such is not required for a meal in a café. I would have debated the subject with him at length, but my recent injury had left me in a weakened condition. I handed him my wallet.

He studied it. "Samson, Albert R.," he said. When he said, "Oh-ho!" I knew that he'd found my license. "This feller is a licensed private detective. Look at this, Mr. Mason."

But Mr. Mason was not keen to look. Without hesitation he said, "Then I'm sure it's all right, Bob. Before you got here, he said that he was thinking about buying old Mr. Lennox's house that he was looking at across the street. I'm sure it's all right."

Bob looked at me and then took a look through the window at Lennox's. "Mr. Lennox was a *de*tective, too, wasn't he?"

"That's right, Bob," said Mason.

"Oh, I see." He turned back to me. "You was thinking that maybe because Mr. Lennox did so good there that maybe now as he was dead you might buy the place and take over where he left off."

Far be it for me to be subtle. "Yes." It was one of the few situations in God's Indiana in which being a private detective actually increased my credibility.

"I'm sure it's all right, Bob," said Mason. "Sorry to have troubled you. You stop in again soon now, hear?"

"Yes, sir, Mr. Mason," said Bob, understanding he was being told to leave. "No trouble at all." He left. I watched. Before he got in the car, he fastened his flap. I sipped coffee.

Mason looked at his wife and sent her back to the kitchen. Time to roast a pork. I would have bet she hadn't been making any progress on my meal. I *was* hungry.

"Friendly place," I said.

"I am sorry about that, Mr. Samson," said Mr. Mason. "Thing is that with houses in town that ain't got nobody living in them people kind of look out, you know, for trouble. We don't really want to let one of these places go and become a co-moon for *hippies*."

"I understand. I saw a German hitchhiking on the road the other day." Well, a girl in lederhosen, close enough.

"We haven't had any trouble from your Germans here," he said seriously. "Not yet. But if you're thinking of buying the place, like you said, why I'm happy to give you any help I can. I don't rightly know who's in charge of Mr. Lennox's estate, but I'll try and find out. Maw!" Her head popped through the swinging door. "Maw, you call up Mayor Paley there in town and see if he knows who is in charge of Mr. Lennox's house now." Her jaw dropped. I saw why he called her "Maw."

"Mr. Lennox is dead, then," I said. "How'd he die?"

"Oh, natural," said Paw without hesitation.

I nodded solemnly. "Did he live in town long?"

"Now let me see. Maw and I took this place in 1951, and I think Mr. Lennox had been here five or six years then."

"You must have got to know him pretty well."

"Not real well. I knew some of the people who worked for him better. Secretaries, you know, would come over here for coffee or whatnot. And for a while there he had some men working for him. Other detectives, I guess. Working on cases and such. But Mr. Lennox didn't come over here very much. Not a neighborly man. I couldn't say he was unneighborly, but I never did know him very well. Kept to himself."

"Did the secretaries live in town?"

He squinted at me, an easy man to make suspicious. "Oh, I see. You're thinking about if you take over the place, you're going to need some secretaries, too." He paused. "Well, sir, to tell the truth, the secretaries as Mr. Lennox had did some of them come from town here. But I don't know if any of them would still . . . well."

"I don't know," I said.

"Mr. Lennox did real well financially here up to 1965."

"What happened then?"

"He lost his license to be a detective. Surely did."

"Really? Do you know why?"

"It was in the papers. I know what it said there. Seems he told somebody besides his client some things he shouldn't have done."

I nodded. "Indiana state law says a private detective can only tell the things he finds out to his client or the police."

"Well, that's what he must have done."

"What happened to him?"

"Well, nothing much. He just retired. Had to let his secretary go, but she said he said he'd been thinking about retiring anyway, and this just helped him make the decision. Well, you never know, but that's what she said he said. But lately I think he was getting a little hard up."

"Why?"

"Well, for the first couple of years he kept driving new cars like he did every year since Maw and I moved in here, but about two years ago, maybe three, he didn't get a new car, and he was still driving the old one till the day he died."

"Does his last secretary still live in town?"

"She does, yes." He thought. He turned. He called, "Maw! Maw!"

After a moment the lady in question came through the door balancing a broad blue plate and a little blue bowl. The pottery she set down before me. Roast pork, mashed potatoes and peas on the side. "Yeah, Paw?" she said. "Mayor Paley says he don't know who owns the place now, but he'll try to find out and call back."

"You remember that girl was secretary to Mr. Lennox before he retired? Where does she work now?"

Maw thought. "Let's see, that would be Janny, the Crocketts' girl. I don't remember what her husband is called. But she went to Mr. Dunn and, right, she works for that lawyer, Cranbrook. The office is down by the bus station." Maw smiled.

"Mr. Samson here is thinking about whether he'll be able to hire local people as secretaries and whatnot to help him in his detective work if he takes over for Mr. Lennox."

"Well, he'll have to see Wallace then, won't he?" said Maw.

"I forgot." He turned back to me. "There's someone you'll have to see. Wallace Ridgelea, the photographer. I know for a fact that Mr. Lennox did a lot of business with Wallace. And didn't Wallace say, right in here, that Mr. Lennox retiring hurt his business? Wallace would be glad to see you, if you was thinking of taking up where Mr. Lennox left off. I'm sure of that."

"He would," said Maw.

"Where can I find him?"

"Well, he's got his store down by the bus station, too. You can't hardly miss it."

"Good," I said. "I'll stop in."

"You ain't a girl, so you'll be safe enough."

Maw was not pleased. I guess it was because she was a girl. "Now you shut your mouth," she told her husband. "Let the man make up his own mind. And let him eat his lunch before it gets absolutely stone cold."

"Another cup of coffee, Mr. Samson?" asked Paw.

"Right," I said handing him the cup.

"No sugar," he said.

I ate my roast pork. Cool.

Mayor Paley didn't call back while I was with the Masons, so before I left, I took down their phone number.

21

It turns out that most things in Selwood are by the bus station. I had a choice of two. I decided to park and let fate decide whether I tried the ex-secretary or the ex-photographer. Fate brought me first to Ridgelea Studios.

It was a somber place not enlivened by a thousand pictures of smiling children crammed into a window whose frame was decaying. People in Selwood obviously paid for the product, not the wrappings.

I suppose there is some tie-in between pictures of children and pictures of making children. I didn't know exactly what sort of photographic evidence Lennox and Ridgelea went in for. Certainly there is not much bursting in on the guilty couple these days. More pictures of people going in and then coming out. Let the happy faces tell the story. At least that's what I've always done on such divorce work as I've had. I'm not really the bursting type. Sneak stealthily, perhaps. Or install remote control equipment in color and porno-vision. But not burst. I'd blush.

Ridgelea looked like he'd blush, too. About five feet ten, maybe a hundred and ninety-five. Arched brown eyebrows supporting hair like amber waves of grain. It was probably touched; he exuded softness. I made him fifty or fifty-five. He sat at a desk in his reception room, behind his reception girl *cum* secretary. I don't know how I knew it was him, but I did. When I asked the girl for Mr. Wallace Ridgelea, she pointed to him. I could feel it, a proper hunch.

"What can I do for you?" he asked professionally.

"The name's Samson," I said. "I'd like to speak to you in private."

He turned to his employee and put a hand on her shoulder. "When's my next, Susan?"

Susan thumbed through an appointment book. "The Drax boy, four fifteen."

To me he said, "That's convenient. I can talk to you now."

"I understand you used to work with Oscar Lennox. I'm a private detective; I'm thinking about buying up his property and setting up in the same business."

He turned on his heel and retreated through a doorway. I followed him. We walked in file through a kiddy playground, which must have been where he did his studio work. He had some neat toys. There were stairs at the back of the room. They went over the seesaw. We took them, passed through a baffle door into a well-equipped laboratory. Out of Susan's eavesdropping range.

He pulled out two high stools and sat on one himself.

"Oscar's death sure was a shock," he said.

"I never knew him. But I understand you worked with him for quite a while."

He looked at me and was silent. I guess that means he was studying me. I sat still, didn't move or change expression. *I* think it looks inscrutable.

"I suppose," he said slowly, "that private detectives tend to keep sort of informal tabs on each other, sort of keep up on what the other fellow is up to."

Sounded like a good idea to me. "I suppose."

"That's probably why you knew to come to me."

"Well," I said. "I've been in the business in Indianapolis for eight years." It was true. I thought it might mean something to Ridgelea. What, I hadn't the faintest idea. He knew things I wanted to know, and the less specific I was, the more he would think me undeceivable. When you are outside a profession like mine, it is a lot easier to believe that there are trade secrets which practitioners share than if you are inside it. I mean, did he think we held monthly meetings at the Atheneum or something?

He helped. "And it's time to think about expansion. That's what Oscar used to say. The big boys have the straight town trade pretty well sewed up."

"You can't help but be interested in the kind of money Lennox made," I offered.

He snorted. "Damn right. You get used to steady money even if you have to work for it." We stared at each other for maybe five seconds. It was long enough for me to think of Cagney. I cracked a little smile.

"This isn't getting us anywhere fast," I said. "Are you good?"

"Oscar never complained. If the pictures were there, I always got them."

"Did you do *all* his work for him?" My intonation begged for salacious detail.

But he didn't quite get what I meant. "Well, I opened here in fifty-six and. . . . Oh, you mean. . . . Oh. Yes. All his work. Plenty anyway. All of it as far as I know."

"Maybe you better tell me exactly what sort of work you did for him."

"It's no secret why he lost his license," said Ridgelea. He tapped a developing tank with his little finger.

"Tell me about it," I said. I tried very hard to act as if I already knew. As if I was the tough guy and he was the dirty rat.

"I'm sure, being in the same business, you know more than I do. Oscar got a lot of divorce work, and most of it he would do straight. But every now and then a case would come in that he figured he could make some extra on. Like sometimes we would get the evidence on a husband for his wife, and then Oscar would go to *him* and say, 'Look, your wife wants a divorce, and I can give her enough proof to get it. What's it worth to you not to be divorced?' Then the guy would pay Oscar to rig a different report to give to the wife. One that had pictures of him working late at the office or something. Something conclusive to give him a clean bill of health."

"For which he'd make a little extra."

Ridgelea smiled. "I used to go out again and take pictures of the same guy in all the innocent places he could think of and Oscar would write these beautiful reports. For which we both would make a little extra. You gotta take the money where it comes in this world." He was corrupt, this chubby photographer. But innocent enough to be unrepentant. It must have been the protected life he led, in Selwood.

"Only he got caught and lost his license."

"Yeah," said Ridgelea. It wasn't a happy memory, many years and dollars gone by. "So Oscar just retired. It's been five, six years now since I did that work for him. And you just don't get Indianapolis detectives that want to use a photographer from Selwood. There's too much competition for the work already."

"So you wouldn't mind if I was to buy Lennox's premises and pick up where he left off?"

"Of course not."

"Not even if I ran it straight?"

"I'm just the photographer."

"Not even if I ran it crooked?"

He smiled. "I might even be able to help." It was a curious promise. He was acting stronger than I felt he really was. Not a very well-defined feeling, but there are some people you come across whom you feel you can control. I felt I could control Ridgelea, probably because Oscar Lennox had controlled him. I felt Ridgelea was a mine of information which I had not fully dug. Yet.

"Right," I said. "I'll let you know if I come up with something."

"I'll be here."

I dropped him off at his desk, where I'd found him. Susan was calling Mrs. Drax to remind her that she had an appointment to have a picture of her son taken.

22

What with one thing and another I'd had quite an earful. I didn't go to the car. I didn't continue on my appointed rounds. I went straight to the bus station café.

When you want to get left alone in this country, you go to a bus station café. I wanted to be left alone. I wanted to transfer what I'd learned about Oscar Lennox to the perfect memory of my notebook. While it was still fresh. While it was still insulting.

It didn't take me long to reconjure the picture. Lennox had made his fortune over the years by systematically selling out his clients' interests to the clients' spouses.

A fairly refined technique, I suppose. I realized that it must occur to most of my fellow tradesmen who specialize in spouse-against-spouse type work. I've got as far as thinking about fiendish schemes to increase the country's divorce rate. To increase the quantity of trade so there would be more for me. But Lennox's angle was different, a way of improving the quality of his trade: more dollars per head.

Neat, yet not so neat. I didn't have trouble visualizing situations where it could backfire. Lennox approaches a guy about controverting incontrovertible evidence and the guy says, "Screw you, let the hag divorce me." And maybe then he goes back to the hag and says her detective has tried to sell her out and she can stuff it up her—

A detective can have his license lifted like that.

It would be a problem of evaluating potential customers. If Lennox knew how to pick the right people, he could be doing them quite a service. It would amount to providing a kind of mistress insurance. Or lover insurance, because it would be worked just as easily by wives cooperating with Lennox against suspicious husbands.

In the right cases it could be worth dinero. If Lennox could pick the right cases out and if he got enough cases to be able to pick.

Which, it seemed, he had.

The waitress finally brought me the two cups of coffee I'd ordered.

I wondered if Lennox had ever been married.

I thought about what a funny town Selwood seemed to be. But you can't judge a whole town because of a dead detective and a semicrooked photographer. Or because they seem to think that shotgun death is "natural." Just your average Midwestern town.

By the end of the second cup of coffee I was convinced again of something I'd convinced myself of before. That the police should already have done the work I was doing. They should have found out about Oscar Lennox right away. Like just what a private detective without a license had been doing in Newton Towers on a Friday night.

I decided to go give the cops a piece of my mind. It's how I'd begun the day, but it was even more deserved now.

Before heading back to Indianapolis, I stopped at the Travelers' Rest Café again. Mayor Paley hadn't called the Masons to report the market situation of Lennox's house yet, so I left my phone number.

I also had another brief look around Lennox's establishment. I saw more peeling paint this time. I noticed that the chimney needed pointing and that the yard had been pretty untended. Retirement hadn't been kind to Oscar Lennox.

I spent the drive to the big city wondering why, in this day and age, people continue to care who's screwing who. Because we're still in the Middle Ages, that's why. And because private detectives need the work.

23

A quarter to five is not the best time of day to find a cop. Not at police headquarters anyway. They're either out giving tickets to tired businessmen hurrying home along Fall Creek Parkway or laying rubber themselves to get home in time to start the charcoal briquettes for the fireman and his wife from across the street.

And what goes for your cop in the street goes double for your newly appointed lieutenant. Unless the lieutenant is lucky enough to work under the guidance of a senior officer who took a long time to make the grade himself, who pleasures himself by showing new appointees that life does not begin with lieutenancy.

Miller always was lucky.

I wouldn't say he was in tears when I knocked on his open cubbyhole door, but his shoulders were clearly sagging under the weight of his new bars. The first day in the full swing of a new job. It either makes a man even more ambitious or makes him want to return to the comfort of underling status. I'm not sure which is the better man.

I tried to comfort him, as any friend would. "Well, how's the big lieutenant? Figured out who done it yet?"

"Go away, Al."

"Hey, cool it. I'm a member of the taxpaying public."

"When was the last year you earned enough to pay taxes?"

Cops know instinctively how to twist balls. It's just that I have a complicated tax situation, with lots of deductions. "What's happening with the stuff you were going to find out for me?"

"Nothing."

I mean, a joke's a joke, but. . . . "What do you mean, nothing?"

"I mean nothing."

"That's not funny, Jerry. I need that stuff. Remember it was you that hustled me for it."

"So you're none the worse off."

"The hell I'm not. I've passed up lines of inquiry I'll never get again." Well, who knows, I might have.

He shrugged. I was getting mad. Burned as it were.

"You lose friends this way, copper."

He looked at me for the first time and breathed out loud as if he were exhaling for the last time. "Yeah, I know. But there's so much. . . ." He shook his head. There were a dozen files spread out on his desk. "Captain Gartland likes his lieutenants to have a working knowledge of all the open cases."

"I know. So in case one of them gets pregnant, the rest of you slobs can cover for him."

"I don't really feel like being called a slob right now, Al."

Even if that's just what he was. Only a dumb slob would take it seriously when a lousy captain told him to learn all the departments' cases "today." He'd be in the office all night, and that fancy celebration dinner Janie was no doubt preparing would get colder and colder.

"All right. You got a lot of work, but you nearly begged me to let you in on my case, so you're in. If you can't do it yourself, stick a little fire in Malmberg's tail, but don't drop me unless you want letters coming to your house telling your wife about you and Policewoman Magillicutty and letters to the *Star* giving details about how improperly you cops have handled the Tomanek case."

He didn't speak. I could see his mind, what was left of it, balancing between telling me there is nothing between him and Magillicutty except a few cups of coffee and getting mad because I accused his precious department of impropriety.

He had at least one more breath to exhale sharply as a sigh. "OK, OK. I'll get on to Malmberg." I knew he was just remembering how he'd come to fill a page with questions to answer. How he'd begged me to let him in. Or maybe that was just how I remembered it. Maybe there was something between him and Magillicutty. Maybe if I went to Janie, she'd hire me. I know this photographer. . . .

Far be it for me to let him go easily. "When?"

"When what, for Christ's sake?"

"When will you get on to Malmberg? Is he here now?"

"How the hell do I know?" We sat in a moment of reverent silence as we considered, simultaneously but separately, that a good lieutenant knows the work schedules. He picked up his phone and rang the front desk. "Mabel," he said. "What is Sergeant Malmberg's schedule?" We waited. He listened. He said, "Thanks."

"Mabel?" I said.

"He'll be back in before he goes home tonight."

"The teenybopper on the desk is called Mabel? I knew a girl called Mabel once. I was sure *she'd* never been in the Army, except maybe overnight now and then.

"Mabel," he said. "Mabel. Beatrice Mabel. Malmberg should be back soon."

"I heard."

"So what do you want to do?"

"That depends on what you are going to do."

"All right. When he comes in, I'll give him all your questions and tell him to get on it."

"If you tell him to give me full cooperation, I won't bother you again."

"Full cooperation! Full cooperation!"

"Right. I'll be back in forty-five minutes."

"What?"

"It's my civic duty to take every opportunity to evaluate the efficiency of our men in blue."

He didn't trust me. He spent a full five seconds over a second's worth of food for thought. "You on to something?"

We both know that it's not like me to work nights routinely. I'm not what either of us would call ambitious. But I sometimes admit to being curious, and I figured I'd come closer to finding out previously unknown things today than I had before. Whether they would help my client or not, I didn't know. I was just hoping it would be my lucky day. "I'm just hoping it will be my lucky day."

He didn't trust me. But he didn't have enough energy to waste any more on me.

I decided to spend the forty-five minutes eating cheeseburgers and catching up on the week's baseball.

Malmberg was neither happy nor unhappy to see me. I suspected he hadn't been around long enough to be actually happy very often. That would come. When he landed his first pot pusher, or baby raper, or Mafia kingpin.

He said, "Lieutenant Miller said there were some things you wanted me to do on the Tomanek case." At least he wasn't bitching because it was late.

"Not so much things *I* want you to do as things which should have been done."

"Oh, I don't know," he said.

"I'm not criticizing the work that has been done. I just think that more work needs doing. Lieutenant Miller agrees with me. It's your case, so either he takes it away from you or he sends me to you with hopes that we will cooperate. It's generous of him, kid. If anything comes of it, that puts it on your record."

Malmberg sat back but didn't smile. "So what can I do for you?"

"You can get the case file again for starters."

"You read it before."

"Only every other line." Not quite true, but I hadn't had time to do it justice. Even poorly investigated cases produce a mound of case report.

"I'll get it."

Which he did. "What do you want to know?"

"What was Edward Ephray doing in the Newton Towers?"

"He lived there, didn't he?" We both knew immediately that Malmberg had made a mistake. A cop should always be sure and positive.

I said, "He has a fancy house out on the East Side. He has a jealous wife. Why does he need an apartment? And how does he get away to use it?"

Malmberg looked through the notes in the file. I knew that he didn't know. He hadn't talked to Ephray, and Graniela in his preliminary investigation hadn't spent much effort on him either.

Malmberg finished his fruitless searches. "OK," he said, "I'll find out."

"I realize," I said, "that you got the case after Graniela did preliminary work and with his recommendation not to put any more into it. But things aren't always the way they seem."

He shrugged. He didn't need my help to justify to himself what he had or had not done. Kids! They're so damned sure of themselves these days. They throw curve balls on three-and-oh. It's the new wave come to wash old bathers like me out for a call on Davey Jones.

"What else you got?" he said.

"Why was Oscar Lennox there?"

"He was serving Ephray with a writ."

That was one question answered, partly. "Ephray works in town every day. Why serve him at eleven at night? And where was the witness to the serving?"

He sat silent.

That was OK by me. When I get going, I can talk pretty good. "What was the suit about? Who was making him come to court?"

"That I have," he said. "The lab put a lot of the pieces together. It's in here somewhere." He found it. "Civil suit. Brought by someone called Robinson Holroyd."

"No kidding!"

"Name mean something to you?"

"Well. . . ." It was too much a coincidence to be a coincidence. "Yes. The guy who runs Easby Guards, the outfit Tomanek worked for, he's called Holroyd."

"That," said Malmberg, with a rattling grasp of the detail, "that explains why Lennox brought no witness. Holroyd would be sure that his guard would testify he saw the paper being served. Save a little money."

"But why at the apartment door? Why not downstairs in the lobby?"

"Maybe he didn't know Ephray by sight. Just knew the apartment."

"Why not ask the guard to point him out as he came in?"

"Maybe Tomanek didn't know him well enough by sight to be sure that he was the guy Lennox wanted."

"If he's suing the guy, he's not sweating the witness money enough to tell Lennox to serve him at eleven at night just because he happens to live, for whatever reason, in a building guarded by an Easby Guard."

"Well. . . ."

"And how long had Ephray had the apartment; does he still have it?"

"All right! All right!" Any deference I had been entitled to had run its course. "Anything else?"

"Yes. Why was Lennox serving papers in the first place? Lennox had always been a divorce specialist. Six years ago he lost his license. Why a paper at eleven at night?"

"I would think that you, as a private detective, would be able to explain little inconsistencies like that better than I could."

Malmberg was not becoming my favorite kid cop. "Right, if it is explainable, I should be able to explain it. But I can't. I can't think of any good reason, and that means whatever relationship it has to Ralph Tomanek, things were going on that night that we haven't begun to explain, and it's not until we know what they are that we can decide whether they *do* have some connection, remote or otherwise, to what Ralph Tomanek did. I don't know what they teach you in cop school these days, Malmberg, but you can never be sure that you've got the right line on something that's happened until you've checked it out from all the lines you can think of. You've got a weird case here, at least strange, and if you don't have the sense to see that, no matter what the guy who passed it on to you says, then you ought to pack up."

We sat frowning. Partly at each other. Partly at the circumstances which put us, respectively, in chairs facing each other across a tidy, dusted desk. He said, "You sound like a teacher I had in college."

"Oh Christ." But I was not displeased. Maybe I should have been, considering my experiences of college teachers, but I wasn't.

"So what else do you think we've been remiss about finding out?" He grinned. I grinned. We both know that cops don't say "remiss."

"I want to know what you've done about Oscar Lennox's records."

"Not much. We locked the house for a couple of weeks. I think some of his stuff was brought here, at least what was on his body. . . ." We paused, remembering I suppose, that Lennox was shotgunned. Malmberg may have seen a shotgunned man. I never had. I don't want to. I've seen rabbits blasted at night, close up, after being frozen with a light. I had this crazy half cousin. . . .

Malmberg went on, "And what was in his car."

"What kind of car did he drive."

"Eldorado. Sixty-eight. Black."

"But you didn't get anything out of his office in Selwood?"

"I'm not sure. I don't think so. We locked it up, and then

after a couple of weeks we gave the keys to the executor."

"Did he leave a will?"

"I don't know. I guess so."

"Who identified the body?"

"Let's see." He wandered through loose pages. "Next of kin was a son, but he's in Methodist. I don't know what with, but I gather it's serious. ID was made by a Tessa Meyer, who was apparently Lennox's lawyer."

"And a friend of the deceased?"

"It doesn't say that here either. Graniela got them."

"I want a key to the house. I want to look at the records."

"All right. I'll try and get it for you. It'll be Monday."

"Monday!"

"I can't help that. Anything else?"

"Only one more thing. If you guys think Ralph Tomanek is so obviously crazy, then why could he get a job that makes him carry a loaded shotgun around every day?"

Malmberg shrugged. "Ask Graniela. I'm only a sergeant."

I resolved to ask Graniela. Someday. I looked at my watch. Seven ten on a Friday night. "What's Lennox's son called?"

"Oscar Junior."

"OK. And before I leave, I want to see the things that you took off the body and out of the car."

He sighed. Picked up a phone.

Lennox's personal effects were stored in an evidence room, kept under a greater degree of security than the rest of cop center. It takes someone impersonating a cop to pick up one of the house phones and say, "There's this guy coming down to look at the bag of Lennox, Oscar," to get a look at evidence.

Oscar's bag. The remains of a private detective. Successful. Dead.

It's depressing to look into a dead man's "bag." At least for sensitive souls like me. Especially if the lout of a private eye was a sentimental bastard. A wallet with pictures, lots of pictures, of a boy. Of Oscar Junior. They depressed me infinitely.

I carry a dozen of my kid, and she's only ten.

I didn't stick around to go through it all. I asked the guy watching over my shoulder what time I could come back tomorrow. He said I couldn't. I told him to call Malmberg back. He said business hours.

I didn't call Methodist to see when I could chat with the kid. I didn't call my answering service to see who had been calling all day to solicit my services. I don't know. I shouldn't let myself get tired. I depress too easily when I get tired. And being depressed depresses me.

I went to visit my woman.

I proposed marriage three times. Two "nevers" and a "no." That sort of thing can depress a fella.

24

By the time I got home at eleven on Saturday, I had realized that things weren't as bad as they had seemed. A "no" after two "nevers" is progress.

Why not?

I took a bath, which was the right thing to do. A bath can do a lot of psychological things. And it can make you clean.

It was my farewell bath. I didn't know when Kapp was moving my new neighbor in, but I didn't want to mess around hanging on to condemned pleasures. Have done with it and move on. I had me one real good bath.

I gathered paraphernalia, the bathroom accumulations of three years, and staggered through the hall into my office. It was a lovely picture. I was feeling better.

Why not?

I walked into my office and found Mrs. Jerome sitting on the front edge of the bench I keep along one wall. She didn't have to sit on the bench; there is a chair. I guess she didn't want to be indebted to me.

She jumped up as I walked in. I must have been pretty. Bathrobe, arms full of dirty towels, and a wide variety of bathing condiments.

I said, "Hi, Mrs. Jerome."

"Well! I heard singing but—"

She was flattering me. It doesn't often get called singing. What a nice lady.

I disgorged my necessaries, piled them on the desk on top of my largest bath towel. It was big enough to hold everything if I had had the sense to put everything in it in the first place. That would have left a hand free. I could have laid some skin on Mrs. Jerome. Ah, well, we remember too late.

"I'm sorry, Mr. Samson. This is just too much."

"What can I do for you?"

"I came this morning to find what progress you are making on behalf of my son-in-law."

"I didn't have the impression that you minded what happened to your son-in-law." I pulled up certain loosenesses in my bathrobe. I was sitting on the edge of my desk, so the hole was covered, but there was no point in wasting flashes of hirsute chest.

"Well, you have the wrong impression. Anything that affects Rosetta I care about. I am just not sure, and have never been sure, that hiring you was the best way to help. If I thought that it would do some good, of course I'd be for it."

"What sort of outcome do you think would do some good?"

She was silent. I guessed that she wanted Ralph committed somewhere, away from Rosetta. Oh, not in jail, but away. She couldn't bring herself to say it. She said, "I'm sure I don't know what would be best for Ralph. That is what you were supposed to be finding out."

"We're going in circles, Mrs. Jerome."

"I want to know what you are doing for the money my daughter is paying you. It may not be a lot to you, but it's everything the poor girl has. She's put all her eggs in your basket, Mr. Samson, and I want to know what you're doing with them."

A burst of poesy. I have a basket, I buy eggs at the City Market.

"I am afraid that by the licensing law of the state of Indiana, I can't tell what I've found out for a client to anyone but the client or, in some cases, the police."

"I—" She stopped. She sighed. She said, "All right, I admit I didn't approve of Rosetta hiring you. But once she decided she wanted it that way, I tried to help. Can I . . . would it help you in your work for her to have more money? The money Rosetta gave you isn't much. I know it doesn't get much; it can't demand much of your time. But if you could find out things that would help if more money were available, I can provide a certain amount of additional assistance."

I never thought it would happen, but I felt sorry for the lady. "Have you told Rosetta that you want to help?"

"I. . . . It's just that. . . ."

"Tell Rosetta, Mrs. Jerome. Tell her you want to help her. That way you will."

"You are difficult, Mr. Samson."

"Yes. But you can tell her that however it turns out, Ralph's case is not as simple as it seemed, and the police are looking into the details again."

She was all attention. "They are?"

"Yes, for whatever it all comes to."

"All right, Mr. Samson. I'll tell her."

"Good."

She left me to my musings. I often muse when somebody shows me unexpected depth of feeling. Humanity. Life is too short to spend it battling the people you care about. If Mrs. Jerome could realize that, anyone could.

I decided to write a letter to my little girl. But I found it hard. My work was on my mind. Oscar Lennox, to be specific. I felt uneasy about him. There is an instinctive recoil from someone who manipulates your own professional standards. Yet there is attraction in someone who finds a better moneytrap.

Maybe I should step into his shoes, buy the house in Selwood. I could call it "Trap-a-Spouse." Specialize.

Most divorce work comes to private detectives through lawyers who are handling the proceedings on behalf of one or other of the married parties. That's what bothered me about Lennox's little gimmick. Once hired, he wouldn't have the opportunity to talk to the offended spouse, and he would only be watching the offending spouse from a distance.

What bothered me was how he decided who to approach for the sellout. How he decided to go to A and say, "Look, your wife has hired me to prove adultery. I can do it. You want to hire me to get you off?" And why he decided not to try the same thing with B. When he didn't ever have a first-hand chance to meet A and B and find out whether they were the type to say, "Thanks for telling me," or whether they would just say, "Beat it, buster," and report him to the licensing board.

The key would have to be some factor other than personality. Like. . . .

Like only trying it with the people you come across who didn't want to be divorced.

Yes.

That's what it was all about, wasn't it? A private detective gets hired because someone wants to divorce his spouse. What if the spouse couldn't afford to be divorced? How many people like that would there be around? Husbands who marry rich wives to get set up in business. Or maybe just the boss' daughter. Politicians for whom divorce would be politically costly. Rotten actresses who marry producers to get parts. Poets married to publishing families.

I suppose there are a lot of ambitious people who marry to get the means to fulfill their ambitions. Who therefore might be more vulnerable than most if the spouse begins to tire.

If he were given a case, could a private detective find out whether the person he was investigating couldn't afford to be divorced? He could. If he was a reasonable private detective.

It gave me pause for thought. I was getting a better feel of the mechanics of Lennox's economic niche, to use Robinson Holroyd's phrase.

"Samson's Spouse Surveillance."

I had a glass of orange juice. I wondered how much mortgage I could get on Lennox's premises. If any.

I had another glass of orange juice.

I wasn't getting my letter done. I forced myself. I write animal stories when I don't have other subject matter that would charm the goodwill of a ten-year-old distant daughter. I have to write something that will amuse because I don't have the money to fly in for the weekend and take her to a wrestling match. The money is all with her Mommy and her new Daddy.

But my letter that Saturday didn't amuse. It was a story of wolves and lions and rats and skunks and lice-ridden porcupines. Of sharks and scorpions. Of creatures each faster and stronger and more heartless than the last.

It scared hell out of me. I didn't know whether to send it or not.

Before I brought myself to a decision, I received a letter myself. More than a letter, because George, the mailman, knocked on the door as he dropped it on the office floor.

I found a manila envelope, which was heavy. It was from Rosetta Tomanek.

Inside was a letter and a book, the yearbook of Arsenal Technical High School for 1966. Rosetta's letter was medium long and handwritten in a clear, controlled script.

> DEAR MR. SAMSON,
>
> I have just come back from visiting Ralph. Mother thinks I am asleep. You said you needed to know what Ralph is really like. You said you needed and I have been thinking about that. Because Ralph has not always been the way he is now, and if you need to know what he is like then I should tell you. I hope you will not mind me writing a letter to you like this.
>
> I met Ralph in high school. I think I will send you the yearbook of the year we graduated to show you what he looked like then. It was in an algebra class and he was always a good student. He

got very many B's. Myself, I tried hard and I think that he saw that. From the beginning we met and he began to help me almost from the beginning.

You also should know that at that time Ralph's father had gone away. It was several years before. Almost from the beginning that we met we spent a lot of time together. He was always kind, Mister Samson. I have never known him to do an unkind thing or say an unkind word. I have tried hard to think of one time, but I cannot. We spent a lot of time walking and he always gave some money to beggers, even when they were so horrible that I wanted to run away from them. I can think of a lot of unkind things that I have done, but not one that Ralph has done.

His mother died in his senior year. We always knew that we would get married because I knew that he had to have someone and because he was willing to have me. Mother never liked him, but Mother's record at keeping a man is not good.

I do not know what information will help you. It is just that Ralph was very different then. He was even chubby if you can imagine it. We used to talk for hours and he always had things to say and he always paid attention to the little things. Even after he came back and was in the hospital at Crawfordsville I still remembered how he was upset when the bus fares went up. I visited him at least three times every week.

The time after he got out was terrible. We had to live with my Mother who did not ever like him. We have never yet had a place of our own. But it was most hard on Ralph when he got out. He just could not find a job. We would take walks on Sundays like we used to do. We would go to the places, but we never talked like we used to. Ralph was thinking about things. About his job and I know that he had bad dreams at nights, I know that. I think I am the only one who knows how bad they were sometimes.

Ralph is not a stupid man, Mr. Samson. My Mother says he is stupid now and he may seem that way. But if he does not talk to you much it is not because of being stupid.

The man at the placement was the one that suggested the job with the guards. He suggested it several times before Ralph went. The man at the placement said that the man at the guards was often helpful about veterans. Ralph did not really want the job, but he took it. He felt pressures. I tried to keep pressures off, but I must say that my Mother did not help keep them off.

That is all that I can think of to say unless you have questions that you want to ask me. I guess that I just wanted to say to someone who would listen that Ralph, whatever he did, could not do anything bad. I know that as well as I know anything. I cannot tell you how much I know it. But I do and it is true.

Yours with respect,
(MRS.) ROSETTA TOMANEK

I picked up the yearbook and opened to the back. I found Ralph Tomanek's name in the index. There was only one reference, the official graduation picture. It showed Ralph smiling, and while he definitely sported some flesh, since lost, I could not have called him chubby without prompting.

Ralph had indeed taken an academic degree though Rosetta, née Jerome, had not. She had graduated, however. Her "ambition" was "to lead a happy, useful life." Ralph had graduated "ambition"-less.

I spent a few minutes leafing through the rest of the yearbook. There is a sense of bustle about yearbooks, a devotion to the poses of activity.

On impulse I turned back to the graduation pictures. I looked for Joe Malmberg. But the hunch didn't pan out. Malmberg might have graduated the same year as the

Tomaneks—he could just be young enough—but it wouldn't have been from Tech. Joe's parents would have arranged to send him somewhere "better."

I crumpled my abortive story and pitched a World Series strike into the wastebasket. My kid deserved better too.

25

Methodist Hospital's visiting hours begin at three on a Saturday. I found Oscar Lennox, Jr., in a private room. It was completely outfitted: television, flowers, books. An expensive proposition. He was lying in bed, making no use of anything except the window. A man about thirty. Like the edge of a page in an old book, he looked slightly yellowed and as if he were about to go up in flames. His hands were large and the fingers long and bony.

He heard me come in but didn't let it interrupt his concentration on the world outside his panes.

It was only after I didn't poke him or prod him that he turned to find out what I was up to.

"Who are you?" he said.

I introduced myself, but I hesitated when, past the name, I was expected to give him some notion of why I was there.

My hesitation irritated him. "So who are you? A tourist? Or did you just come in to check me and see if I was still alive because you've got someone else who wants dialysis at five. It's OK. I don't mind if you put someone else on it. What's a little dialysis here or there?"

"I'm not hospital staff. I'm a private detective."

If nothing else, it surprised him. He did a stagy double take. "I'll be fucked," he said. "A visitor. A real goddamned visitor." He thought about it. Maybe he didn't like it. "A private investigator like dear old Dad," he said. "Would you be so kind as to allow a brief examination of your license, my good man? That I may verify your authenticity."

I showed him my ID.

"Well. Has someone named me as correspondent in a

divorce action?" He waited for a moment, for me to laugh, I guess. Then he frowned. "That's an example of ironic humor, my thick man. Consider that I have been in this bed for nearly a year and that my health severely hampered my activities for some time before that."

"You'll excuse me if I don't laugh."

"No, I won't," he said, and turned back toward the window.

"I stopped to see you on the off chance that you would be willing to talk to me about your father."

"About my father!" he said. But did not turn back to me. "What in heaven's name could concern you about my father? Now there's a riddle. Riddle-me-ree. What was the last thing that dear old Dad expected from this life? Riddle-me-ree. To die before me!"

I just sat and waited.

My reward was another look at the pallid face. "That is an example of stylized so-called black humor. What sort of humor does appeal to you, my thick man?"

"Humor intended for the audience rather than the actor." He turned away again. I said, "I don't know how bad your medical problems are or any of your personal history, but if you are willing to talk to me, I like to talk. And if you're not, I'll go. But I am not going to hang around and play games. If you're not willing to talk about your father, just tell me so. I'll go away."

He exhaled heavily. He coughed. "Working on a Saturday, too," he said. "Go home to your wife and your family. Stay by the fireside bright." This last he sang. The tune was "Irene." He didn't have a bad voice, what was left of it.

I left my card and closed the door behind me.

From his end room, I walked slowly back to the nurses' station by the elevator. A rather pretty nurse had directed me to Lennox, Jr.'s room in the first place. She still sat at her desk as I walked back. It was nice to have an excuse to talk to her again. I said, "Mr. Lennox asked me to check that his dialysis is still set up for five."

She spoke in a singsongy accent, West Indian I guessed. "Oh, dat Mr. Lennox. He's always frettin' about somet'ing.

I wonder he t'ink we don't take good enough care of him."

"It's not that. He's just worried about himself. He worries about where the money's going to come from now that his father's dead."

"An' haven't I told him not to worry about dat? But he's always worse on a Saturday. You come back durin' next week. Then he'll be more jokin'."

"Did he take his father's death hard?"

"How else can you take the death of a father but hard? An' his only relation. Why, sure he took it hard, man. But you come back durin' the week."

I lied that I'd try and then ambled on my merry way. I knew that I should be doing things, that I should be resolved to be doing things. But I came into the daylight utterly devoid of resolve. I felt I had shot my daily wad. I felt fuzzy-headed. Not on top, unable to make forward progress. I thought too much about the question of who, Ralph Tomanek or Oscar Lennox, Jr., was the more in jail.

I sidestepped, as well as one can in a '58 Plymouth, over to my woman's. No one was there, so I waited on the doorstep. Looking at the trees blowing in the breeze. Watching the sun peek out from behind a passing cloud.

Cloud? No, a passing sheep, king's head, lion-woman, airplane, chimney, and blob.

Mentally I cleared my desks of the seasick letter I'd written to my little girl. I wrote a new story, with a cast of clouds.

26

It was six o'clock and I was in the middle of a bowl of canned chili before I remembered that I had an appointment to go back to police headquarters and look at Lennox's impounded personal properties. It's what I get for not referring to my notebook. For letting myself indulge my self-indulgence. I left the chili mid-bowl.

And didn't remember that I was supposed to turn up "in business hours" until I was more than halfway there. It didn't turn out to matter. Cop business hours are different from yours and mine.

Lennox's personal possessions were not all that helpful. First I took a closer look at the snaps of Oscar Junior. A less sentimental look now that I knew the gentleman. I deduced he had graduated from college somewhere old enough for graduates to get their pictures taken in front of an ivy-covered building. There was also a picture of a younger, much heavier Oscar Junior gesturing proudly toward a theater front. I couldn't tell whether his name was somewhere on the marquee, his stage name, or whether he owned it or was an usher. But the picture was there. And some others. Miscellaneous to me, except of a young boy with a rather attractive blond lady. I presumed Oscar's mother. Where are you today, mother of Oscar?

Otherwise, six gasoline credit cards; $478.60; a gold watch with no inscription; a gold wedding ring, no inscription; driver's license; miscellaneous identification, including a Navy separation card, 1946; ring of keys.

The cop in charge watched me very closely. No doubt because of the money. For his benefit I counted it slowly and checked my total with the itemization total on the outside of the bag. It checked. But it was the keys that were of most interest to me.

I felt saucy, but I skirted the temptation to palm the key ring. There was not only one house key on it. There were three. A great temptation indeed. But I rarely steal before midnight.

Malmberg was drinking coffee when I plopped myself down at his desk. There were crumbs and sugar specks scattered on his blotter. It looked like two doughnuts' worth. I was proud of him. A good working cop's dinner. You look desperately for signs of humanity in any college grad cop.

He even greeted me. He said, "Hello." Things were looking up. I knew it.

"Hello yourself," said I.

"You were interested in looking around Lennox's house, as I remember it."

"You remember it, Sergeant."

"Well, I've checked it out. The estate is in the hands of Lennox's lawyer, who says nothing's been done about it yet. It all goes to Lennox's son, and he's in the hospital. But we can go and have a look at the house whenever we want to. It turns out that we have keys, in Lennox's bag downstairs."

"When did you find all this out?"

"Well, I made some calls after you left last night. I figured it was worth a try. I got lucky."

Not lucky enough to try to give me a call, natch. "How you doing on the other outstanding questions?"

He smiled. "I've started on them. Ordered preliminary information, and I go out to see them tomorrow."

"Sunday?"

He shrugged. "Tomanek at least. Maybe Ephray. Maybe Mrs. Tomanek. Maybe Holroyd. Some neighbors at the murder scene, maybe. I don't know."

"Do you have any way to justify opening the case again?"

"Not yet. Graniela's my man. But I don't need justification yet. I guess you wouldn't know, but as long as I get some results, nobody bothers much. The captain deals with monthly arrest statistics. The lieutenants go more week by week. We're pretty much on our own. Besides, tomorrow's the beginning of a new week."

"Whatever you say. But anyway, I appreciate your not fighting me about this."

"I had a little talk with Miller."

"Oh."

"He told me about your last little outing here."

"You want to make lieutenant, too, huh?"

He smiled. I felt a bit more uncomfortable.

"If you go downstairs, I'll tell them to give you Lennox's key ring."

"That should do it."

The patrolman on the property bags was particularly pleased to see me again. He got the key ring from Lennox's bag in only ten minutes and made me sign a minimum number of receipts for it after examining my identification. He especially liked my private detective's license.

Without further kazoo I took the keys and called it a day.

27

Sunday broke clear, early summer hot. The kind of day to lie in bed and think about vacations, afternoons in the bleachers and cool showers. So I was up at eight.

Things to do. I'd puttered for nearly a week. Pushing two hundred dollars' worth. What I'd found probably wasn't worth ten cents on the dollar.

Yet. . . .Yet certainly things were not settled. I dawdled over breakfast, but once I was through, I made straight for the chariot. And drove to Selwood. To my great surprise the Travelers' Rest Café was open for business. I suppose travelers have to rest seven days a week.

Maw and Paw Mason greeted me like a long-lost son. "Why, Albert!" said Paw. "Come right in, boy. Set yourse'f down. Maw!" he called to the back room. "Maw, look who's here!"

The notion of someone being "here" brought Maw in a flash. She wiped off the blood on her hands on her apron. Beef, I presume. "Why, it's Albert!" she said, as if I were one of the few pleasures in life. "How nice!"

"You open every Sunday?"

Paw drew himself up a little. "The Sabbath was made for man, not man for the Sabbath."

"Every little bit helps," said Maw.

I ordered a second breakfast. A light one. I was willing to forgive and forget. Forget that at their first sight of me they had called the cops. Though Selwood doesn't have the best reputation in the world for acceptance of new people and new ideas, I guess once you pass certain tests, you're in. It seemed like I was in. Maybe because I purported to have enough money to be thinking of buying a house.

Still, it was nice to be welcomed.

"We've been meaning to call you, Albert. Haven't we, Maw?"

"That's right."

"Only we just found out on Saturday, late. And we just haven't had a chance yet today. What with one thing and another."

"That's right," chimed Maw. "We only heard late Saturday."

"Heard what?"

"That poor Mr. Lennox's house *is* for sale and that the keys are kept by Mr. Lennox's lawyer. The office is up in Southport. Not here in town. That's why it took Mayor Paley so long to track it down."

I took the name and address down.

"That's where you can get keys to the house, I reckon."

"I already have a set of keys."

"You do?"

"Yes," I said. "I saw Lennox's son over the weekend." True but irrelevant.

"His son?" said Maw. "I didn't know he had a son. I didn't never know he was married."

"It's why I stopped in. I'm about to go over to the house and have a look around. I didn't want you getting worried."

"Oh," said Maw. "We ain't worried."

Relieved of that anxiety, I ate my breakfast and then drove across the street into Lennox's driveway. It's funny how you see new things each time you look at something. I could see how much the house was neglected. Yard overgrown. When I bought it, I'd put in roses here, radishes there. Sigh.

I got out Lennox's key ring and went to the door. There were three house keys all right. Lennox had three locks on the front door.

Fascinating, since I don't have any on mine.

I went in. Hallway. I went into the room on the left. Office. Desk. Half a dozen filing cabinets.

I started with the desk. Very little of note, except, peculiarly, an Indianapolis Board of Education stapler. And a box of staples. And a light with a metal shade suspended low over it from the ceiling. Otherwise, perfectly ordinary business trappings. Interesting only in that Lennox had apparently been doing all his own trapping, for the last six years. Secretaryless. Licenseless. It was interesting that the room had been maintained as an office at all.

From desk to filing cabinets. Little keys on Lennox's ring made them easy.

Six filing cabinets, all in a row. A cabinet meeting. A man's professional life and, in the detail of its recording, a man's whole life. The first one that I opened was "Number 1. January 19, 1947. Married woman. Southport."

Apparently in 1947 Lennox had been working in Indianapolis. Where he had come from, what he'd been doing before, both unspecified. He wasn't that young. He was fifty-nine when gunned down. In '47 he was about thirty-five. Maybe savings from his Navy career had staked him? Whether he'd come from the area originally, I didn't know.

I began my serious work. Carefully drawing out each file tray. Examining the files as they lay. Looking for . . . peculiarities. Obvious gaps or familiar names. Maybe Tomanek's or Ephray's or the mayor. Mr. and Mrs. Mason, me. Mrs. Jerome.

A fella is entitled to daydream, on a dreamy day.

All I found was that the files were chronological. It occurred to me that it's not the easiest way to maintain files if you want to go back to them frequently. Normally you keep them alphabetically. That way, if you want to look up Bella Berzerk, you just look under *B*.

It was sufficient occasion to have a sit down in Lennox's desk chair.

Why keep files chronologically? Well, you can put new cases in at the end of the last available tier; you never have to shift piles of folders from one drawer to another when you get a rash of *Q*'s divorcing one another. But if business was so good, you wouldn't mind making occasional room for new records.

And I suppose chronological filing is somewhat easier for computing taxes owed. If you want to make it easy to compute taxes owed.

Somewhere I noticed a quiet humming bell. Outside or upstairs. Or in my inner ear.

I picked up the telephone on Lennox's desk. It was dead. I should have remembered. I'd tried to call it.

Chronological filing. Maybe the man had himself a good memory for cases, knew his files like his sexual fantasies. Or maybe he didn't. Maybe he just had a cross-reference index somewhere. That's all it would take. A little alphabetical card file matching names to dates. Not bad. And if it came to it, a nonalphabetical file also was a degree of safety against random snoopers. Like me. At least someone couldn't just drop in for a look at the way his favorite divorce investigation was progressing. Not without having the cross-reference index.

I never had the vaguest suspicion.

Behind me and to my right windows shattered.

Instinctively I dropped to the floor.

Over my head I heard a voice saying something about hands. In panic you don't listen too good.

For no apparent reason an explosion happened. I heard a clanging. I didn't look up, but I knew that it was a bullet embedding itself in the filing cabinets. Filing cabinets only stand about four and a half feet off the floor. Much too close.

A voice rang out. "Now cut that out, George; I'll tell you when to shoot him."

"I was just trying to scare him a little, Bobby."

"Well, cut it out!"

"Yes, sir."

"All right. Now, you there, under the desk. Are you going to come out with your hands up or do we—"

"I'll come out," I screamed. I wanted them to hear me.

"Now y'all relax. If you don't make no trouble for us, we won't make none for you. Just get them hands up."

I came up, slowly, hands first. Very slowly. Hands very first. So high and straight above my head I stuck my fingers into the light above Lennox's desk. It would have burned my fingers if the light had been on. I got my hand off the bulb but kept my elbows straight and high.

My visitors were Bobby, the state cop, and a colleague. Bobby recognized me, too.

"I thought it was you," he said. "But I couldn't tell too good from the window. I'm nearsighted, you know, but I don't like to wear my glasses because they make over my nose hurt."

"I know what you mean," I said. I find it a lot easier to be brave when I have a chance to work myself up to it. And easier to be angry, too, if I get some preparation time. Off the cuff like that, I was feeling nothing but relief. Especially when Bobby put away his pistol. George was less easily convinced but acquiesced.

"How'd you happen to be in here?" asked Bobby. Casual, but not friendly.

"I have keys," I said. I picked them up from the desk and brandished them.

"Where'd you get them?"

"From the Indianapolis police." I began to regain my emotional footing. "Just what occasioned this little visit? Or do you always knock on the window when you want to come in?"

"Is there anybody in Indianapolis I can check with?"

"Try Detective Sergeant Malmberg. Or if he's not there, Lieutenant Miller knows me, and he can check about the keys. Now what's this all about?"

"I guess they didn't tell you about the silent alarm."

"No, they did not."

"That's pretty funny." He had a little laugh. If you can't join 'em, wait for 'em to finish. "Well, old Mr. Lennox, he had a couple of devices put in. One of them rang upstairs in his bedroom, and the other one connects directly to our office in town."

"And I guess no one bothered to turn them off."

"I guess so."

"That's very sweet."

"Should I go in and search him, Bobby?"

"Shut up, George. I guess I should take down your name again, mister. Just to check everything out and make sure it's all OK."

Slowly and carefully I reached under my jacket to get my wallet and brought my card to the window for him.

"Albert Samson. That's right. I remember. Your middle initial is R, isn't it?"

"That's right."

"What's it stand for?"

"Robespierre."
"Robs-pee-air! What kind of name is that?"
"It's the French for Robert."
"Can we go now, Bobby?"
"Shut up, George. Would you say it again for me, Mr. Samson?"
"Robespierre." I did it just like they used to on Baby Snooks.
"Sound kind of like you got a frog in your throat."
"I think you're getting the hang of it."
He shook his head. He could shake if off for all I cared. My knees were beginning to shake, my heart to flutter. The adrenalin was just catching up with me. I wanted to sit down, but as an act of will I remained standing until they left. An act of personal courage.
They left. Presumably to check things out. With my luck, Malmberg would be out, and Miller would deny he ever heard of me. Big lieutenant. Too good for the friends he knew on the way up.
I sat down. I breathed. The combination helped, eventually.

I was in no mood to hang around Selwood. But I was also in no mood to come back soon. Of course, I should have looked for alarms when I came in. I even know about them. But it had just not occurred to me. It made me feel that I didn't have my heart in things or something. I gathered myself, my resources, and turned back to the files.
The open file, 1951, had a bullet hole clean through it. I leafed through the flawed file folders. Hole after hole. I finally found the bullet embedded in the dent it made in the back of the tray. Solidly indented, but not through. If anyone ever asked me now what would happen if a state cop shot a filing cabinet, I could tell them.
I went on to the next tray. All nameless. Somewhere there must be a file connecting names with file numbers.
I did notice there were missing case numbers. For whatever reason.
I thought about that for a minute.
I couldn't think of any good reason.
I thought of some bad ones.

But enough was enough. It was pushing noon, and I was very tired. More relaxed, no longer shaking. But extremely sleepworthy.

I decided to leave. But at the front door I had a little unfinished business. Disconnection of two wires. One of them was definitely the silent alarm to the state police office branch in Selwood. I couldn't tell for certain which, though I thought I could guess from the difference in wire quality. But for kicks I pulled them both.

Somewhere in the background, upstairs, a little bell stopped ringing. Didn't someone say that Lennox had an upstairs alarm?

It had been ringing all the time I had been there. Boldly, I opened the disconnected door and marched to my vehicle. Sabbath is made for man.

28

I was on the Indianapolis side of Homecroft before my conscience caught up with me. Not that I acted directly on it. I used the occasion to pull into the first diner I came to. I had a doughnut and three coffees.

And I checked my notebook. It seemed stupid to yoyo endlessly between Selwood and Indianapolis. I really ought to get the most out of each trip. I could try. What can't be done can't be mourned.

What I wanted to try was Janny née Crockett. Married, legal secretary to Mr. Cranbrook by the bus station. Formerly detective secretary to Mr. Lennox. If anyone knew the place that the cross-reference index was usually kept, it should be Janny.

If I could find the place that Janny was usually kept on a Sunday. This I did by phone. There was only one Cranbrook listed in Selwood. I called him. He had only one secretary. She was called Janny, it turned out. After a little chat he told me her last name. Huddenlocher. There were only two Huddenlochers listed in Selwood. My dimes lasted long enough for me to locate the right one. I explained who I was, that I wanted to talk about Lennox. She said, "Sure," and gave me directions. Simple as pie.

Before I left the diner, I had a piece of pie.

It was about twelve thirty when I rolled back into Selwood. Past the Travelers' Rest. Past Lennox's. Past Ridgelea's. Past the bus station. But not too far past. Left, left, right.

A little fifties-built ranch-style house. I knocked on the door.

I was rapidly invited to enter. I did and found a rather gorgeous plump young lady tickling my purview. Fantastic hair of a rich mouse brown, shelved in tiers of tiny swirls. Eyes like limpet pools. A unique specimen. Speciwomen? Coffee notwithstanding, I was tired.

"I'm Janny Huddenlocher," she said. "My real name is Jan-ellen, but my friends call me Janny." She led me to a comfortable chair. A lawn mower rattled comfortably from the back of the house.

"Well, Janny, my name is Albert. I understand that about six years ago you worked for a man here in town called Oscar Lennox. Is that right?"

"Oh. yes. Poor Mr. Lennox. I did. I did. What can I tell you about him?"

In my business a question like that is red-carpet treatment.

I said, "I got the keys to his house at the Indianapolis police department"—I showed them to her—"but in looking over Mr. Lennox's effects, I'm having trouble finding some of the things we need."

"Ooooo," she said. "What?"

"The most important one is the cross-index file. The one which connects all the names to the numbers in his filing cabinets."

"The blue card box. I remember it."

"Good. Do you remember whereabouts he used to keep it?"

"No."

"Oh."

"That is, he never kept it in just one place. When he was in his office, he kept it in his office. When he went back into his kitchen to make lunch or something, he locked it in his desk. Then, when he went to bed, he used to take it upstairs—at least some days when he'd come down late from upstairs, he'd be carrying it."

"But he kept close track of it?"

"Oh, yes. It was very important, you see. It's the way he got from the files to the names of the people involved. He needed it so he could know where to send the bills."

"Of course."

"Does that help?"

"I think so. He must have been pretty upset when he lost his license."

She bounced on her seat. "Oooo, not nearly as upset as I was. I liked that job. He was a real nice boss. Very considerate. He didn't get angry if I did happen to make a little mistake in a letter or something. He's probably the best boss I ever worked for."

"I can see you wouldn't want to lose a job you liked."

"I didn't. But Mr. Lennox wasn't upset about his license at all. You see, that's the kind of man he was. He just took things as they came, like. He said to me that all it would mean was that he would retire a couple of years earlier than he intended. He said to me, 'Those are the breaks, Janny.' That's exactly what he said. I remember the very words. It's funny how some things people say stick with you like that."

"Yeah," I said.

"He was real good about it, too. He had to let his operatives go too, but he said we could all stay around for a few weeks until we found another job."

"How many operatives did he have?"

"Lessee. There was four full time and four more that he used sometimes." Shouldn't be hard to track them down if they were needed.

We were interrupted. A head entered the room from somewhere in the back of the house. A tiny head. It was followed into the room by a body of considerable bulk.

"Oh, there's Oliver. Come in, honey. This is Albert what called up half an hour ago. He's come to talk to me about Mr. Oscar Lennox that I worked for. You talk to him for a minute will you, honey? I got to go to the john."

While I shook hands with Oliver Huddenlocher, Janny trip-tropped to another part of the house.

"How'd ja do?" asked Oliver.

"Fine," I said untruly. "Did you know Oscar Lennox?"

"No, sir," he said with finality. "But when you live in a town this size, you hear about people like him."

"Oh?" I said.

"You know, a private detective and all. Not that Janny had to do anything bad while she worked for him. But people like that, well, you're not really surprised when they die by the sword."

"I guess not."

"Excuse me, will ya? I got to go finish mowing the lawn."

Which he did, leaving me alone in the room, in the world. To think about the necessity of sword control legislation in a civilized country.

Janny took her sweet time, but it's a lady's prerogative. "Hi," she said when she did come back. She fluffed her hair up and settled back into her chair. "That feels better. Where were we?"

I stayed another half hour. I found out relatively little about Oscar Lennox. To be fair it was because I didn't have many specific questions to ask. But about Janny Huddenlocher, née Crockett, I learned quite a bit. I'm an expert. Go ahead, ask me anything.

29

It wasn't a long drive back to Lennox's house. I didn't have time to resolve the different impressions I'd got of Lennox, the man. Kindly, understanding boss, philosophically inclined and rich enough to retire. Loner who didn't deign to sup with the Masons. Divorce detective who people called, but didn't have much nice to say about to the little girl who'd been given his phone number. Paper server who'd menaced Ralph Tomanek and Eddie

Ephray so effectively that Tomanek had thought he ought to shoot him.

The trip wasn't even long enough for me to ask myself what I was doing sweating so much about a dead man. At least not long enough to answer it. To do that, I had to sit in my car in the dead man's driveway.

I checked my notebook. I remembered why I was checking Lennox out. To find out if there were any mitigating circumstances associated with Lennox's occupation which could help Ralph Tomanek. More generally to see if there had been some connection between Lennox and Tomanek, or Ephray, or Mrs. Ephray or Mrs. Jerome. I could imagine connections, but none of them helped Ralph.

Does a private detective always have to work for good guys? Isn't it enough for him just to be a good guy?

On the other hand, I wasn't working for Ralph. I was working for Mrs. Ralph. Surely she was a good guy. Maybe things would be better for her, whether she knew it or not, if Ralph was snatched from her bosom. Childe Ralphe.

Lennox's house looked worse with smashed windows. It seemed an age since a bullet had whined above my head. Far enough above, true. But think of the possibility of richochet. . . .

I wondered if Bobby and George would arrange for pane replacements or at the least boarding up the windows. May is an unpredictable time in Indiana. Or rather predictable; you can be sure that there will be flash thunderstorms, deluges, damage. In between the balms. I found myself caring what happened to Lennox's house.

I opened the door with the three keys. Three keys? To serve notice that he cared about security. It should warn the wary, presumably, that there might be more to his defenses than door locks. An excellent gentleman and scholar, Oscar Lennox. True blue. Honest, hardworking. Never bluffs.

I checked Lennox's desk. The lower drawers were open and empty.

I went upstairs, oblivious, this time as before, to wires on the door. Knowledge allows great liberties to libertines. On occasion.

I was tired.

Only at the top of the stairs did I realize just how big a place Lennox's house was. There's something about coming to a long landing with six doors leading off it.

It left me a problem. I was looking for Lennox's bedroom. Which one? A dicer's chance. I went to the closest.

It was locked. The key ring gave no relief.

The next room was locked, too, and the one next to it.

The fourth was a room with a toilet, the fifth had a bath tub and a shower as separate fittings. Quaint.

I took pause before the sixth. Three locked rooms. What does a private detective keep in locked rooms in Selwood, Indiana? Bodies?

I decided that I was glad the doors were locked. Bodies neglected for so long—just one month after Lennox's decease, would surely not be pleasant. Bodies need watering every day.

The last room was unlocked and contained a double bed. The bedroom, perchance. It was intricate, human. Lived in. Filled with useful space. The sort of room a man who lives in one room and an office can appreciate.

The bed was firm and comfortable. I would like taking this place over.

I lay down for a while.

I went to sleep.

It was very dark when I woke up. It was about nine thirty. I lay on the bed for quite a while. Computing the odds of my sanity. How in hell could I fall asleep in this particular place? Danger somehow lurked everywhere. I doubted the wisdom of turning a light on. One of Selwood's kindly neighbors would see the unaccountable light on in the late Mr. Lennox's house and, thinking it was a black family moving in under the protection of dark, they would call the Army, Navy, and Merchant Marine.

I didn't feel much like running into George and Bobby again.

Nevertheless . . . I didn't feel much like coming back to Selwood again tomorrow. The eternal problem.

I was also cold.

In the dark I closed the blinds. I thought about putting blankets over the windows, but as I soon discovered, there was only one blanket and there were two windows. The blanket was electric. I tried its controls. It worked.

So I got in under the blanket and warmed up.

I was no longer tired. My arm didn't hurt. My afternoon shock didn't send chills up and down my spine anymore. I couldn't, in short, think of any good reason not to look over the room for a blue box.

Right. I got up, switched on all the lights so no one could conceivably think I was being coy about it, and searched the room.

No blue cross-reference file card box.

I did the room pretty thoroughly. It was nearly eleven by the time I finished. Time to go home. Time to go to bed. A good, safe, simple bed. My own bed.

30

I slept the good sleep. Moody and deep, I was out for nearly eleven hours. Up just in time to see the last wisps of morning sun change into the first wisps of afternoon sun. The change wasn't dramatic. I was surprised that a big manila envelope didn't come across the sky to finish off morning followed by a second envelope from which poured the afternoon.

The absence of this sort of thing actually surprises me rarely. But a fella wakes up in moods.

Wakes up, but doesn't necessarily get up. I found I wasn't hungry. I just lay and watched my friends, the clouds, through my window.

I thought about Oscar Lennox. I thought about the day I had just finished sleeping off. I didn't quite believe the sort of things I was thinking about. The sort of things that don't happen to a fella. Things that didn't add up. The more I thought about it, the more I wanted one little blue box.

By twelve thirty I realized that my ivies were dying. I keep them in my window. They keep themselves, actually, but they do need water. I'd been spending less time with them than they had grown accustomed to over the winter. They were poorly.

So I got up. I watered them. Then I went out for a little walk.

Doughnut and coffee from a stall in the City Market.

Chat and coffee with Malmberg in the Homicide Department.

"Tried to call you yesterday," he said.

"I was out getting shot at by a couple of trigger-happy cops," I bantered.

"Ten years ago that might have been a joke, Mr. Samson, but these days a crack like that is taken down in triplicate and sent to the police review board."

"Would I lie to you?" A holy pause, in reverence. "What did you want?"

"We've done a little background work on Tomanek's problem. Thought you might be interested."

"I'm interested."

"You want the report or the gist."

"Start with the gist."

"All right. I went to Newton Towers to have a chat with Ephray. He no longer has an apartment there. Then I went to the manager of the building. Apparently Newton Towers has been open, officially, for about a week. It's a residential upper-income building. Ten floors, luxury fittings. It's only just started taking the people on its list in. But five of the apartments were used briefly at the end of April."

"And one of the users was Ephray?"

"One was Ephray. Others: a Woodrow Ivydene, an Adrian Hall IV, a Robinson Holroyd, a Roger Millwald." He sat back with his eyebrows raised.

"OK. I recognize Ephray and Holroyd. Who are the others?"

"Hall and Millwald I don't know. They may or may not be local. But Ivydene is the husband of the sister of former Mayor Cawley's wife, and the funny thing about him is that we had an inquiry about him from Camden, New Jersey."

"Why?"

"Seems his name appeared in some documents they took away from some nasty people they ran across there."

"No kidding."

"We couldn't help them. He hasn't been of any interest to us here. All we've had is some rumor that his suits get paid for by local talent who don't pay for everybody's suits." He pulled at his lapels. "'One other thing. It's perfectly possible that the guy who runs Newton Towers was there, too. A Malton Markenbuch. The building is in his name."

"Any taint on him?"

"None that I've heard of. He's got money, that's one thing."

I thought about it. "Well," I said. "This is all very interesting, but I can't see what it has to do. . . ."

"Damn it, Mr. Samson, it was you that wanted to know what Ephray was doing in Newton Towers. Now you know. Some sort of business conference. I've probably given you even more than that—a plausible case why Tomanek was there. Holroyd decided to break him in easy, considering his record. He puts him in a building that's empty except for five or six guys who are having a meeting. Should have been a piece of cake."

"I suppose Holroyd even sent Lennox up there at eleven at night to test Tomanek, to see whether he would pull the trigger or not."

"At least it shows how Holroyd knew Ephray would be in that particular building."

"To have a paper served in the middle of some joint business negotiation?"

Malmberg shrugged. It didn't bother him. I wasn't sure that it bothered me, but I certainly wasn't sure that it didn't. I said, "All right. I want to know about a blue box."

"Oh really?"

I explained about Lennox's filing system and what Janny Huddenlocher had told me about the way Lennox always kept the box near him. I omitted the detail that the description was of habits six years out of date.

"And you couldn't find it when you looked around."

"No. But there are three locked rooms, and there may be a basement. I think they should be searched."

He sighed. "If it's not where he usually kept it, why should it be in the other rooms?"

"I don't think it is. I just think they should be checked so we can be sure that someone has it who shouldn't have it."

"All right," he said in such a way that he made clear he was mighty tired, so early in the day. "But have you considered that maybe if it's missing it's nothing to do with Tomanek or with Lennox being killed? Maybe someone just heard he'd died and went in and picked it up."

"The thought had occurred to me," I lied. It hadn't, until he said it. It should have occurred to me. I was just being stupid. The goddamn box didn't have to relate to my goddamned client at all.

"What do you think? The secretary or maybe one of his former clients?"

"Hard to say. But there's a photographer in Selwood called Ridgelea who worked with Lennox. He dropped some hints. If he has it, he'd probably offer to sell it to me."

"At which time you tell me and we can drop in and collect it."

"Are all cops bullies?"

"Yes."

"All right, Sergeant. You take a couple of flunkies who are tired of traffic duty out to search the Lennox house to make sure the box isn't there."

He sighed yet again. "OK. This afternoon. Stop by about four or four thirty at Lennox's house."

31

I remaindered the early afternoon by going home. On the way up I tried my neighbor's door. It didn't yield. Tenants.

I went to my own door and carried myself across the threshold to an old age with nothing but showers. No longer to lose sight of my toes beneath the murky water.

The hot and cold ran brown for a few minutes. Corrosion in the pipes from disuse. I'd liked my baths. After a while it ran clear, and the new era began.

It was while I was drying myself that I heard the first bangings on the wall. My luck, a wall-sculpting neighbor. You'd think with all the vacant offices in this building—there must be a dozen—my presence would reduce the desirability of my specific neighborhood. It reflected on the people who had taken it.

I sighed, aloud, to myself. At my age one shouldn't be constantly subjected to the whims of hostile outsiders, aggressive landlords, and the like. I don't like change as much as I used to. I never liked it forced on me. I would campaign to get whoever it was out. I would become a ghost. Clank my chains.

I practiced by rattling my towel. The pounding on the wall continued. There was some question as to who was haunting who.

To pretend I was doing something, I called Maude Simmons.

"Well, well. Albert Samson. A voice from the past. I figured you had wised up and quit your seedy racket. I heard you became someone's valet."

Laugh a minute, Maude. She knew damn well why I'd been out of action. "I'm on an urgent case, no time to quip. A big bunko operation. I need the full rundown on a corrupt newspaper editor called Maude Simmons, but I need it fast because the police are about to make a raid."

And so we went on, for maybe five minutes.

Maude's real function in life is the sale of information about who's who in Indianapolis. She just edits in her spare time. Ultimately I asked her for outline information on Woodrow Ivydene, Adrian Hall IV, Roger Millwald, Malton Markenbuch, Edward Ephray, and Robinson Holroyd. With attention to what they might be up to together.

A fast twenty dollars.

I wonder how I'd like being a valet.

* * *

At three forty-five someone knocked on my door. That is a rare occurrence since that particular door is my lone advertisement, and it says plainly to walk right in.

Only illiterates knock.

He, it, they knocked again. With missionary zeal I roused myself and answered it. I was going out anyway.

A mustachioed gentleman with a bum-length braided queue hanging over his left shoulder said, "Hello. I'm your new neighbor."

"Hello." Behind him stood two young ladies of the gentleman's approximate age, give or take five years. Their backs were three-quarters turned, and they were marveling about the intricate pattern the cracks in the hallway make beneath the cobwebs.

"My name is Danny," said my neighbor. He pumped my hand for water. "I'm a Harvard dropout, and these are my wives, Lucille and Ena." That disappointed me. I was sure he'd brought one for me. Sort of a get-acquainted gift.

"How do you do, one and all. Would you care to come in?"

"That's mighty neighborly of you, but we have to get back to work." His accent was All-Eastern, but he seemed to be trying to overlay it with rusticisms. Imagine a Kennedy saying "mighty neighborly."

"You starting some sort of business?"

"That's right. We're opening a car transport service. Like you get transferred to your company's New Mexico branch and you want someone to drive your car out there because you're too old. See, we drive it there for you."

"Sounds good."

"What do you do?"

I gestured to the door. "I'm a private detective." Ena's head turned sharply toward me, but it still looked like a three-quarter back profile.

"Groovy," said Danny.

"When do you open?"

"Oh, we're open now. Mighty open. Got a blackboard on the wall to keep track of the comings and goings of all our cars and drivers, and we got an ad in the afternoon paper."

"If I were you, I'd advertise in the *Star*. Not only a bigger circulation, but it's read over a larger area of the state."

"Thanks for the tip."

"Any time."

Conversation failed for a moment, until Danny said, "Well, dollies, back to work. We just wanted to stop in and say 'Hello, Albert!' like, and let you know that we won't be hammering on the walls all night."

"That's plum friendly," said I. A jest, like, but taken seriously by Danny as a sample of local dialect.

"We'll see you around, Albert."

"I'm sure."

They left, and I gathered my belongings and left, too. Bound for Selwood. I had a date with some police gentlemen and, I hoped, with a blue cross-reference index file box.

On the way out I decided that I liked Danny and his harem. If I ever got rich, I'd have my car transported to Evansville or somewhere. And back. Just to be plum neighborly.

32

The police gentlemen were not on the premises when I arrived. I wasn't sure whether to call Malmberg or go on in. I went in.

The police had been there. They left me a note on Lennox's desk of yore.

> *Re* missing index file.
> Mr. Samson.
> The file is not on the premises. Sgt. Malmberg requests you keep him informed of your progress.
> Search leader: Patrolman Charles Plzak.

Cops are funny. You get all kinds. Trigger-happy beef. Ambitious traditionalists. And nowadays bank clerks. There's been quite a change in the police force the last few years, as the veterans they hired after World War II have come up for retirement. Vets were given preference then. But not now.

Before I left, I took a stroll through the rooms that had been locked on my previous visits. They were open now, and I found out why there had been no busy reception waiting for me, laid on by Cops, Inc. The rooms were utterly empty. There had not been much to search. No drawer bottoms, no chair stuffings, no globular lamp shades.

I left and drove into Selwood center. Near the bus station. It was about a quarter to five. I parked at a meter and studied my notebook to remind myself about Wallace Ridgelea.

Then went in.

"Hello, Susan. Is Mr. Ridgelea in?" She looked at me funny. Then screwed up her eyes.

"My name isn't Susan."

I can't help it. My notebook said her name was Susan. That is, that Ridgelea's front lady was Susan. Come to think of it, this wasn't Susan. I'd been preoccupied with figuring just what I was going to say to Ridgelea and had been showing off that I keep such detailed notes in my little book. Which I do. I live everything twice.

But I guess I've got to start taking pictures.

Or paying more attention to faces.

Or stop taking opportunities to show off.

"Gee, I said. "Are you sure?"

"I'm sure."

"Is Mr. Ridgelea available?"

"He's in the back doing a sitting. He'll be done at five. He might be able to see you then. Is it about a portrait?"

"It's about some candid photography. But he'll know my name."

I left it and then went window shopping along Selwood's high street.

I bought a doughnut. Honey dipped.

At ten after five Wallace Ridgelea was sitting at his receptionist's desk doing nothing but waiting for little old me. Not-Susan was gone. Apart from the flaxen butterball in the chair, the place looked lifeless in the way that only large collections of still photographs can. Even Ridgelea didn't move visibly till I knocked.

He unlocked the door and let me in and hardly let me pass through before he was shaking my hand and grinning.

"I'm glad to see you," he said.

"Good," I said. "Can we go somewhere a little less on display?"

We went through to his studio, and instead of going up to the lab, we sat on a pine bench he apparently used as seating for crowded family portraits. Formal family portraits are coming back into fashion, and Wallace Ridgelea was at the forefront.

"Can I take it," he said, "that your coming back here so fast means that you have been thinking about taking over poor Oscar's endeavors?"

"I've been giving it a lot of thought," I said. "But I'm a careful man."

"Wise." He was grinning like he was the only cat in town and I was the only mouse.

I raised my voice enough for pussy to notice the increase in volume. "I'm a careful man, and on reflection I consider it stupid for me to go into an operation like this on the word of a small-town photographer I've met once and don't know anything about. A baby photographer at that."

I turned away to look over the room and to let his optimism evaporate and to let him get to the point of wondering just what the hell I had come for.

When I looked back at him, the grin was gone, but he wasn't in shock. A quizzical frown. He was waiting for me.

"Especially when that small-town baby snapper has not exactly played it straight down the line." Now I was doing my ocular best to bore through him.

The theory was simple. If he had the blue box, he would know just what I meant and would, should, be impressed that I knew it. One of the ways to find out whether something is true is to act as if it is true and watch the results. If he didn't have it, it wouldn't matter. I had no intentions of taking over Lennox's enterprise or ever having dealings with Wallace Ridgelea again. I'd gone thirty-eight years without him. I'd manage the take away.

"I. . . . What do you mean?" If there were time, my coy mistress.

"When I do business with somebody, Ridgelea, I do it man to man and cards on the table. I don't like it when someone holds out. Do you understand? I don't like it." I edged closer to him on the bench and raised my voice. One of my better performances, helped by the fact that I'd put on some winter bulk. When I'm not in motion, I can look threatening.

He shook his head in confusion. He was the sort of man who would take a bent opportunity if it came along, but who didn't have the fortitude to make a bent opportunity or habitually keep bent company. Certainly he wasn't used to being threatened. Not many people are. "I. . . ."

"Now look, damn it. You want to get back on the gravy train? You've got a little box of goodies rightfully belonging to the estate of our late mutual friend. It's something I should have a look at, and I don't much care for the fact that you didn't volunteer it the last time I was here."

It was crunch time. Did he or didn't he?

For quite a while he just didn't speak, and I began to get bored just sitting and boring through him. Masters of human quirk are supposed to tell worlds from mysterious lengthy silences. This one just remained a mystery to me.

But then it happened. . . . "I'll get them," he said and he turned toward the stairs to his mezzanine lab. But he stopped. "How?" Hesitation.

"Yeah?" Rough, tough, and hard to bluff. Arrr.

"How did you know I had them?"

"I am a detective, you know."

He went to his lab.

I nearly choked trying to keep from laughing. How do you get something? Ask for it.

Though, to be fair, there was a dangling artificial carrot during the query. Tell me all, said the carrot. Show me proof of everything that Lennox did and pass on his active files, and then I'll go into business and pay you enough to buy you lots and lots of whatever a donkey buys with money.

While I waited, I looked around the studio. I have more

than a passive interest in photography, but I didn't learn a lot walking around. I suppose there was not much about studio photography that I wanted to learn.

After several minutes I began to wonder just what the hell he was doing. Where the hell was the man? Why the hell had I let my mind and attentions wander.

I was getting senile, no doubt. When you do a job, you do it. No folderol till it's bloody well done. Dumb ass, old bean.

I heard a creak from somewhere. Building noises as it settled in for the night?

I just didn't know whether to go up to the lab or not. Was he waiting up there with some surprise? Did he want me to come up? Or had he gone out the back? Phoned for some muscular assistance? Maybe even the obliging state troopers *d'antan*?

I went out of the studio to the reception room. Through the venetian blinds I looked over the street. A lot of cars. It was not yet 6 P.M. The daylight outside reassured me. Perhaps the most striking thing about a portrait studio has nothing to do with the trappings people pose on. It's the control of light. If you're thinking midnight thoughts, it's one of the quickest places to simulate midnight light.

I stood, indecisive, in the doorway between office and studio. I was sure he was gone. Certain.

The door to the darkroom opened, and I jerked backward into the reception room/office. I felt a blow at the back of my left knee. For all my will it caught me by surprise and I couldn't help falling. Into the arms of my assailant. An armchair for impatient kiddies' impatient parents.

"Mr. Samson?" Ridgelea came slowly down the stairs. "Is everything all right?"

Who was the donkey now? "Yes," I said. "Just peachy. Where the hell have you been? I've had half a night's sleep in this chair here." Rain or shine, the show must go on. At least now I was genuinely grumpy. The key to method improvising is to adapt your own feelings to the situation you've been set. It was getting easier and easier.

"I'm awfully sorry," said Ridgelea. "But I keep them

very safe and out of the way. And it's been so long since I added anything to them that I'd moved a lot of things in front of them."

I was beginning to come back to the real world. It was six in the evening in Selwood, Indiana, and Wallace Ridgelea was standing mousy in front of me. But not holding anything that could remotely be called a blue file card box.

I could see it was an envelope. I almost gave in and asked, but I reached for it instead.

He placed it delicately in my hand. Score one for Samson, but one what?

"All right. Now where is the blue box?"

"What blue box?"

"Lennox's cross-reference file that matches names with cases."

"I'm sorry, Mr. Samson. I don't know anything about it. All I have is what I've given you."

I thought about it. If I went on pleading for information without having thought the thing out, I would lose my image. I had to assume that Ridgelea was telling the truth, that my game had eliminated all the petty artifice he possessed. That he was really just a shallow pool.

"Where will you be the next few days in case I want to call you and ask you some more questions?"

That made him nervous. "Why, here. During the day."

"And at night?"

It took a little more bluff and bluster. But I got his home phone and another phone. One or the other would work.

I gathered my wrap from the bench.

"I . . . just didn't mention those before," he said, referring to the plural contents of the envelope, "I want you to understand. Oscar never knew I made them. That's the only reason why I didn't, well, mention them before."

I grunted and left him to stew.

My vehicle was overdue on the meter, but unticketed. I got in and, without looking back, drove off. I didn't want Ridgelea to watch me look over his gift. If he was looking after me from his window or from his doorway, I wanted to show a decisive state of mind. I didn't look back to see if he was watching. I turned around and drove off toward the big city.

When I was out of Selwood, I stopped by the edge of the road. It was a fat envelope, and the insides crinkled. I pulled out the contents. A great wad of negative folders. Filled with photographic negatives. What else would you expect from a photographer?

I picked one of the packets and pulled out a sample. Just a snapshot of a couple of people. A man and a woman.

A car passed me, perhaps not the first since I had pulled over, but the first I'd noticed. The last thing I wanted was a visitor. Did the car slow down as it went by? What if a cop came by? Especially a cop from this, my favorite part of Indiana. How many times must a man get shot at to be gun-shy? Or shotgun-shy?

I packed the negatives back into the envelope and put the envelope . . . where? Where would be safe? Nowhere. So I settled for inside a tear in the car's roof padding. It made the tear bigger, but what the hell.

I pulled back on the road and hustled, under the speed limit, all the way home.

The only thing that happened was that as I stopped at a light a hop, skip, and a spit from home, the envelope fell out of the ceiling and hit me on the shoulder.

But I'm a big boy. I didn't cry.

33

When I got upstairs about ten to seven, I had a fair idea of what I would do. First I took an aging TV dinner out of the refrigerator and put it in the oven at about two-thirds the recommended temperature. To coax it into eatability.

Then I set to making contact prints of the negatives Wallace Ridgelea had been so kind as to contribute to the cause. The big envelope contained twenty-nine negative sheaths, each of which bore a code number, but no other identification. They all contained 35mm film, but they had different numbers of frames. The fewest was fifteen, but one sheath surrounded more than seventy separate exposures. I didn't spend much time examining the negatives. I'd spend my time when I had positives.

It took ages to get contacts of them all. In the middle of the printing I came out of my closet briefly to turn the oven off.

I ate while the contacts were rinsing. There's nothing cooler than a cool TV dinner. I washed it down with a tot of bourbon and a beer. I didn't rinse the pictures for the full time. I wasn't aiming for fifty-year keeping quality. I dried them in the oven.

It was eleven fifteen by the time I was relaxing in my dining-room chair studying the snaps. I didn't have any trouble catching the drift of what they were; there wasn't much question. They were rather standard divorce-evidence-type pictures. Couples going here and coming there. Only seven of the twenty-nine series contained pictures set in relatively explicit indoor circumstances. They were probably the product of hidden cameras of one sort or another.

But as divorce pictures they were schizo. Each set included a sequence of noncompromising pictures. Man taking walk. Woman working late in office.

Ridgelea had explained the setup in my first visit. In certain cases Oscar Lennox would get positive evidence on somebody and then conspire for lucre with that somebody to rig negative evidence.

In twenty-nine cases, I dared to say after examining the pictures. Ridgelea had given me the photographic part of the fake evidence Oscar Lennox had used in his little hustle.

I was quite astounded; it was like looking into someone's special closet, the one he keeps his skeletons in.

I walked around the room a couple of times. I'll admit to a furrowed brow. I had no doubt what the pictures were. I had other questions.

Lennox made a successful deal with Mr. 592, and together they compiled evidence that satisfied Mrs. 592 that her husband was faithful and true. Most of the evidence would be Lennox's written report, but the new set of rigged pictures would be convincing icing. Mrs. 592 would be satisfied; Mr. 592 would be satisfied; Lennox would be richer. And satisfied. But the question was what Lennox did with the two contradictory stories he'd collected. Which would include the two contradictory sets of negatives.

Mrs. 592 would get the rigged report. But surely, *surely*, there would be some assurance to Mr. 592 that the incriminating report and set of negatives would be destroyed? Wouldn't he demand it as part of what he was paying for?

I would have thought he would.

What I couldn't see was how Ridgelea, of all people, came to have the negatives of *both* sets of pictures.

It was a problem. I didn't solve it by walking around. I sat down and had another look over the contact prints I had made. That solved it.

I should have noticed it before, perhaps. Each negative strip was made up of pictures that were numbered in series. The numbering is not something that the photographer puts on; the numbers come on the film. The key to my problem was that in each group of negatives the numbering was consecutive.

That meant the pictures had already been edited; the rigged pictures continued right on in number from the end of the candid pictures. They would not originally have been shot on the same film. So the negatives I had were edited, abridged copies of the original negatives that had been shot.

Moreover, only Lennox would have been able to edit them properly, to pick out which pictures were damning and which weren't.

And that meant that Lennox, on each of these cases, had had Ridgelea make a continuous set of negative copies. Presumably for Lennox to keep in the files, so he could dramatically present the originals to Mr. and Mrs. 592 for respective destruction.

That suggested that after making edited negatives for Lennox, Ridgelea had made a second set for himself. It's easy enough to do, if you have the means to make the first negative copy. But why? To keep a little evidence on Lennox?

I laughed out loud to myself. It was perfectly possible that if I went to Lennox's files and picked the right cases—presumably they corresponded to the index numbers on the negatives I had—I would be able to come up with Lennox's copies of the same negatives.

34

I woke up early. Too early, full of anxieties about all the things I had to do and all the things I had left undone. Mature people realize that useful occupation should be strung out, played for its satisfactions. But when I get something live, I want to jump for it, devour it.

As I lay in bed before getting up, I'd realized that the first thing to do on a Tuesday morning was *not* to jump in the landaulet and trot off to Selwood for another look in Lennox's files. There were other things of interest to do. Like try to identify some of the personnel in the negatives I had. If I could find some familiar faces, it might prove something. Maybe. If Rosetta had been trying to divorce Ralph. . . .

Before breakfast, I went off to buy some more photographic paper.

And I came back home and got to work. I printed wallet-size close-ups of the faces in each set of negatives.

Breathing chemicals in the darkroom so early in the morning gave me a headache. It made me impatient. I gave my wallet snaps even less rinsing time than I'd given the contacts. I'd be lucky if they lasted a month.

I toweled them off and rushed them to the oven. I steadfastly triumphed over the temptation to look at them. But I turned the oven up a little higher than usual.

I felt special to have such a good file of nearly divorced persons.

For the first five minutes while they were drying I looked out my window and twiddled my thumbs.

Then I made myself useful. I wrote down the code numbers from the twenty-nine negative sets. When I did go to Lennox's, it would facilitate my investigation.

Then I put on a pot of coffee. Then I looked in the oven. The pictures were dry.

I took them out, cooled them down, flattened them. The coffee burned. I turned it off. And finally I had a look through the cast album.

And I found a familiar face. Or two. No lesser faces than Robinson Holroyd, impresario of Easby Guards, *and* Edward Ephray, antiquarian. Messrs. 394 and 516 respectively.

I was sure of Holroyd's identification, though less definite about Ephray's. The close-up was a little blurred, and he hadn't had the beard he sported now, but I was pretty sure.

The others—there were seventy-nine different people in all—I couldn't identify. At least the girls with Holroyd were not Alice. Or Marie.

Ephray was a cute notion. It certainly tied up with his wife being on the jealous side. Though her continuing suspicion suggested that Lennox hadn't been completely convincing in his reassurances to her.

I was pretty sure that it was Edward Ephray. I really needed to know for sure. But I didn't feel like going back in the closet. Not when there was an option. Not when I already had an excuse to go to the man and look at him again. I had been supposed to meet him Monday or Tuesday. I would go now and explain how it was that my mother, overcome with pangs of remorse at the thought of selling her precious objects, had decided to sell her soul instead.

35

Finding Eddie Ephray on a Tuesday morning is easier said than done. At the auction gallery there were a lot of people, but nobody who worked for him except two porters helping purchasers clear out their new fineries.

I considered showing the picture I had of Mr. 516 to them, but my natural discretion stopped me. Nobody comes up to a stranger and says, "Do you know this man?" without advertising to all the stranger's acquaintances that somebody was showing pictures of the boss around. If it turned out to be the boss.

What I wanted was to see the man himself. So I could show the picture to myself. I knew I wouldn't gossip about it afterward. I have no one to gossip to.

"Can you tell me where I might find Mr. Ephray?"

"No."

Off to real estate office number one.

Thence to real estate office number two.

I decided to have a word with the man, about how he'd be smarter to have his enterprises centralized. But maybe having to travel around made him feel important. When I got to number two, I was told that the man had just gone to lunch. I nearly got mad, but before I could, Ephray came back.

"You better gimme a map, Mrs. Turner," he said to the aged darling behind the desk in this, the third of his establishments I had visited. I could see why he went wandering around with a furbelow now and again. A man who is confined to his office needs staff he can fantasize about. That's my theory.

When I am in my office, I fantasize about having staff.

"Mr. Ephray," I said.

"Oh yeah. You're the guy who came to the house. Was I supposed to see you yesterday or something?"

Why not? "You were indeed."

"Sorry. I'm *usually* in the auction office on Mondays, but this important piece of business broke. I can't even stop now. You see Morton, my auctioneer. I'm sure he'll be able to help you." If his memory had been better, he'd have known that that's what he'd told me Thursday. Of course, it's not everybody that keeps a notebook like mine.

"That won't be good enough," I said. When I get up early, I am not easily pleased.

After all, the man had put me to an inconvenience the day before. Hadn't he?

"Well, screw it, then. Mrs. Turner, I said I wanted the map, didn't I?"

"Which one, Mr. Ephray?"

"County."

The county map was blue and thick. I suspected it showed the location of every hundred-dollar bill in town.

I stood my ground and watched Ephray while he waited for his map. I felt like a dumb ass, but I felt also that I had a certain right. Special rights come from special knowledge. After all, I knew he was definitely Mr. 516. And not everybody knew that.

He took the map and left without further adieu. For no special reason I followed him. Out the door, and then later and at greater distance, in my car. I was curious to see just where all this big business was going on.

He headed south through the center of town and out the southwest on Route 67. But not too far, just a bit past the Municipal Sewage Disposal Plant and Maywood, to Mars Hill.

But before we got to Mars Hill, I was feeling stupid. Curiosity is all well and good. Call it hunches. But when a man has specific things that he wants to find out, wasting time on indefinables is self-indulgent. I wasn't thinking properly when I set off after Ephray. It just took me several miles to admit it to myself. My morning discoveries had made me feel a godhead. It's not a head I can keep up with after noon.

It's horrible to find yourself in the middle of a hunch project for which the hunch has run out. It's like watching a horse you have twenty bucks on go into the starting gate and remembering that he *lost* by ten lengths last time instead of winning by ten as you thought at first. There is an engulfing sense of waste. What in hell's name are you doing, Samson?

Which was a pretty good question all around.

At Rybolt Street Ephray turned left, but I let him go. It was too farfetched to think that anything he was doing out there was anything to me.

I stopped at a diner and got two coffees to take out and took them to my car.

Just what the hell *was* I doing? I was a long way from searching for extenuating circumstances on behalf of Ralph Tomanek. I had been working more on Oscar Lennox. Promiscuous curiosity again? The words I had been using were that I should know the participants better, that I should have a better idea, at least in general, of what they were doing, where they had been. Did I have such things? And wasn't it getting a bit past the time for general information?

Did I know what everyone had been doing there? No. In fact I wasn't satisfied with what I knew about any of them in Newton Towers on April 28.

I had a professional opinion that Ralph Tomanek had known better than to take a job that involved carrying a weapon and that he might well have been able not to fire it under stress anyway.

But he was there, and he had fired it.

I had the image of Edward Ephray, nervous and paranoid, telling Tomanek that he was in danger and inciting Tomanek to kill. Yet the Ephray I knew was pretty gross, but not overnervous.

And I had Oscar Lennox, trade-mate, who had been a first-class divorce man for decades, who had retired comfortably, even elegantly. This is the man out at night serving legal papers and getting shot in the bargain.

All of it, every single bit, reeked to high heaven.

Christ, no wonder I was following people around the world's sewage plants. None of it made sense.

That upset me. I had finished my coffees and truly didn't feel like more, but I wanted to go in and get more to . . . to break, to rest.

But I didn't. There are times when a man has to follow

his stomach, not in the hunger way, but from what he feels in his gut is right. It was right that I drink no more coffee. It was correct, right, that nothing in the whole case fit. And it was right that I go ahead slowly and make sense. Clients be damned. You get to a point in the world where something comes to represent all the gut-rotting slime of human endeavor and you have to mobilize yourself.

When your basketball game is going sour, go back to fundamentals.

Fundamentals in my game are facts and questions. I went back to my notebook and read. And asked questions.

The first good fact I found was proof in one particular that Edward Ephray was a liar. He'd told Graniela he didn't know Lennox. The picture of Mr. 516 made a liar of him.

The first good question I asked concerned the paper that Oscar Lennox had been serving. I had noted that it was on behalf of Robinson Holroyd and to be served on Eddie Ephray.

Which was uncredible, for two reasons. First, they were, in a fashion yet undetermined, business associates. Ephray had a suite in Newton Towers because he was to negotiate with four or five other men, including Holroyd. In fact, it was by no means unlikely that Holroyd had a room in the Towers within gunshot distance of Ephray's.

The second reason that it was unlikely was more one-sided. Holroyd hated private detectives; at least he had hated me when he found out I was a private detective. If that was true, why had he hired one to serve his paper? He could have done it himself if he was meeting Ephray daily. Or he could have had Tomanek do it. Or anybody else, for that matter. Alice even. Why, in God's name, Oscar Lennox?

Of all the people in the world.

It was a decent question.

Mars Hill is reasonably convenient for Selwood. Mann Road to Interstate 465, which lets you off on Selwood Road. It's not scenic stuff. But it was becoming familiar.

I made only one call in Selwood. Lennox's house and files. I checked the twenty-nine case numbers I had. Or thought I had.

Not a single case file was there.

I wasn't really shocked to find them missing, but I didn't know immediately what it meant. I decided to go through the entire file system to see just how many entry numbers *were* missing. Whether it could be coincidence that my twenty-nine were gone.

No coincidence. Mine were the only twenty-nine missing entries. It was worth thinking about. It was my day for thinking.

36

I parked at home and went upstairs to use the phone. The answering service informed me that a Maude Simmons had called in my absence, but I didn't call her right back. Instead I gathered the whole of my close-up collection, and I walked over to my friendly men in blue.

I had my choice. Malmberg or Miller. Things must have been quiet. I took Malmberg.

"I expected to hear from you again yesterday," he said.

"Us working men don't always have time to drop in for a gossip."

He said, "Oh?" Malmberg was not turning out to be the most mirthful of men. But an unaccustomed confidence, resulting from my few poor ideas as to how the irreconcilable reconciled, helped me shift styles midturn, quell my quippery, and get down to work.

I said, "I've been busy."

"You're not the only one. Say, did you know that Tomanek's case has been assigned? For a week from Friday."

"No."

"Well, it has. How did you find things at that photographer's?"

"He doesn't have the cross-reference file."

"Are you sure?"

"Absolutely." Well, quite reasonably sure. "But I'm on to something else. I want you to have the fingerprints taken off Lennox's filing cabinets. There are twenty-nine case files missing, and I think that whoever took them has the box. It's the only way someone could know to take just those particular files. There's a chance, just a chance, that there might be prints."

"Oh yes?"

"Another thing, Lennox's front door had a silent alarm direct to the state police office in Selwood. I want you to check with them and see what record they have of the alarm being tripped since the last week in April. That can't be hard."

"I mean no disrespect, Mr. Samson, but are you in possession of all your faculties?"

"It's no big deal, Malmberg."

"I'm going to have to check with Miller."

"Fine, fine. But let me finish first. I want a picture of Oscar Lennox."

"As a corpse?"

"As a private detective, if possible, but as a corpse if you can't come up with something better. Maybe from the licensing bureau, or something. Oh, and while we're at it, take a look at these." I spread out my close-ups. "Do you recognize anybody?"

He looked at me more unbelieving than ever. But he didn't ask me where I got them. He just picked them up one at a time and studied them. Like a good identifier does.

"This is your friend Holroyd," he said, looking up after the third picture. "I saw him yesterday. He gave me his file on Tomanek." He interrupted his perusals and got a folder out of his drawer. The one I had missed my chance at stealing six days before. He pushed it over to me. Everything comes to him who waits.

I wish.

He went back to the pictures. He pulled out a woman, then a man, and then another man, Ephray, whom I'd put back on the bottom of the pack after I'd got home from my jaunts. A man and a woman to the good.

"This one," he said, "is your friend Ephray. I had a little chat with him, too. This one is a guy called Brian Jones who ran for Congress a couple of times and lived on the same street as us. And this one, the woman, I arrested for soliciting when I was on probation. The others I don't know. Never arrested any of them. Help you?"

"I guess so. What does Brian Jones do for a living?"

"I don't know. He isn't in Congress."

I threatened to haunt him forever if he didn't move his ass on the things I wanted. But I don't think he was impressed.

37

My next step was Ralph Tomanek. It was just past four thirty. I didn't know what sort of hours visitors were restricted to, so I hit them with everything I had. Tomanek was coming up for trial; I was his lawyer's representative; I wanted to see him now. A sledgehammer for a fly. I was within general visiting hours.

They took me again to the isolated glass-divided room reserved for legal consultations. I felt kind of bad while I waited for him. My real client.

I seemed to wait a long time. It was a cold place for the soul. I haven't exactly taken life and tweaked its cheek, but that glass wall makes you realize there are people worse off than you are.

Ralph Tomanek, for instance. He was even paler than I remembered him, if that was possible. A kind of blanched butterfly, floating to death's light.

"Hello," I said.

He peered at me through the glass before he sat down. Not that there was any glare or the room was dark. More as if he had just been brought out of a darkroom or reverie.

"It's you then."

"That's right, Albert Samson. I talked to you a week ago."

"I remember." He sat down slowly.

"Were you expecting someone else?"

"No." As if he never expected anything. He waited, looking at the little counter which supports the glass divider.

"Are they treating you all right?" I don't often feel motherly, but. . . .

"All right."

"Ralph, do you remember who I am? Do you remember anything about me?"

"No."

"I'm a private detective. Rosetta hired me to try to help you."

"Rosetta is my wife," he said. "How is Rosetta? Have you seen her?"

"Not in the last few days," I said, feeling some regret. "But I'm sure she's all right."

He was quiet, outside, but I felt inner chattering. Or maybe I just wished that, inside, he was a communicator.

I said, "Rosetta comes to visit you, doesn't she?"

"Yes."

"Often?" Pause. "Most days?"

"Yes. Most days."

"Well then, you can tell me how she is. How is she?"

"Rosetta's an angel. She's always deserved better than me."

"There's nothing much wrong with you, Ralph."

He lifted his eyes briefly. "Yes, there is," he said. He flicked the corners of his mouth up on each side. I suppose you could call it a smile.

"Oh? What?"

"I'm a degraded person," he said, now lip-flickerless, but at least looking directly at me.

"Why do you think that?"

"I am. I know it. It's the only thing I do know anymore."

"Has anybody told you that?"

"Yes. But I knew it before."

"Who told you something like that?"

No answer.

"Rosetta?"

"No! Never Rosetta. She's an angel, I told you that."

"She loves you. Would she love you if you weren't good?"

"That's why she's an angel."

"Ralph, who told you you were degraded?"

He didn't tell me. "Was it Dr. Grue?"

"Who's Dr. Grue?"

Was he guileful enough to act as if he didn't remember his psychiatrist if he really did? No.

"Dr. Vurst?"

He was silent. He remembered Dr. Vurst. And if "Vurst" had been quick to try to get on top of a hapless visitor, what kind of hell must he ladle onto the lives of other patients?

But Tomanek said, "It wasn't him."

"But he was bad to you."

"I . . . he agreed with me."

If he kept at it, everyone might agree. I tried something else.

"Look, Ralph, when did you start thinking that there was something wrong with you?"

"It didn't come out until I went over there."

Over there.

He went on. "Rosetta helped me."

"And she will again. Rosetta doesn't think there's much wrong with you. Dr. Grue doesn't think there's much wrong with you. I don't think there's much wrong with you. And I'm doing my best to try to help you get out of here."

"Out of here?" Flicker again. Oh, hell, get what you came for.

"I need to know something, Ralph. I need you to tell me again how you came to take the job with Easby Guards."

"I answered an ad in the paper."

"Did you see the ad? Did you decide to go?"

"No. The man at the veteran placement showed it to me. He said that Mr. Holroyd there did his best to give us a job. I needed a job. I tried and tried, and I couldn't find one." He was remembering struggle.

"And then you went over to Easby Guards. Who did you see there?"

"Mr. Holroyd."
"What did he say?"
"He looked over my file, and he talked to me."
"What about?"
"How I'd feel about being a building guard."
"How did you feel?"
Looked down below the counter. "I wanted a job."
"But how did you feel about being a guard, about carrying a gun?"
"I didn't want to. I knew I shouldn't do it."
"Why shouldn't you do it, Ralph?"
"It wasn't something I should do."
"What did he say about that?"
"He said that I should go home and think about it and come back tomorrow."
"What did Rosetta say?"
"That it was my decision. That I should do what was right."
"And what did Mrs. Jerome say. Her mother."
"I. . . . She doesn't like me." And maybe if we heard the chattering inside, we'd learn that you don't like her.
"But what did she say about the job?"
"She said I was crazy."
"But then you went back to Mr. Holroyd?"
"He said to. Yes, I went back."
"And told him what?"
"That I didn't think it was right. Wasn't there maybe something else that I could do?"
"What did he say?" It was like pulling teeth with a pair of scissors.
"A guard was the only job. That I shouldn't worry. Things would be all right. He took me out for a ride with him."
"A ride? Where to?"
"To the building where it happened."
"What did he say about it?"
"That that was where I'd be working, and that it was a nice new building. And he gave me some money. He. . . ." A frown. Tomanek's facial expressions were so rare I had to take note. "He said . . . said not to worry."

"Do you worry now, Ralph?"
"No. Only about Rosetta working."
"She has to live." That fact passed him by, so I got back on the track. "What happened then?"
"He took me home."
"Did he come in?"
"Yes."
"Was Rosetta there?"
"Yes."
"So it was after six."
"Yes."
"And what did he say?"
"That Rosetta and I should go out for a walk and I should tell her about the job."
"Did you?"
"Yes."
"And what did she say?"
"That it was my decision. So I decided."
"Do you think you made the right decision?"
"Yes," he said.
When I left, it was closer to six than five. I was extremely sober. Why is it that you go for days with nothing happening and then all of a sudden you start getting so much to think about that you can't balance what you have, you can't decide what should count and what shouldn't?
When you feel like that, it's time not to drink. I had intended to go over to see Maude. But that would have required flippancy which was not sober. I just didn't feel like it.
I walked around for a while and then went home.

38

There was a stranger in the office, an immaculate middle-aged man chewing gum. For some reason it never crossed my mind that he might be a client. I knew that he wasn't. I think I'll change my shingle to "Private Detective and Psychic."

"Mr. Samson?" he asked as he pitched forward off one of my chairs, his hand extended like a prow.

I shook it to avoid being gutted.

"Unless I am mistaken you are the owner of that gizzard green fifty-eight Plymouth that is parked behind this building."

"Yeah."

"Well, I'd like to buy it from you. Would you consider selling it?"

You get them all in this world. A Plymouth collector. He left his card in case I decided to sell.

If only I could find someone who wanted to reconstruct me into a life-size working model of a private detective. But no one would. All they'd do is break me for spares.

I put my evening's work down on the dining-room chair and put on water for a pot of tea. I looked over the cans on my shelves, but hunger didn't direct my hand to single out one can from among its fellows. Hunger seemed not to have his clock set right, so I settled for tea and files.

File, to be more precise. One Easby Guards employment file on Ralph Tomanek, trainee guard. It was not very full. In fact, it was, for me, empty, save one short typewritten note on veteran placement stationery. It was written, it said, to introduce Ralph Tomanek:

> Mr. H.,
>
> You asked us to try you with our difficult placements. Ralph is that; he has been having a very hard time. His high school grades were good; he graduated in the top third of his class. He's married, but really needs a job to complete his reintegration into ordinary civilian life. We had in mind some sort of desk job or clerkship, if it is conceivably possible. We're sure that in such a post he would soon respond, and develop into an excellent, loyal employee.

To this note Malmberg had clipped a note to the effect that veteran placement said they'd received and filled a request from Easby Guards for a summary of Tomanek's medical history.

Which, presumably, had been ignored. Or in which, perhaps, the optimism of psychiatrist Grue had been stressed. But it was a technical question. Holroyd had been warned about Tomanek, had ignored the warning.

Robinson Holroyd was morally responsible for killing Oscar Lennox. I was perfectly satisfied about that.

39

I was pouring a cup of tea into my giant-sized seaside prize mug when I heard my office door open.

I was too depressed to think about the possibility of danger. I barged through to the office, where I found, not pillaging barbarians, but my client, Rosetta Tomanek, and her pillaging mother, Mrs. Jerome.

"Good evening, ladies," I said. "May I offer you a cup of tea? I've just made it."

I should have been surprised when they accepted, but I wasn't. I left them sitting in the office, strolled back to my kitchen counter and poured tea from my mug into the two proper coffee cups I own. I have them for the little candlelit dinners *à deux* that I dreamed about when I was young and had just moved in. I knew little of the ways of the world then.

I brought the two cups and the mug out on a plate and carried cream, sugar, and spoons in the other hand. A proper gent I was. It's my hobby actually. Being a gent.

"We've just been to see Ralph," said Mrs. Jerome. "He said that you'd been there to see him."

"That's right."

"Well?"

Rosetta burst out before I could say anything. "He's going on trial, Mr. Samson. We just found that out. I just have to know how we're going to help him, how I'm going to keep him." She didn't break into tears, which would have been too easy, maybe.

"Have you talked to Ralph's lawyer about the hearing a week from Friday?"

"No," said Mrs. Jerome. "We just received a formal note from him this morning. That is, I received it and kept it for when Rosetta came home."

She showed it to me. It gave the court and date and time for the hearing.

"I will be going to see Lubart," I said, "but I'll try to give you some idea of what I've done."

"That would be something," snorted Mrs. Jerome.

"I never promised that I would be able to do anything for Ralph. You know that. I have been working hard and have made some progress, but whether anything will get a result that you want, I don't know."

"I just have to have him back home," said Rosetta. "He was doing so well. I don't think that I could bear it if he was put away in one of those places again."

"Or in jail?" I asked.

"They're all the same to me."

"So you came to me because there was nothing else you could do. But no one could guarantee to do anything."

"I think he's preparing you for a letdown," said Mrs. Jerome to her daughter. But even then Rosetta didn't cry. I suspected the well had long gone dry.

"In the eight days I have worked on this case I have done some positive things. I have been able to get the police to take interest when they thought it was already wrapped up."

"To what effect? What did they say?" asked Mrs. Jerome sharply. If nothing else, her interest had perked up in the last week.

"It's not finished. I've been finding out other things. The general line is this. There is good reason to believe that the man who hired Ralph acted irresponsibly in doing so. That Ralph shouldn't have been hired to carry a weapon." Rosetta was looking at the floor, but Mrs. Jerome was giving me her full attention. "The important thing is that

Ralph knew this and didn't want such a job. Holroyd urged him to take it. And therefore, this man should bear some of the responsibility for what happened."

Rosetta was nodding. "I knew he shouldn't."

Mrs. Jerome was shaking her head. "I don't think you fully understand the circumstances at the time Ralph took that job. He had been unemployed for months. He needed a job desperately, and all of a sudden he had one offered to him. That's what he knew."

"Oh, Mother!" said Rosetta, with a harshness which I had not heard her use in her mother's presence.

"Well, that's the truth. There he was, out of the Army with a wife and no job for months. No red-blooded man could turn down any offer in a situation like that. So what if he had killed people in a war and he had dreams about it? Lots of men kill people and come back normal. It was normal for him to take that job, for him to set aside any little sniveling objections he had. He could perfectly well have taken that job and kept looking for something he liked better."

"You're just making excuses," said Rosetta factually.

Mrs. Jerome stood up and shouted at her daughter. "I'm doing no such thing. I told him what I thought then, the same as I'm telling you now."

"Well, why did you tell him not to take that part-time job in the undertaker's when it was offered in November?" Rosetta's eerie voice was at its most passionate when it was most under control.

"He didn't want that one either, did he? Did he?" screamed Mrs. Jerome. "He was just a lazy, crazy good-for-nothing, and he still is, and that's the truth whether you like it or not."

Rosetta ran out of the office.

"Well, it's the truth," repeated Mrs. Jerome, basically to herself. And then for my benefit she retrenched. "You see how much all this upsets her. I'm only grateful that it will all be over in a couple of weeks and that Ralph Tomanek will be where he belongs. Where he always did belong as far as I'm concerned. I never liked him. Never. I always thought he was funny. I'm not saying that I knew he was a killer from the beginning, but I never liked him. And I'm glad that it will all be over soon."

"I'm not so sure it will, Mrs. Jerome."

"Whatever do you mean?"

"She seems pretty attached to him. She might just waste away."

"Ralph Tomanek is a degraded person, Mr. Samson. When he is locked in a prison or put into a lunatic asylum for the criminally insane, I trust my daughter to have the common sense to get over him and go on to have a decent life."

"Well, I'm not an expert on your daughter."

The little woman looked flushed and excited, but she made gestures of fatigue with her hand. She rubbed her forehead, for one thing. "It's hard being a parent. It really is," she said. "But I don't suppose that you would know."

"I've never been a mother."

But she wasn't listening. She was fishing around inside a large black purse. Finally, she found an envelope and drew it halfway out.

"Those things you said about Mr. Holroyd don't sound much to me. And you see how much this whole business upsets Rosetta. I would appreciate it very much if you would just take this and let the whole matter drop, please. Rosetta would want it this way, if she really understood things. I'm sure that it is more than enough to cover both your time and your expenses. Take it with our thanks. I'll explain to Rosetta."

She gave the envelope to me and left.

It had been a busy day. An emotionally exhausting one. I didn't know whether I had the energy to open the mysterious envelope. Yes, I did. I had the energy, but it offended me that I was supposed to open it, now. That my script was being written by Mrs. Jerome.

But I did open it, then and there. Just a pawn in the game. It was four crisp new hundred-dollar bills. Not a fortune, but. . . .

I gathered the still-full cups and my empty mug, the sugar, the spoons, the milk, the plate. I carried them and myself through to my living room. My haven.

I put everything except myself down on the sink top. Me I put down on the bed.

Life is too complicated. It's a loom of loose strings. Silvery threads which you are expected to tie together, one pair at a time, with lead mittens on your hands.

And so you do manage to knot a thread or two, against the odds. What do you get? A whole new frame of loose threads again.

I hated it all. Hated it.

I had so many miscellaneous facts floating around in my head I like to choke.

The thing that I hated most, maybe, was that even if I figured out correctly what in hell's name was going on, I would never be able to prove it to anybody. Least of all a court.

I lay on my bed of hate.

I didn't go to sleep. I didn't sift through things. I didn't go over anything. I didn't get back to fundamentals. I didn't do anything but hate. Resent what thirty-eight years of life had brought me to. Things had to be better than this.

The best thought I had was an impulse to burn my notebook. But that would have been too much effort.

The only outside interruption I had was from next door. I heard a gentle tapping on my door, my inner door. And Danny's face intruded itself into my line of vision.

"Got the birds fighting over you, eh, Albert?" And he gave the thumbs-up sign. And vanished again.

Saying he'd heard the ruckus between my client and her mother.

But it was easy to deal with in my frame of mind. I hated him, too.

Kids. Who needs them?

40

I suppose in my younger days I would have wallowed in discontent for days. Now I can make do with hours. There wasn't much chance of my chucking the case. Four hundred dollars is not the high point in a lifetime's temptations, but even if I wanted to forget the case, I couldn't. It shows how little else I have to think about.

By nine thirty or so I'd doused the fires of self-destruction and was on the road. Off to see Maude. If you can't grasp all the strings at once, then grasp one. Or two.

Of course Maude was in. She has a couch in her office, and though it's a little narrow for her these days, she uses it. She has a four-room house on the southeast side, but if she could get another room at the *Star*, I'm sure she'd move in permanently and sell the house. Money is a powerful mover with Maude. At least income is. She never seems to have a lot of capital—like for a fourth round of drinks.

But who does?

After greetings, she gave me the rundown on the people I'd asked her about. Woodrow Ivydene, Roger Millwald, and Malton Markenbuch were all local development people. Progress with a profit. Put Eddie Ephray and Robinson Holroyd in that club, too. Though neither of them had yet got into anything big, it was known that they were interested.

"Together?" I asked.

"Not as far as being partners," she said. "It's hard to say for sure."

Markenbuch, Millwald, and Ivydene were partners in Newton Towers, though Markenbuch was the only one actively involved in its operation, and was the only one who had had any considerable experience in construction before, though not, primarily, in buildings. He had been one of the men who had been made rich by Eisenhower's highway programs.

"What about Adrian Hall IV?"

"He's something else," said Maude. "No one really knows." "No one" being Maude's economic correspondents. "Except that he's from out of town. I can find out. I can check and see if he talked to any of the banks, and I can track down what part of the country he is from. But it'll take a little time." And cost some money.

"Not right now. But if I told you all six of them had gotten together for four or five days for chats, what would you think it was about?"

"Some project. A big one maybe. Let's see. If Hall is the representative for an outside interest, maybe Ephray has the line on the real estate. It's hard to say."

"Is there any hint in what you've heard that any of the six might have unsavory connections?"

She raised an eyebrow. I knew that meant the answer was not a straight negative. "You think you've stepped into some sort of criminal conspiracy?" I didn't respond. "Thing is that if Hall *is* somebody's representative, he isn't in the usual lists of big boys."

"Hoosierland bewares a stranger."

"Well, you asked."

"I have heard rumors about Ivydene."

She just nodded. "So have I."

We had a little drink to rumors.

"How would a security outfit work in?" I asked.

"You don't know about Holroyd? His wife has bundles. Her maiden name was Easby. The security outfit was just one of old man Easby's ventures. But it was the only one Holroyd didn't sell when the old man died. He must have something on the ball, though. The place has grown phenomenally in the last ten years or so."

"He does have a few ideas about the future of the business," I said. "What about Ephray?"

"He's another one. Only his money comes from the mother-in-law."

"Nice work if. . . ."

"Here's to ladies with money," said Maude.

We had a little drink to other people's hundreds of thousands.

I pulled out my collection of photographs and spread them on the desk top in front of me. "How about these? Can you identify these lovely people for me?"

Maude gathered them and glanced through them quickly. "Some of them I'm sure. If you can wait about half an hour." While she showed them around.

"All right. Just show me the way to the advertising department and put in a good word for me."

"They won't cut rates down to your level," she said with a mildly malicious grin.

"I just want to look up a few of your more successful advertisers to see how they do it."

She rang downstairs saying that I would be coming, and we went our separate ways.

There was no one actually on advertising at that time of night. It's only in business hours, except for some technical people. But I found my way to the advertising records.

I was interested in looking over the Easby Guards advertisements of the past few months. And there they were! No muss. No fuss. Why can't everything be simple.

Moreover, they were quite interesting. For the seventeen months before April, 1971, Easby Guards had run the same advertisement for staff. Not explicit about the vacancies to be filled, but with an explicit statement of preference accorded to Vietnam veterans. The ad had run every week over that period—from the end of November, 1969—until it had been "suspended" on May 3, 1971.

It was a thing of beauty. Circumstantial beauty, to be sure. It also kicked my curiosity a bit. I was interested in what had happened in November, 1969. Maybe I should go and ask Holroyd. "Was it then you decided?"

While I was there, I had a look for some more old ads. I looked under Lennox.

There was nothing under Lennox. Either they are quick to pull accounts which are permanently closed, or the good Oscar had never advertised his unique services in the local paper.

There are quite a few detective agencies in Indianapolis, but not many spring to mind at the snap of a file drawer.

Not even to my mind. But I looked up three I've had dealings with. Two didn't ever seem to advertise. The big one, which was also in the security business, had advertised that side of things. Nobody advertises that they are private detectives. Nobody.

Except me. I looked myself up, and, by God, there I was. Ten weekly ads of beauty. The first ten weeks of my detectivehood. I'd wanted to get off to a fast start. I was even eager. I designed the ad myself. "Trustworthy private investigations," it read. April 17, 1963.

A long, long time ago.

I walked slowly back up to Maude's office and waited about ten minutes.

"I've got some of them for you, Berrtie," she said, coming back much too chipper. Or maybe I am too subject to depression. "Thirteen men and seven women."

"That's pretty good," I said. Twenty out of the seventy-nine would be a start.

"I've written them down on the back of the pictures. The names and occupations. Do you want me to go over them?"

"That's enough, if you've written clearly."

"Then it's enough. What's wrong with you?"

"Ahh, just a doppelgänger striving to be free," I said.

"You cry about yourself too much," said Maude, setting in again behind her desk. "Sometimes I think you're crazy."

"I just don't wear well on close acquaintance."

She shrugged. "Maybe you don't feel so good yet."

She meant in the body, but my tears are for my soul. Boo-hoo. I shrugged.

"Why don't you go off and do something brave so you can brag to yourself in your old age?"

That wasn't bad advice from someone who knows you well but not intimately.

41

I got back home elevenish. There were a lot of things I could have done. I could have called the police to see if Malmberg was staying up late waiting for me to call. I could have studied the identifications Maude had given me on the pictures. I could have watched television.

What I did was pull my dining-room chair over to the window and turn the lights out. Symbolic, like.

It was getting to crunchtime. My problem was that I just didn't know what I should do next.

Life is full of ifs. In my job you spend more time on them than most people do.

If Ralph Tomanek was not really responsible . . . and not insane. . . .

Point one: I had caught Edward Ephray in one lie.

Point two: There was more to Oscar Lennox's shenanigans than had yet appeared. Ridgelea had been able to keep copies of edited negatives; that meant that Lennox had had copies of the same negatives. Where were they? In the missing files, presumably. And where were the missing files?

Suppose some of the people who could not afford to be divorced when Lennox had been hired to get information on them were no more eager to be divorced now? *If* Lennox had needed money but didn't have a license to earn it with. . . . Mightn't he consider blackmail? Some of the people he'd rigged reports for should still be willing to pay to avoid being divorced. Was that what Lennox had kept negatives for?

If the blue cross-reference file and the twenty-nine case files *had* been stolen, didn't that suggest that Lennox had been doing bad things with them?

And *if* Lennox had been blackmailing. . . .

I turned on a light. To look over the pictures Maude had

identified for me. Twenty faces. Twenty names and occupations.

I recognized a few of the names. A major local restaurateur. The wife of a basketball player. A wealthy lawyer's wife. As a group the twenty had attained a high professional standard in life. Several business executives with fancy-sounding titles. Couple of doctors. You name it. The real question for each was the extent to which each depended on being married to continue his or her success.

I turned out the light again.

If I had wanted a way to get rid of Oscar Lennox. . . .

42

Morning bypassed me uneventfully. At first in sleep, then as I occupied myself with the details of business life which I had been neglecting for days. Threats to disconnect the phone. Offers of splendid employment. That sort of thing. I was stalling. The only thing I did on the case was phone Malmberg. He had a full frontal face of the corpse for me. And he'd checked with the state police. There had been no alarm triggerings at Lennox's house in 1971 except for one on May 28 when an authorized person had failed to inform officers that he was going on the premises.

They didn't tell Malmberg they had taken a potshot at this authorized person. Could it be that they felt shame?

Just before lunchtime I went out. I picked up the picture of Lennox from Homicide. Then I drove to Easby Guards, parked across the street, and waited. I knew three people who worked there. One of them I didn't want to see, but either of the others would do. Stand and deliver. Your answers or your life. I was in an inauspiciously unserious mood.

Lunch at Easby Guards does not commence on a whistle at noon. I know. I was there.

Six people left the building before any of my three did. They trickled out over thirty-seven minutes, during which I thought about approaches. The best one was a special for Upstairs Alice from the File Palace.

"Hi, baby. Wanna fuck? Well, how about looking at these pictures instead?" Bound to get results.

In fact, Alice was the first familiar face to come out. She looked up into the sky. She stretched her arms. And she turned back toward the doorway, from which emerged the solid, square man called Robinson Holroyd.

I dropped in my seat below the line of vision. I didn't want to meet Robinson Holroyd just then; I had been thinking bad thoughts about him. I stayed down so long that they were out of sight when I came back up for a peek. I didn't know whether they'd gone off arm in arm or foot in mouth.

I wondered if Holroyd's wife knew he lunched with the help.

I was disappointed with Alice. I'd hoped my conversation would be made with her, but in a way it was a break. This way I could stride in and ask Marie in perfect comfort.

Marie, looking plodgier than ever, was sitting behind the reception desk eating a sandwich. Her days of sunlit lunches with the boss were over. I put on my most official voice, the one I'd practiced when I picked up the picture at Homicide.

"I've come to see Robinson Holroyd. Tell him I'm here," I said.

The voice was perfect. Spontaneous, yet rehearsed. It flustered her. It made her uncertain how to respond. She half turned to the doorway of the hall to Holroyd's office. I smiled and said sternly, "He's not out, is he?"

"Well . . ." she said.

"Damn it," I said passionlessly. A Congressman's dammit. "It was important."

I began to withdraw the pictures from the envelope I'd put them in. The one Malmberg had left Lennox in. Bigger than the snaps I'd made, but the police can afford bigger pictures than I can. I was going to show them to her. She could identify Lennox as well as anybody.

"Maybe," I began to say.

There was a rustle, and in the doorway behind the reception area Alice appeared. She walked straight out and didn't notice me. I noticed her all right and was kept in painful suspense for seconds, years. When Holroyd finally appeared behind her.

As he inexorably had to. He had a bundle under his arm. Something to have been mailed, at first forgotten when he set out for lunch. The o'ercautious detective had not had the wherewithal to make certain he had walked off.

I turned my head away from him, but what can a fella do? My face became too hot to hold. I would have given something to be able to change into a handsome frog.

"What is it, Marie?"

"This gentleman came in while you stepped back to your office, sir. I didn't know whether to say you was out to lunch because you was, almost."

"Well," I said, facing the damned because there was nothing else to do but play out the horrible scene, "if you're going out to lunch, I can come back."

Holroyd definitely remembered me. He looked down at my half-exposed photograph collection.

"He did say it was important," droned Marie in the background.

What can you do but make the best of things? Confrontation. For all I knew I might have decided to do just this. Tomorrow. Or next year.

Holroyd made his decision. Without taking his eyes from me, he said, "Sorry, Alice," and he turned his body back to his doorway.

"Oh, shit," whined Alice, and presumably pranced out. I didn't look. I did hear vaguely what in the old days would have been a rustle of skirts; only I knew it was the rustle of legs. I realized that I really preferred to follow Holroyd.

Which I did.

My knees were none too steady. I don't take surprises very well, on the whole, but I was, in mind if not body, beginning to take this one better than my average.

Holroyd was sitting at his desk when I came in. I didn't

knock. On the other hand, the door was ajar when I got there.

I scratched my back, on the high left shoulder side, and sat down.

"I'm a private detective," I said.

"I know," said Robinson Holroyd.

"You don't like me," I said.

"I know," he said.

Things were going swimmingly. What did I do for an encore? I leaned back and almost put my feet on his desk. He was ill at ease, and I liked that. I really did. What could he do to me? I was just beginning to raise my feet when it occurred to me that he could kill me. Mid-raise, I settled for crossing my legs.

"Do you know this man?" I asked. I pulled out the picture of Lennox as a stiff and flipped it to him.

Holroyd glanced at it. The briefest of visual flickers. Me he studied.

"I can't quite figure what you think you're doing, Mr. Samson."

"If that picture is too hard, then try these. They *are* just faces, I know," I said. "They are selected close-ups from a much more complete photographic record."

Holroyd gave more attention to these pictures. He was putting two and two together. Associating the picture of Lennox with the seventy-nine individual portraits.

For a moment I thought that I might have been smarter to keep his picture out. But I decided it was best off where it was. He would know it was coming, but it couldn't help being a shock when it came. It was. I sat proud.

He did not, in fact, go through all seventy-nine. After he came to the picture of himself, he put the pile down. He looked at me again, his chin resting on his left fist, his left elbow resting on the back of his right wrist.

He was thinking about killing me. I knew it for a fact. Who had seen me come in; who would hear? Point by point he was evaluating the odds. There was nothing I could do about it.

I decided I didn't like Robinson Holroyd.

But I wasn't dead yet. After a few moments I didn't think I was going to be.

He kept looking at me and said, "What exactly is it that you think you want?"

I wanted just what I'd got—acknowledgment of recognition of the pretty pictures.

"A wise man," I said, "doesn't want things that he can't get. There's no point to being thirsty in a desert."

"You are being needlessly mysterious, surely."

"I wanted you to see these pictures," I said, gathering them up, putting them back in their envelope. "I thought you might be interested in knowing that there is still a set of them outstanding. That I know what they are and I know what Oscar Lennox did with them."

"And you want to pick up where Oscar left off." Statement, not question.

"I'd rather not commit myself to specifics just now," I said. "But I'm sure we can work something out." I got up to leave.

"I hate this sort of thing," said Holroyd.

"What?"

"Being put under the gun by somebody. I've never liked taking orders from anybody."

"We all have to live with it," I said gaily. "You can tell your friend Ephray about my visit, if you like. He'll commiserate."

He didn't laugh. He just said, "I'd better not."

"He's hard to control, is he?"

I left him in his office and made my way along the hall to the reception desk. Marie was still eating sandwiches.

She said, "Mr. Holroyd coming out now?"

"In a minute. Before he does, I want you to take a look at this picture. Do you recognize him?"

"Sure. That's Mr. Lennox."

"He worked here?"

"Never did regular work, but he was on the payroll. He used to come in and out from time to time. He probably did special assignments or something. 'Course he's dead now."

"Of course."

"Everybody's time comes sometime."

"Sure does." I was hopeful that mine wouldn't be coming very soon.

43

When I left Easby Guards, I found myself a '58 Plymouth with a flat tire. It was just about the limit. I considered finding some lunch and then coming back to deal with the tire. There were only two objections. I wasn't sure I'd be any more in the mood for tire changing after lunch than I was now, and I was also afraid that I might run into Alice if I went off looking for food. I didn't feel like running into Alice. Call it prejudice against other people's women.

So I changed the tire. Slowly.

Maybe it was therapy. I found myself thinking. That made things even slower, but I got it done. I had extra incentive at the end. From my vantage point next to the trunk I saw Holroyd march down the front steps of Easby Guards. He walked up the road.

I got the impulse to follow him and find out where he was going. I tightened the last nut, flipped the jack's ratchet catch, and lowered the old darling as rapidly as I could to fourwheeldom.

Holroyd got into a black and tan Chrysler and drove past me. My jack stuck when I tried to pull it out from under the car. Because I tried to pull it out too soon. I kicked it. Then I put the handle in again and lowered some more. Out it came. I tried to put the hubcap on the new tire with the grace and speed of a gazelle. I hurt my fist, and it took more patience than I had. So I left it off, threw the hubcap into the passenger seat with my notebook, primed the car for starting, and, yes, started it.

I'd lost sight of Holroyd.

I sped three blocks, then got caught at a red light. On impulse, or was it half a visual memory, I turned left.

I drove for some fifteen minutes. Looking desperately.

There aren't very many black and tan Chryslers in Indianapolis. None to be exact.

I made the best of a bad job at last and pulled into a diner for a celebratory lunch. Celebrating not the missing of Holroyd, but the fact that I had, in fact, done something active. I'd stuck a pin in Holroyd. I hadn't planned it enough, perhaps. But it would be interesting to watch which way he jumped.

44

Miller and Malmberg didn't want to get a man from the prosecutor's office in right away. They wanted to hear what I had to say first and then decide whether it rated passing on. That annoyed me because it meant that I would have to go through the whole thing more than once. If it had been up to me I would have had prosecutor, Sidney Lubart, and a stenographer there first time. I'm not all that keen on repetition of things over and over again. It's why I never became an actor. That and no talent.

We chatted in Miller's new office. There was just room for three chairs. I tried to make it concise, but circumstantial cases never are. And all I had was circumstance, for the moment.

"Let me get it on paper," said Miller at the beginning. "And take your time."

He had been keeping up with the case since his promotion better than he'd led me to believe. The problem was convincing him that there really was a case.

"I'm just going to tell you what I know. I can't swear that you'll be interested."

I began by explaining how I thought Oscar Lennox had been blackmailing people. Edward Ephray, for example. Ephray had married his wife for her money, and eventually he'd started grabbing himself a bit of extra skirt. Edna had suspected. She'd gone to Oscar Lennox. She could afford the best.

Oscar had read the situation correctly. That Eddie had a whole way of life to lose, not just a wife. So Oscar made his approach, Eddie bought it, and between them they wrote and documented the story of how Eddie had not, after all, been getting it elsewhere. Maybe he just hadn't felt much like getting it at all.

Whatever it was, Edna believed it enough to stay married.

Then, as the vicissitudes of life would have it, Oscar lost his license. And before many years of retirement had passed, he found that he needed money and had no way to ply his trade to get it. I guessed that the need for money concerned the sick son, but it could have been anything.

How does a licenseless private detective get money? My version had Oscar digging up his copy of the records of the cases he'd rigged. Like Ephray's. Twenty-nine in total. He must have checked out the people he'd rigged cases for to see how they'd been getting on in life. Like Ephray. Oscar would approach them and say, "Remember me? If you don't start paying me money again, I'll go to your wife and tell her some things she'd like to know."

Of the original twenty-nine Ephray was one of the lucky ones. Still dependent on his wife for his standard of living. And his wife still caring about certain standards of his living.

I was sure that Holroyd was one of the lucky ones, too. Not that I'd met his spouse, but because Lennox had been on the payroll at Easby Guards. Considering Holroyd's distaste for private detectives, it seemed to me that it added up.

It added up for Lennox, too. If Holroyd was an example, Lennox didn't hit these guys for lump sums, just got put on a modest salary. Five thousand dollars a year from a half dozen lucky fellows pays a lot of hospital bills.

Miller was interested. So was Malmberg. Blackmail is something that interests cops. "How many people do you think Lennox was tapping?" asked Miller.

"I don't know. But identify the people in those twenty-nine picture collections and ask them confidentially. Some of them should tell you."

In fact, the blackmail was neither here nor there. Lennox was dead, and unless I took up where he'd left off, there'd be no one to prosecute. I had other things I wanted to tell them about.

Like about Holroyd's ads for veterans. And how everybody, *everybody*, knew that it wasn't smart for Ralph Tomanek to carry a loaded gun around, but Holroyd had given him a job with one anyway.

I told them how Holroyd's ads for vets had been suspended the week after Lennox had been shot.

I explained that Lennox had been in the process of serving a writ on Ephray for Holroyd.

It was getting a little complicated for them.

"So Tomanek was set up," I said. "I think that Ephray told Tomanek just what Tomanek says he did. That Ephray came into Newton Towers knowing that Lennox would be there and that he tried to work Tomanek up to just what happened."

Dawn broke for Miller. His jaw dropped, momentarily. "You are trying to tell me that you think Holroyd and Ephray worked together to get Tomanek to kill Lennox?"

"That's it exactly," I said. "Of course, I haven't got all the details."

Malmberg and Miller looked at each other. Miller, his lieutenancy rising and falling with his deep breaths, spoke for them both.

"You're crazy."

To be frank, I'd expected better. "No, I'm not. It's the only thing I can think of that fits."

"Fits!" exclaimed Malmberg. I think he was having one.

"I don't want to underestimate you, Al," said Miller in reflective contrast with Malmberg. "What else do you have?"

"I know that when I showed Holroyd those pictures, he nearly had a rupture."

"OK."

"I know that there are twenty-nine file folders and a blue index box missing from Oscar Lennox's case records."

"So?"

"So those twenty-nine cases are the ones that Lennox used for blackmail."

They still didn't seem impressed. "Look," I said, "Lennox didn't take them with him."

"How the hell can you say what happened to them? When did you find they were missing?"

"Monday."

"So how do you make sure they weren't taken some time in the month before?"

"And how do you know that your photographer friend didn't take them?" piped in Malmberg. I think he was sore that I never called him in to rummage through Ridgelea's stuff during some dark night.

"I am certain Ridgelea doesn't have the box and files or he would have given them to me, but"—I raised my voice to stifle their objections—"but I can do better than that. When I first went to Lennox's house, using the key you got for me, I tripped a silent alarm to a state police office outside Selwood. Before I'd been there long enough to have a bath, I was looking down the barrel of state hardware. Ridgelea could not possibly have got into that house without tripping the alarm. He just doesn't have the talent."

Miller looked reasonable, but it was the sergeant's turn. "Christ, Samson!" said Malmberg. "I called the Selwood state police office myself, and they said *nobody* but you'd set off that alarm since before Lennox got shot. If we listen to what you're saying, we have to figure that you stole that box and the files."

I just shook my head.

"Well?" said Miller.

"That just means that nobody without talent got into that house."

"And who has talent?"

"The only person with a motive to take that box and those files, the only person is Robinson Holroyd."

"Holroyd?"

"What business is he in?" I asked. "Guards. Security. Look at his other ads. He's not just a shotgun-armed night watchman purveyor. He's in the whole security setup. Someone in his position may not have to know how to break into a house, but he sure as hell can find out if he has a reason to. I say he had a reason."

They weren't saying yes, but at least they weren't saying no. Cops are reasonable folk, as long as you hit them on the head with it. I'd never said it was anything but circumstantial.

"If," I went on, "if I could get one of them to give me the blue box and the files?"

Malmberg still didn't like it, but Miller, my old pal, my old beauty, he was beginning to look more like himself.

"All it would prove," said Malmberg, "is that when they heard Lennox got dead, they said, 'Here's a chance,' and went down to his house and got the blackmail evidence."

"They were in a position to hear about it pretty quickly."

"Ephray realizes what's happened and calls Holroyd?"

"No. He just goes down the hall and knocks on Holroyd's door. Holroyd had a temporary suite in Newton Towers, too. You know that, Malmberg. You found it out."

Miller said, "It looks like too many coincidences, but there are some things that don't feel right." He reflected for a minute. "Like, how do the two of them get together in this thing?"

"My guess is that Lennox bragged about it, about who else was getting tapped. Or maybe one of them didn't like anyone putting pressure on, but realized that Lennox wasn't putting it on hard enough to live on what he was getting in the one place alone. Anyway, if you ask right, you might be able to get some of the other candidates to admit that Lennox was blackmailing them, and maybe more to admit that Holroyd or Ephray came around some time and sounded them out about getting out from under. At least you can check it."

"I suppose," said Miller. "But what I want to know is this: If they want Lennox dead, why do they go about it this way? Maybe they wait for a year before they finally find a freak like Tomanek. How can they be sure that the guy is actually going to pull the trigger for them? How do they know that it's not all going to be for nothing, all the plans, all the setup?"

"The way I see it," I said, "that's just the point. If they can't guarantee that the trigger will be pulled, they figure that no matter what happens, they can't be touched for criminal responsibility."

He thought about it.

I continued, "If it doesn't work, they can always try it again. It doesn't have to be cut-and-dried, now-or-never. Lennox isn't that big a pain for them. They can put up with it if they have to. They just don't want to have to."

"You're trying to say. . . ."

"I'm trying to say that the way this war has gone, there are enough disoriented vets that if they try often enough, they're bound to get lucky."

"I see," said Miller. His class on the kid Malmberg was showing in spades. "And if a setup doesn't work, Lennox doesn't even have to know they were trying."

"Not if they do it right. Remember, that ad for veterans didn't get canceled until after Lennox was dead."

Miller nodded his head. Malmberg watched him and then didn't shake his, but raised his eyebrows in resignation. "I still don't like it very much. But it's possible there's something in it."

"Possible or not," interrupted Miller. "It's checkable. There are points that we can check out."

"Even so, even so," continued Malmberg, "it still sounds too much like a guy who gets hired to walk on water. He gets a case, and he's not allowed to try to prove Tomanek's crazy, and he's not allowed to prove that Tomanek made a deal to gun down this guy in cold blood, and he's got to come up with something else. Now he's done pretty good, but I'm not convinced that he's done better than just saying that Tomanek is crazy and letting it go at that."

"I'm not saying that Tomanek isn't crazy," I said, "when he's put into a situation like he got put into. What I'm saying is that there's a good chance, as far as I can see, that what happened just wasn't his fault and he damn well shouldn't be taken out of society because of it."

"Save it for the witness stand, Al," said Miller. "Just let us have a crack at checking this all out."

I agreed. There was some conflict between us, however. I wanted to do some of the checking, too. Specifically, I wanted to stop in on a few of the people I had pictures of. I wanted to ask them myself whether Holroyd or Ephray had come around asking them to help kill Oscar Lennox. I wanted to be in on it.

But they said no. I could see their point. If anything went wrong, a lawyer or a judge could ask why they let a civilian do cop's work. I just made them promise to pick their most delicate men for the job. Sensitive, refined, yet incisive. The cops most like me.

And they sent me home to sleep it off. For a day. That was all I agreed to stay out of it for. Twenty-four hours, but I went away pleased. The kind of pleasure I get when I think I have done right by the job I'd been hired to do. The kind of pleasure you get when you walk on water.

I'm not often that buoyant. I wanted to share it. I think my woman gets the best out of me.

45

By the time I got home the next morning, I felt great. Still. My best sleep comes between the hours of one and ten, provided I have been properly peppered.

And even the weather was good. Warm and sunny. And a breeze. I like to have your zephyrs on your ideal first day of June. I know there is some as prefers your zephyrless days, but not I, I says. Not I.

How do you spend a day on which other people are taking care of your cares?

I went out to play basketball. I almost wished to find a little kid of my acquaintance. But no joy. I didn't even get into a game. Toward the end of a week the standard of play in a park goes up. Even a star works into condition gradually.

I came home about one, showered, and dressed in a gaudy shirt. I don't know what the design is called, but I dubbed it Tangerine Fantasia, and the name itself had been enough to keep it under wraps for months. I got it for Christmas from a sort of foster daughter called Eloise who hasn't put on enough age to realize that aging detectives don't really dig the same threads that look groovy on the pimply kid next door.

But today I wore it and wasn't afraid.

I even stopped in next door to see how Danny and his ménage were doing.

But they were out.

I'm not sure why, but in the middle of my second cheeseburger plate I started thinking about my various business acquaintances again. I had reveled in the instruction to cool it for a day, but it was only with my lip covered with ketchup residues that I realized a few details. First, that the whims of Miller and Malmberg didn't mean that I had to stay away from work.

Second, and probably more important, I remembered that I'd started something yesterday. Just because it was accidental didn't mean that it didn't happen. I'd told Holroyd that I possessed certain pictures, certain negatives which he might be other than eager for me to have.

What would he do? That was a reasonable question to idle away a second cheeseburger plate with. And a piece of apple pie, almost as good as Mother serves.

What he would do depended, of course, on what he had already done. If he wasn't a murderer, then he wouldn't worry about that being found out. If he was, he would.

And what then? Almost certainly he would tell Ephray.

But hypothesizing that they did kill Lennox, what would they do to Samson?

Kill me? Surely that depended on the degree of danger that they expected from me. So what danger could I be? If I was setting out to blackmail them in Lennox's place, at least there was no rush.

Or was there? Something occurred to me on the last mouthful that hadn't before. Since when was fear of being divorced a killing motive? Especially when the means for paying the blackmailer existed readily—a job with the firm which required no work. Or little work. What is the need to end the arrangement dramatically?

Was annoyance with being under the gun so odious? Or was there any reason to believe Lennox had been putting extra pressure on? That he had come in one day and said that instead of an annual salary he wanted some undeliverably large amount of cash?

It wasn't possible. They had spent too long setting things up. The planning for Lennox's death had been spread over months. Look at those ads.

Maybe there had been something special happening to Holroyd and Ephray that made it essential, all of a sudden, to be rid of Lennox. They had picked the time and place for it to happen. Why April 28 instead of April 27? Or instead of next August.

And for that matter, why pick Newton Towers as the place?

That was an interesting thought. Why Newton Towers when there were meetings going on?

Things struck me as sinister. I began to despair of getting proof of what I thought had happened. It was not the sort of "crime" which left any direct evidence, unless it be overheard conversations or a confession. It was a crime of circumstance. In a sense it was a circumstance that had been committed, not a crime. They had committed, created, a circumstance from which the crime followed. Was it therefore their crime?

For me the answer was a simple, moral yes. But legally I didn't know. It wasn't conspiracy in the usual sense because the operant arm, my client's jailed hubby, hadn't been in on the plans. What Ephray and Holroyd had done, as far as I could see, was conspire to create a circumstance which maximized the probability—but did not guarantee, require, or request—that a violent act would take place.

I decided to go back to the office to spend the rest of my waiting hours. Perhaps to call up my friends at Homicide to see how they were getting along with things.

To see if perhaps they needed me.

I ran into Danny on the way in. He was unencumbered by chattels. He liked my shirt.

"I like your shirt, Albert," he said.

"I'd forgotten I had it on," I said, and made feeble efforts to cover up. Tangerine Fantasia indeed; I looked more like a pile of orange peels underneath a juicing machine.

"Don't do that, man!" hissed Danny. He held the door for me. "You're the most cheerful thing I've seen on Ohio Street the whole day long. Man, when I'm not working, I sit on that window ledge and I watch the world go by, so I know."

I asked him how business was.

How is it that some people can just walk into a strange city and begin to make their fortune while established residents have trouble scraping along?

I wasn't exactly being rushed off my feet, but when I rang the answering service, as is my wont each working day, my little friend Dorrie had a cheerful note in her voice.

"Oh, Mr. Samson, there *was* a call for you this morning. And it sounded like business. A Mr. Holroyd wants you to call him back, and he left his number."

Holroyd, eh. I wondered and I hesitated.

But I called.

"Mr. Samson," said Robinson Holroyd in tones purely dulcet.

"My service said you called."

"I'd like to continue our conversation of yesterday. I wondered if you could stop around this afternoon."

"I'm pretty busy. Perhaps you could stop in here about five." No reason not to push a little bit.

But he sounded pleased enough. "Fine, I'll be there about five. Good-bye."

"Uh, wait, wait."

"Yes?"

"You will come alone?"

"I had intended to, yes."

"Fine. Come alone."

"Really, Samson, I think you are dramatizing things more than they are worth."

"Then don't come," I said as malevolently as I could.

"I'll be there at five," he said.

"Cheerio," I quipped. Having said good-bye once, he didn't feel it befitting to repeat it.

So I was going to have company. Time to tidy house.

One thing that it occurred to me to tidy was the matter of my most important possessions. Some negative copies, to be exact. I had left them around the office and had just wandered out, last night and again this morning. Not very clever, considering they were virtually the only lever I had on Robinson and Eddie. But for all I knew they would presume that I would have taken careful steps to protect my toys, so they shouldn't bother trying to steal them. That would be Holroyd's approach. In this case a more reckless notion would have helped them, but as long as Holroyd seemed to be calling the shots, I guessed that I was in safe enough hands, for the time being. This afternoon he would be coming over not to do anything, but just to find out exactly what I knew or had and to find out more exactly what it was that I wanted.

Fair enough. I had the afternoon to protect my negatives, maybe delve into a little fabrication about how it was if anything happened to me, then the cavalry and a band of wild Indians would descend on Easby Guards.

46

It was a busy afternoon.

The hardest part was tracking down Sidney Lubart. That's the problem with lawyers. When you want one, you can never find one. I had to settle for leaving a message with his answering device. Call Samson. And the number.

"This message is high-grade, top-class, urgent, important," I told his recording machine. "That means that when he plays you back, you've got to tell him you won't take any more messages unless he calls me back right away."

Bleep.

I stayed home for the call.

And I was lucky. Not that the timing mattered in the long run, but it saved some boring hours. Lubart called about one fifteen.

He said, "You called."

"It is important that I see you as soon as possible."

"I. . . . How important?"

"I know better than to ask for time to talk about the weather," I said.

"Will it take time?"

"It may."

"Then be here at three thirty. I'll be back as soon as I can."

Which left me nearly two hours to idle away. I made lists of options and obstacles.

And before I left for Lubart's, I had the best bit of hunch play that I'd had in decades. Things were breaking right. I could feel it.

The hunch was calling Maude.

"Well, well, well," she said. "Don't tell me that all of a sudden you want a receipt?"

"No," I said. "What I called about was to ask if anybody has been asking you for information about me?"

She was uncharacteristically quiet. "Yes. As a matter of fact, someone has."

"Did you tell them anything?"

"Of course I did. What do you think I'm here for?"

"Who was it, Maude?"

The crunch. "I don't really think I can tell you, Al." Business instinct triumphs over friendship. Fair enough, we aren't that good friends.

"Suppose I guess."

"So guess."

"Robinson Holroyd?" Silence. "Well?"

"I'm not telling you to guess again, am I?" she said.

"What did you tell him?"

"I told him you're a nosy private snoop, that you i timidate old ladies, that when you're intemperate, you' incontinent."

"It's important, Maude. I'll pay for it. I'll pay you for report on Albert Samson as long as it is the same as yo gave him."

To Maude, money talks. She heard me. "Well, no one i going to report me to the Better Business Bureau for that, suppose. Look, really all he wanted to know was genera stuff, like what sort of work you do, how business is, how honest you are, if you made a deal, would you stick to it, whether you were cozy with the police."

"Nice sorts of question. Am I honest?"

"Yes. I had to say yes."

"Much as it hurt you. Am I poor?"

"Yes."

"Am I cozy with the men in blue?"

"Well, you never used to be. But my information says you've been in and out there a lot recently."

"I've been getting a lot of parking tickets. All right, since I'm paying, you better give me the whole thing."

Which she did. And even that didn't depress me. I was riding high. I figured I had my white horse; all I needed was some armor and a sunset.

At three o'clock Miller called me. It was a busy afternoon.

"How've you been doing?" I asked. For all I knew it was his day off and he'd been chasing Janie around the living room trying to get her between himself and the couch.

"We have been learning a little," he said. "It comes slowly. We've been identifying the people in those pictures. Malmberg has been out talking to the ones you ID'ed for us."

"Any results?"

"I had lunch with him. He confirmed that one of the three he'd seen was being blackmailed by Oscar Lennox, but he hasn't had any confirmation that anybody tried to get them to conspire to kill Lennox."

"Not even a hint?"

"Well, I don't know. He does seem to be less skeptical about the whole notion now. Have you been doing anything?"

"Eating, sleeping, washing my car. Pulling weeds; patting the children's governess on her behind."

"I don't like the sound of that."

"The sound is the best part."

"Give it a rest, Al. Not just today. Tomorrow, too. There's time. Tomanek doesn't come up until next week."

"You can hardly keep me from talking to his lawyer."

"I'd rather you didn't."

"So put me in jail. Whose case is this anyway?"

"Mine," he said.

"Not as far as Ralph Tomanek is concerned. Just tell me where you're likely to be come five or five thirty today. In case I want to call you."

"Suppose I call you."

"You'll forget. Besides, I might be out."

"I'll probably be in the office, but I'll leave a number."

"And tell them to give it to me when I ask."

"And tell them to give it to you when you ask."

"What a nice cop you are!"

"You've been drinking. Or just keeping bad company?"

"You won't tell the revenuers if I tell you the truth, will you?"

"I don't like the sound of this, Al."

"I'll talk to you later," I said. "I have to go now."

Which I did. Thinking happily that it doesn't do for a successful private detective to be too cozy with the police. It's a matter of reputation. You have to be neutral. Even the law respects that to a degree. You aren't required to report everything you find out to the police. Just to your client.

47

Lubart was at his office door to receive me by three forty-five. I was charged up with banter about how he ought to leave his door open like I did and such irrelevancia. But he was all business. I often take my mood from the people around me. I became all business, too.

And explained, as I had done for my police friends, what I thought and why.

It was a matter of interest to Sidney Lubart. Speculative interest. Interest in what he would be able to prove in court.

"That's all well and good," he said. "You maybe get the prosecutor to prosecute on a mass of circumstantial evidence. Perfectly reasonable. But what has it got to do with Ralph Tomanek?"

He wasn't serious, surely. "Shouldn't it get him off?"

"What you have is an alternate theory for what happened. As it stands, it's not strong enough to avoid being called fanciful and slanderous. Failing a confession from these people you accuse, you'd have to have everything added up, verified, double supported by expert witnesses. You'd have to have independent people stake their reputations on the fact that Tomanek wouldn't have done it on his own. Maybe you could get it all together. But even if you did, there would still be a decent chance that a jury would say, 'He pulled the trigger when he didn't have to. Lock him up.' If you have the time and the money, maybe you go for the chance. But the problem on top of everything is the fact that if the prosecutor thinks that the police might come up with enough circumstantial evidence in the long run, he's never going to let you use a part of it in a lesser case before he's ready."

"But," I said, "if we were to have some evidence that wasn't circumstantial?"

The problem was getting it. We had quite a lengthy chat. He knew a man he thought might help. A private detective, a specialist, called Roger Alexander. "He's absolutely reliable," said Lubart, "absolutely."

It was about five after five when I left Lubart's office.

48

Usually I am punctual. Today I dawdled. I looked in shopwindows and daydreamed. I felt a little giddy.

Within reason. I was home by five twenty. I walked into the office without a second thought. I never considered that Holroyd might not be there or that Ephray might be or there might be a gang waiting for me, or a cement strait-jacket, or a bomb.

Robinson Holroyd was relaxing in my client's chair. He was moderately slouched and puffing on a cigar. He was supposed to be nervous, but he looked comfortable.

"Sorry I'm late," I said as I strode around him to my desk. I made myself at home. After all, I was.

Rather ostentatiously I put my notebook down on the desk, opened it, and leafed through to a blank page. I don't get too many chances to be ostentatious, so I made the most of it.

"Quite all right," he said. "I walked right in. Hope you don't mind."

"Which just about takes care of civilities."

But not as far as he was concerned. "I had pictured you in slightly more elegant surroundings," he said.

"You never can tell."

"You have hopes of doing better in the not too distant future, then?" So maybe he wasn't civilifying.

"Maybe it'll burn down and I'll get the insurance."

"The building is coming down, you know?"

"No, I didn't."

"It's part of a city plan."

"That's not the one that is supposed to take down the City Market, too, is it?"

"I think it is."

"It'll never happen. City Market is a historical landmark. I belong to a preservation group." I don't, but maybe I'll join.

"Well then," he said. "No worries." He shrugged. He had no stake in it. "I want to talk about those pictures you showed me," he said finally.

"OK."

"I'm interested in your plans for them."

"We're agreed as to what they are, then."

"I suppose."

"Well," I said. "I have some interest in their history before I decide what I do with them. If anything."

"You wouldn't have them if you weren't aware of their history," he said. He was not amused. It was a little hard to tell exactly what he was.

"If you're suggesting that I was in the confidence of Oscar Lennox, I wasn't. I never met the man."

"How did you get hold of the pictures if he wasn't a friend?" The word was not friendly.

"There was a copy of the negatives that Oscar didn't know about."

"There was?"

Perhaps I imagined it, but I read a combination of expressions on his face: disbelief, bitterness, a dash of irony.

"His photographer made an extra set when he made Oscar's copies."

"Oscar led me to believe he took his own pictures."

"He did well enough to afford an employee."

"So you have a set of negatives."

"I do."

"They are the only outstanding set?"

"They are. I might add that they are in a safe place."

"No doubt. And do you have copies of Oscar's reports as well?"

"No. You have the only set of those."

"I do?" he said, but it didn't sound like a denial.

I didn't want to make a federal case of it. Yet. "In a safe place, no doubt."

"Which brings us to business. What is it that you want, Mr. Samson?"

"Money," I said sweetly. And sat up. "Lots of money."

"What do you figure is lots?"

"I'm not sure," I said. "But more than Oscar got. I have decided that his rates weren't worth the risk."

He sat quietly for a moment. He must have been squirming inside, but it didn't show. He couldn't threaten me without giving away more information than he wanted to.

I continued, "You see, I am at a little disadvantage because I don't know what Oscar was tapping you for, so I have a notion of how I want to go about things. Assuming you have no objection."

We paused; he grew impatient. "Yes?" he said irritably. He was striving to control himself. He succeeded.

"I want to have a little meeting. I want you and Edward Ephray to bring me the financial records of your respective companies which show how much Lennox was getting. And in order that you don't take liberties in the presentation of these records, I want them tonight. When I see them, we'll come to the crunch about what I'm going to cost."

He was breathing hard, but he just said, "I don't see how you expect me to produce records at the drop of a hat. It's already after business hours." Which it was. Past five thirty.

"I'm sure you'll manage. I'm willing for it to be a late meeting, say, ten o'clock."

"I am hardly in a position to guarantee that Edward. . . .

I was impolite, I interrupted. "That's not all. I want to have a look at Lennox's cross-reference file. The blue box of index cards."

He shook his head. "The what?"

"Please don't waste time." At which point the phone rang. I considered leaving it, but I reconsidered. Holroyd was not, in all likelihood, going anyplace.

"Hello?"

"Miller."
"Well, how's life been treating you, sweetie?"
"Not too bad. How about dropping over now to have a chat about some of the scraps that Malmberg and I have picked up."
"Gee, I'm afraid I can't. I'm on a case."
"What the hell are you talking about?"
"Tonight is out, honey." I smiled sweetly at Holroyd. Who, considering, was enduring pretty well. "I've got an engagement. But maybe tomorrow."
"Let me guess," said Miller. "You aren't alone?"
"So it's arranged then?"
"If you've got somebody from this case there, I'm damn well going to see you tonight."
"Oh, you mustn't be so impatient, baby." I whispered to Holroyd, "They can't leave me alone." He was not amused. I can see why. I wouldn't want to be waiting for orders from a thirty-eight-year-old teen-ager like me.
"You call me back," Miller said firmly. "When you're free. Baby." He hung up.
I cooed on for a little longer and said a sweet good-bye to the dial tone. Kiss, kiss.
"Where was I?" I asked.
"You were going to tell me where you wanted to hold this meeting you've been talking about."
"No, I wasn't. I was telling you that I also want to see the blue box."
"And I was saying I didn't know about any such box."
"So you can learn before tonight. Understand, I need that box. You weren't the only fish that Lennox had. I have pictures, and I need the names of the other people in the other pictures. What luck for me that two of the people Lennox was blackmailing happen to be involved in the accident that killed him."
Holroyd was definitely not on cloud nine. "Not here," he said at last.
"Where?"
"I have a house on Indian Lake. I'll talk to you there at ten tonight. I'll see what I can do about arranging what you want."

"OK. As long as I'm not crossed, you'll find me a most obliging fellow."

He drew me a map of how to get to his particular house. He gave me the phone number, too, in case I was delayed.

He was about to leave, when I added a dash of salt to the wounds. "By the way, have Lennox's full case records there, too, will you? Except for yours and Ephray's. They'll be very helpful when I start to approach other members of your select group."

We didn't part close friends.

To be on time, I should have left right away. But I sat on the bed for a while, thinking about life. The jaws of death. Little girls. And I changed my shirt.

49

Lubart was waiting in his office to take me to his detective friend, but on my initiation we talked for a few minutes first. I was worried about going to see Holroyd and Ephray without some sort of cooperation with the police. I was afraid for my life, to be specific.

Lubart's contention was that Holroyd and Ephray were the last people who would kill me themselves. That the point was other folk did the work for them. Rationally I agreed, whatever emotional reservations remained.

But he had a more compelling point. "We are trying to induce them to give us evidence which will help Ralph Tomanek. If the police are involved with us, we would have to go by police rules in order to have that evidence accepted in a court. Do you want to walk in there and say 'By the way, anything you say may be used as evidence against you'?"

Lubart's electronics man, Roger Alexander, was in his sixties and had been in the business through many a technical revolution. I guess technical revolutions keep you young; he was physically fitter than I was. He had been expecting to outfit me under a tie. The problem was I wasn't wearing one. Not the only problem. I was worried that if the device was as sensitive as he said it was, my pounding heart would be so loud as to drown out the whole exercise.

We settled for underneath my right lapel and discounted the interference from excess oozing of my bile juices.

He was not pleased when he learned that we were going to Indian Lake instead of Chez Samson. It meant an independent power source. But by eight fifteen Alexander and I were ready, and we bid Lubart adieu. He would wait by the phone in Alexander's lab.

The original plan had called for setting up in my office closet with about an hour for testing. Instead, we took the whole show out to Indian Lake to see what kind of arrangement we could make in the dark. It was not impossible to receive transmitted conversation at half a mile, but it would improve quality to place the receiver somewhere closer.

He brought what seemed to be masses of equipment. "To keep our options open." I considered bringing a camera, my sole contribution in technological fields, but abandoned the idea. It just wouldn't fit. Walking into a nervous group to grub for money. Then saying, "Hold it," as they extended wads of fifty-dollar bills. "A picture for my mother."

Lubart wanted me to take a gun, but when he learned I don't have one, he just shrugged.

It was a clear night. A bit of moon. We took the scenic route to Indian Lake, along Fall Creek Road to Seventy-first Street. Turn right.

If there is a snooty section of Indianapolis where the younger very rich buy houses, it is the area around Indian Lake. It sports a certain kind of wealth. Elite, very Hoosier, but the type who doesn't want to build a house for himself. It's a cluster of such people, people perhaps more cosmopolitan than the rest of the city, but at the same time more exclusive. It's a rather closed little group, the homeowners of Indian Lake. Not that many Indianapolisites know that a pleasant wooded lake exists between the city and Geist Reservoir. But it does.

Holroyd's foot up on Cheyenne Way was not one of the most aggressively moneyed structures in the area, but it was pretty good size. It was set closer to the road than I expected, but the road close to which it was set was narrow and winding. Sort of English-like. The house looked like it belonged to one of the lesser plantation owners of Virginia. On the Jefferson pattern, but with dimensions reduced by 20 percent. And no flurry of outbuildings like came in the traditional package.

The front was spotlit, toothy white columns grinned down a moderately sharp slope to the edge of the road, and the only privacy was given by a stand of tall, thin trees not yet in full leaf. A driveway led up to the front of the house. We paused to look things over. Tourists.

The first problem was finding a place to leave the car while we scouted. We couldn't be sure that everyone who was coming was already there, so we couldn't park by the closest available side of the road.

We settled for a side of the road around the first corner. Whence we walked back to the edge of Holroyd's property.

There was a wide band of lawn running on the two sides of the house, but skirting each was a thicket of trees. As far as we could see. We came up from the road on the left side of the house as we faced it. The trees were fairly thick, but wouldn't have provided any encumbrance in daylight. Or much protection. We made our way slowly up the slope till we were opposite the side of the house.

"You don't think there are any animal traps in here, do you?" said Alexander.

"No," I said. "I'd be surprised."

We had a look. He could receive well enough from the woods, but we talked about his getting closer to the house, like outside a window. The contours of the house made it possible. It depended on how likely he was to be discovered. And whether it would hurt reception if he was sitting by a window on one side of the house and they took me to a room on the other.

"Wouldn't really matter," he said. "It's just a question of recording quality. The closer we are, the better we get."

I decided to nip across the lawn and see if I could find the room that was likely to be the center of action, so we'd know better where to place the receiver. Maybe the people were already there. Maybe they were waiting for me. Maybe baking a cake.

I ran across the grass to the shadows of the side of the house. Christ, for all I knew there would be servants and guards and mines in the yard. But at least there were no rose bushes. I caught my breath. And I listened. I didn't hear anything. Not a thing. It was music.

I edged toward the window nearest to me, the left front room; there was a light shining brightly through some very lightweight curtains. I gradually eased my head up at such an angle that my eye would be one of the first parts of me to pass the windowsill.

It was a dining room. There were dirty dishes for one on the table. But no people.

I dropped down and tried to figure what to do next. Why not try to locate where folks were, what they were doing.

First I held up my hand, as arranged. "Testing," I said. "Five million, two hundred and ninety-eight thousand, one hundred and sixty-seven, hike!" When I went back to Alexander, he would tell me whether he'd caught it or not.

I decided to go around to the other side and see who was home.

I almost went around the back, but the balance of reason sent me around the front. There is no place less visible in the dark than the area behind a light. If I ran behind the spotlights, then even if someone in the house looked out, he couldn't possibly see me.

I crawled up to the front corner of the house. There were three lights in a row across the narrow band of lawn between the house and the circular parking area that the driveway widened into. I ran a wide arc through the yard and crossed in front of the house through the gravel parking area. There were two cars there. They were cars I recognized. Ephray's gray sports sloop, and the black and tan Chrysler I'd seen Holroyd drive past me in when I was changing the tired tire on my own stately vehicle. Which reminded me. I had to have that flat fixed. If we got another flat tonight, there would be problems.

I passed quickly to the other side of the house. The side lawn was narrower, the house closer to trees. A patio, an outside table with an umbrella, which was down. A birdbath. I didn't see any gnomes, but the light wasn't too good.

Before I got close to the house, I could hear people talking. This was the side on which I was to be entertained. I worked my way to the edge of the patio, where I could see half the living room and could hear all.

I heard too much.

50

Paranoia comes easily to me.

From out of sight, a man was saying, ". . . if you don't want Maxwell to shoot him, why the fuck did you bring him?"

Holroyd was sitting by French doors. Three-quarters of his back was to me. "I brought Maxwell in case it becomes blatantly hopeless. The man talks in great dramatic mysteries, but I have a feeling that he doesn't know nearly as much as he wants us to think he does. If he just wants to try a little blackmail, fine. What's that to us? We just put him on our list."

The other voice had much more nervousness in it. Which was why I hadn't recognized it immediately. It was Ephray, of course. "You may not have thought about it, but he might perfectly well be coming here intending to harm *us*. He's a petty hustler, and he might be crazy enough to kill us and settle for what he can find around the house."

"You're too afraid private detectives are going to harm you," said Holroyd pointedly.

"Ha, ha," said Ephray.

"And if we do have something to fear, Maxwell will be something of a surprise for him."

"I don't see how you can be so fucking calm," said Ephray.

"Practice," said Holroyd as he lit a cigar.

"I know, I know. I'm going out for some fresh air."

"He's due soon. Why don't you go out front?"

I didn't stick around to find out why or why not. I ran like hell for the cover of the trees. I passed a rabbit in the grass so fast he thought he was a tortoise. Gave him nightmares and identity problems.

The same sort of phenomena I was experiencing as I pinioned myself against a tree that I feared wasn't thick enough to hide my thickness.

But I had decisions to make. Fancy self-inflating schemes for entrapping villains is one thing. But I'd overheard a discussion in which two men had been calmly discussing the merits of putting me out of my further misery on this planet.

Show me the way to go home, friend. Just call the cops, and let them drop in and pick up what evidence they can. Let them make the case if they wanted to.

All I wanted was out.

I tried to see what time it was, but the dial on my watch isn't radiant.

When it became clear that Ephray wasn't coming out on the patio, it meant he was somewhere out front. I started my trek back to Alexander, round the back. I wished like I have never wished for anything before, that we had brought the police with us.

I made my way slowly until I saw the backyard. The trees didn't complete a simple rectangle behind the house. There was no straight and simple wooded passage back to Alexander. The backyard opened up like the mushroom of which the house and side yards were a stalk.

So I crossed to the back corner of the house. The room against the outer walls of which I was pressing was illuminated like a stage. Light gushed out through a glass door and through a broad window. I didn't really mind the light. What I objected to was the implication that someone was in there.

They were bad, bad people to have talked about me like that.

The window wasn't much of a problem. It was high enough that I could pass under it easily. The door worried me. It was at the top of two concrete steps, which left about eighteen inches to slither under.

I considered tripping into the middle of the backyard, but that put me in sight of a viewer in the window. It was dark in the yard, but the light from the window and door was bright enough that I would reflect light back. As earthshine illuminates an otherwise dark moon. Enough to be seen.

I caught my breath, passed under the window, and crawled up to the edge of the door. The glass didn't go down as far as I'd thought it did. It gave me the eighteen inches of the stairs, plus about another two feet of solid door. I was in.

I listened carefully for a minute at least. I didn't hear a thing. Courage was slowly ebbing back. Not a positive courage exactly, but something to fill in the cowardice that had been for those few instants my life and soul.

I guess it was curiosity. I decided to have a look in.

I crouched like a sprinter and prepared emotionally for an emergency start. I slowly pushed my right eye along the bottom edge of the door's pane of glass, so that I could see an increasing amount of the room. A kitchen.

It's not the best angle to be introduced to a room from, but it wasn't the room that took my attention.

Sitting at a table facing the window under which I'd just passed was a thin boy. I couldn't say how tall, but he was spectacularly thin. He looked very young. Late teens at most. He sat at the table with his back against the wall behind him. His head was bowed forward to keep from hit-ting shelves above. The shelves had piles of dishes and bowls on them and a rather fancy portable radio. It seemed a most unnatural place to be sitting, and before long, I realized the table was originally under the shelves, that the boy had moved it out specially to take this awkward position, back against the wall.

He was cleaning the stock of a double-barreled shotgun.

This had to be Maxwell.

It had to be Maxwell, and I knew that I should get the hell out of there. No self-respecting coward would dawdle watching Maxwell tidying up a shotgun.

But I did.

I even dropped out of my starting stance to sit on the lower step and watch this, this boy.

It was all wrong. Everything. Not just cleaning the goddamn gun. Everything about him was wrong. In retrospect I suspect that there was a glaze to his eyes, but the thing that struck me first was the radio. It should have been on. Any normal kid would have had the radio on. For company.

But Maxwell had no company. He just sat, backed up against the wall, cleaning his shotgun with absolute attention.

It was all wrong, and before I could say, "Pull the trigger" I knew why.

Maxwell reminded me of someone. Someone I had just abandoned to his fate. The only other person of my acquaintance that I could imagine sitting in Maxwell's place was Ralph Tomanek.

I realized at last what I should have realized before. Ralph Tomanek was no more a unique phenomenon in the world than a '58 Plymouth. Holroyd's *Star* ad had not been searching out one destroyed person, one degraded person, to set up to kill Oscar Lennox. It had been used and would be used again to assemble a collection of skeleton men, desperate men, no longer fit for ordinary life. Men to be interviewed and evaluated. Men to be selected for their low thresholds in emergencies as tested and established in war. Men to be kind to, to make loyal, and then to use. Because they are destroyed and consider themselves expendable, they are made expendable.

Ralph Tomanek was *made* to kill Oscar Lennox, not because there was any overwhelming need to kill Oscar Lennox, not because Lennox was making unfulfillable demands. Holroyd and Ephray just didn't like the notion of anybody having a hold on them. So they trotted out one of their nonmen, Ralph Tomanek. End of the Lennox problem.

For all I knew they had tried others on Lennox before. Or they had already killed other people. Or considered it, planned it as an option, like they were doing now, for me.

For all I knew, the very meeting in Newton Towers had concerned selling the use of more of these Tomaneks. It was possible that Oscar Lennox had met his end at that time and place merely as a demonstration.

I sat by the door for fully five minutes. Staring out into the backyard. Well lit close to hand, but getting darker and darker the farther before me I looked.

I've never thought of myself as a self-sacrificing person. But at the end of those eternal minutes I was worrying less and less about the certainty of personal danger and less too about Ralph Tomanek's particular circumstances. I concentrated on a vision of an endless stream of borderline youths, bucked up, as it were, by getting a job with Easby Guards. Given, briefly, what appears to be a chance to pull the disheveled threads together to make of a life a wearing weave. Then, in deft hands, they are used and destroyed, for the last time. For profit, at the whim of Robinson Holroyd and the likes of Eddie Ephray.

I was very careful as I crawled under the sight line of the door and window. And then I walked to the position in the edge of the woods where Roger Alexander waited.

51

I was about ten minutes late for my appointment. Not that much time had passed during my reconnaissance, but we lost the difference squatting in the woods, whispering about how we ought to go about things. I explained how I intended to avoid the Maxwell problem, but Alexander expressed hesitation about going ahead without some kind of protection.

Finally, we decided that we would cover ourselves by having him in the car with me. He would crouch out of sight as we came in. I would turn the car around when I parked, so it was aimed for a quick exit. He would sit on the ground next to the car and monitor the conversation as he recorded it. If the conversation began to get threatening, I would show my lapel microphone and reveal to all assembled that I had not come alone. Hearing this, Alexander would get the car the hell out of the driveway. My fellow inmates in the house would hear him leave. I would be protected from any but insane danger because they would know they couldn't kill me without the world knowing. Alexander was also to deflate the tires on the other two cars as soon as I was in the house.

Whether Ephray had remained out front to watch for me or whether they heard the car come up the gravel hill I do not know. But the door opened as I walked up to the porch, and my host, Robinson Holroyd, escorted me in. I had the presence of mind to let him show me which way to go. He turned me to the right, to the living room *cum* patio.

Ephray was waiting there. Holroyd began proceedings. "I have gathered the interested parties as you requested. So please let us get down to business so we can see if we have any grounds for talking to each other." Ephray just glared.

"I'm sure we do," I said. "I'm not an unreasonable fellow." We all sat down. I took the seat Holroyd had had before I came, the one next to the patio. The french doors were close at hand, and their latch was opened. Holroyd sat opposite me. Ephray was at the other end of the room altogether.

"Do you have the documents I requested?" I asked as sweetly as I could, considering I knew Maxwell was in the kitchen.

"Yes," said Holroyd. "They're on the table." He gestured to a coffee table on my left. It bore a stack of papers held in place by a large blue file box. Actually I would have called it aqua.

I picked up the file box. Several hundred index cards arranged in a row. Apart from a few odd blue ones, the cards were white, and there was a separated section at the front of the box. I pulled one of the front cards. It bore consecutive numbers followed by names. The rest of the file was the names in alphabetical order, with addresses and particulars of billing.

I looked up Ephray in the alphabetical file. Eddie's card was blue. No. 516. I didn't count, but I was sure that there were twenty-nine blue cards in the file.

I closed the card box and thumbed through the files which corresponded to the blue cards. They were fat. I pulled one out, leafed through it. Lots of words in there. And pictures. And negatives.

"Now, I take it these bottom papers are the financial details of Lennox's employment with each of you."

"That's right," said Holroyd.

"I'll look them over more carefully when I get home, but you can tell me now what salary Lennox was drawing off you both."

Ephray jumped up. "Nothing was said about you taking those fucking things home. He just said you wanted to see them. I never thought you was going to take them home with you."

"I promise I'll give them back," I said. "Cross my heart and . . ." I stopped. I couldn't bring myself to say "hope to die." "I just need to study them, that's all."

Ephray sat down again. Holroyd shrugged.

I waited. They waited.

I took a breath. "There is something else you can do for me now, though."

"Yes?" said Holroyd. But he was not enthusiastic.

"I want to know more about how you set things up to kill Oscar Lennox."

"How the hell did—" Ephray jumped up again.

"Shut up! Shut up, Edward!" shouted Holroyd.

Eddie shut up, but kept standing. I was afraid of him. Even Holroyd was on the edge of his chair.

I said, "I'm sure you wouldn't try the same thing with me, but if any others among Oscar's clients were involved, I'll need to be reassured about them. I need to know how many of you got together. How you decided to set it up. It's not that I give a damn about Oscar Lennox. I just need to know."

Restraining himself, Holroyd said, "If you think you know so much, what is the point of our talking about it?"

"Call it curiosity," I said. "Just a few details. For instance, did Lennox know that you and Ephray did business together?"

"Not," said Holroyd carefully, "that we knew we were both on his list. He was rather amused on the unfortunate night of his death that he was to serve a paper on Edward. I think that's why he was willing to serve it."

"Or why you happened to arrange for a paper to be served," I chipped in. "Did you know any of the other people Lennox was blackmailing?"

"No," said Holroyd.

"How did you and Mr. Ephray get together?"

Mr. Ephray interjected again, "I don't like it. I don't see why we should tell him any goddamned fucking thing."

"Shut up, Edward," said Holroyd forcefully, harshly. I decided I was more afraid of Holroyd than Ephray. "You see, Mr. Samson, Edward was the one who got the bright idea to follow Lennox around for a few days to see just who he was blackmailing. That's how we got together."

"And whose idea was it to look for a borderline case like Ralph Tomanek to bump Lennox off with?"

Ephray was really heated, but Holroyd kept his cool. "Ralph Tomanek was a *hopeless* case, Mr. Samson. He knew it as well as anyone, once he thought about it."

"You helped him think about it; you helped teach him that he was a degraded person, for instance."

"Well, it's obvious," said Holroyd. He was rising to his

favorite subject: how Robinson Holroyd manipulates people for his own ends. "He could never be expected to survive in a competitive world. He's happiest under care. And he knew it."

"What do you mean he knew it?"

"He knew what was going to happen to him."

"For God's sake shut up!" shouted Ephray. He ran over to stand in front of his partner in crime. He was hysterical. "You have no right to tell him things. No right. I'm a part of this, and I say you have no right!"

Ephray pulled Holroyd to his feet, and they stood glaring at each other for a second or two. A silence, just long enough for us all to hear footsteps coming up the hall. Attracted by the commotion.

Just long enough for us all to realize whose footsteps they were.

I didn't stick around for dessert. But my mistake was to try to take the pile of files and the index box with me. You can't take it with you; if you try, you lose any time edge you may have had.

Ephray got to me before I got to the patio doors and he was only a second ahead of Holroyd. They spun me, the papers went flying, everywhere. Ephray had me by an arm, Holroyd by the jacket. I didn't do much.

"Ouch! God damn it!" said Holroyd and shook his finger. He turned back the right lapel of my jacket. The microphone pin had stuck him. At a glance he knew what the microphone was.

The three of us knocked over a floor lamp, and as it fell, the bulb popped with a bang. Momentarily we stopped in place, a tableau.

In the hallway entrance was a tall, thin figure with a stick.

Maxwell looked puzzled. His head was twitching slightly. Both barrels of the shotgun were clean and ready. I could see right down them.

"I . . . heard . . . uh . . . something."

Eddie Ephray let go of me and stepped aside. "Kill him," hissed Ephray. "He's trying to kill Mr. Holroyd. We said it might happen. Kill him! Shoot!"

The message sank in about the same time for all of us. About certain things everybody is equally smart.

Maxwell's right hand steadied the shotgun, and the left index finger found the trigger.

"Shoot!" urged Ephray, edging toward Maxwell along the side of the room.

I was a little bit slow. I had seen this all somewhere before. In a play or a nightmare. I just wished that I wasn't cast as the private detective.

I tried to spin Holroyd in front of me by his shoulders. But he was aware of what was going on, too, and resisted. My jacket tore. It gave me brief advantage. Who says cheap jackets aren't worth the money?

Holroyd and I rocked and spun. I knew my only protection was to keep Holroyd with me. Close. Extremely close.

We wrestled for a week, back and forth. It was a one-fall contest. Unfortunately we were equally matched; only I was the one not at the peak of my training. My right arm was still weak. I felt it begin to slip.

I pushed when I could no longer pull. I shoved him away and broke his hold on me momentarily. I jumped for the french doors, two or three strides.

Holroyd should have left me clear. I don't know whether he was afraid I would get away or whether he didn't want what was going to happen to happen. But he dived for me as I half smashed, half opened the door. Holroyd hit me from behind and knocked me forward a little. The gun fired.

It was very loud. It hurt my ears. I broke through the door. I felt stinging, but I ran. I ran as fast as I could out of the light of the living room. I sprinted, yet again, across the grass toward the trees.

Until my foot caught on a long-eared stone rodent. I fell hard and fast. On my nose. The trees passed me as I fell. Barely an arm's length away.

52

I'm sure that I lost consciousness for a minute or two, because I remember the gradual way my awareness returned. But even by the time I began to hear things and get my wind back I realized full well that there were things I did not hear. Footfalls near. Thunderclaps.

What I heard was a wail, like a dog chiming with a distant siren. But the sound was human, and it was pathetic. It was what I had risked my too precious neck for.

I just lay and hugged the earth and kissed the grass

I might have stayed there all night, but I heard Eddie Ephray whining in the distance. "Get up, damn it! He's out there in the woods. Get the fuck up!"

It was Ephray who reminded me I was not at home snuggled by the wall in my double bed.

How long before Ephray successfully brought Maxwell back to the hunt? Or took the gun and duty into his own hands?

I crawled to the nearest tree and used it to pull myself up. Ephray was silhouetted against the light from the room I had recently left. He was standing over a crouching figure. He was kicking and swearing. I guess Maxwell didn't feel much like a moonlight prowl. He was still wailing for his fallen master.

I didn't think about where I should go; I just went. I ran for the front of the house. I kept near to the trees but ran on the grass. No track records this time. My left leg hurt in its power muscle.

I didn't stop to look back.

Down the gravel hill to the road. I don't remember falling. I do remember sliding to the bottom, getting up and wondering which way to turn.

I turned right and ran down the road. Maybe I should be hiding in the trees. Maybe this, maybe that.

I ran. And when I came to a crossroad, I turned left and

ran for a while there. I didn't see any cars. I wanted to know why. Surely a '58 Plymouth would come up over the hill, and I would hop upon its back and ride off into the moonset.

After I ran, I walked.

I passed at least three houses before it occurred to me to go up to one and knock on the door and try to convince whoever answered that I wasn't just trying to break in. In a neighborhood like Indian Lake everybody is very suspicious of strangers.

53

Mona Paul is a very unusual lady. The sort who never makes the papers. The sort who makes a fella believe that the monied classes aren't all bad. I was quite lucky, because a fella like me rarely gets to mix with any but the bad ones. Maybe I should go knocking on rich people's doors covered with blood at eleven o'clock on a Thursday night more often.

When I knocked—ignoring the electric bell—Mona Paul answered the door right away. And when I asked to use the phone to call the police and then fell on my face at her feet, she let me lie and went to call the police herself. It turned out that she thought I was dead, shot through the face. But I wasn't, and what she saw that made her quickstep to the phone was the least of my worries: the broken nose I'd gotten falling over the stone rabbit.

My real problem was that I was bleeding a lot from cuts on my hands and chest from breaking through the window and from an assortment of shotgun pellets in the left buttock and leg.

But Miss Paul was clever on that score, too. After calling the police, she called an ambulance, too. She told them, "I think he may be dead." I know. I was listening. Granted I had felt faint and had been lying on my face. But I wasn't unconscious, just resting. So I heard her. I didn't really disagree with the notion. I felt like maybe I was dead.

After several minutes' prostrate relaxation I knew otherwise. I was bleeding, and I was hurt, sure. But I just didn't feel dead. More out of breath. That's what comes from having to run the mile after training for the ten-yard dash.

When she'd made her phone calls, she went away for a few minutes and returned to sit next to my face, such as it was.

She wiped off the parts that needed wiping, and that's when she heard me breathing. "Are you awake?" she said.

I didn't answer. I was saving up.

"My name is Mona Paul," she said. "Is there anything I can do for you?"

I decided to open my eyes.

"Can I help by turning you over or something?"

I tried to shake my head, but the floor it was resting on wouldn't let me. She started dabbing around on the carpet. That's when I knew I wasn't dying. If I'd been puddling blood, she'd have had to go back into the kitchen to get a mop and bucket.

"My parents will be surprised when they get back," she said. I found out later she was twelve.

I made my big move. "Please excuse me if I don't offer you my seat," I said. She giggled. I loved Mona Paul with all my heart.

I stayed there quite awhile, and the whole time before the police got there she just sat beside me and dabbed my face and the floor. I felt safe.

The only other thing I said to her before the police came was "Thank you."

A sheriff's patrol car was the first to get to us. I didn't see the flashing lights, but my earth mother got up to greet them, and I did hear clomping feet.

"What we got here, young lady? A stiff?"

"No. He's alive."

A face, big and round, a moonhead, bent down close to mine.

"Hi," I said.

"What's the problem, pardner?" he asked. I could sense that I was being bathed in a bad breath which must have been powerful considering the condition of my nose. But it spurred my mind back to what had been going on. The minutes I'd lain on the Pauls' doorway had been cut out of the context of my life. I hadn't given the most fleeting thought to how it was I came to be there. I'd lost time, purpose. A sense of urgency returned to me in a jolt. I began to breathe heavily again.

"Up . . . the road," I struggled to speak. "Shootings. Go arrest them. Hurry."

"Now you take it easy and tell me about it, pardner."

So I did. Enough to get them moving. I didn't remember the number of the house on Cheyenne Way, but they looked up Holroyd in the phone book. I also mentioned Miller and the city police.

By the time the ambulance came I was feeling better. Willing to sit up and have a cup of tea. But they wouldn't let me. I didn't know where Mona had gone to, because I don't remember seeing her after the emergency services began arriving.

They took me out on a stretcher. It hurt more lying on my back than it had on my front. During the entire ride to the hospital I remembered with lunatic fondness the calm, cool voice of my new friend. Mona Paul. Right then and there, as they wheeled me through the emergency doors, I decided to go and visit the lady. Thank her again. Marry her.

Life problems settled, I returned anew to the problems of the day. When the doctor came in and asked me what happened, I asked to speak to a cop. I wanted to talk to Miller. I also wanted to talk to Lubart. I wanted confirmation that Alexander had got away. I wanted to hear the tape. I wanted to find out what the sheriff's people had found at Holroyd's place.

But the doctor, for no reason I could see, wanted to talk shop. He was insistent. I had a broken nose, glass cuts all over. Some bruised ribs.

"You seem to have some holes back here," he said, as he tried my flip side.

"Yeah. There would be. Shot from a shotgun."

"Not very many of them."

"How many?"

"About fifteen, twenty. I'll have to count them later. As I take them out. Whoever it was wasn't a very good shot."

"I was running," I said.

"But you're bigger than a rabbit," he said. "Did you know that there is still a law on the books in Indianapolis which prohibits shooting rabbits from the back of a trolley car?"

We were interrupted by a nurse who asked the doctor if what he was working on was serious because they had another gunshot coming in.

He covered me up and left me alone. I felt neglected. I thought about asking for morphine to kill the pain but decided I needed a cop instead. I shouted, "Hey! Help!"

Another nurse opened the door. "Shut up in there, fat mouth!" and slammed the door. I was offended. It was an emergency ward, and I was an emergency, wasn't I?

After about ten minutes the doctor came back. "I found the rest of that shot," he said soberly.

Holroyd. Of course they'd bring him in, too, if there was any life in him when they got there. "Is he dead?"

"Not yet. But he got it, two barrels, real low. He's unconscious, and he'll die in a couple of hours."

He went about his work without further chat. I didn't talk either. Clearly whatever was to be found at the house had been found. Now any impatience I felt would be self-indulgent—just eager to know quickly the things that I would know soon enough. It gave me a moment to think about how many inches away from lying next to or in place of Holroyd I had come.

Life is a game of inches.

54

As he finished wrapping my nose, the doctor told me, "Try to get some rest the next few days. You haven't really hurt yourself badly, but you're bound to feel off color for a while. It's like falling off a roof without breaking anything.

There is trauma when the body is attacked, even if the body repulses the attack."

"I'd like the pellets," I said. The fourteen little doodads he'd removed from my posterior. Maybe I could melt them down into a tiny toy soldier.

He found them on the table and handed them to me. That's when Miller came in. I'd prepared myself not to expect him. It was almost an additional trauma.

"I want to have a little chat with you, Al. Are you done with him, Doctor?"

"He can go."

So we went. I wanted him to drive me home, but he said he'd be in better contact with what was going on if we went back to his office first. I thought I could hold out.

But the ride in the car made me regret it. I was getting tired. My shock. And I realized that there were things that I wanted to find out before I told everything even to my friend in blue.

"I didn't really expect to see you," I said. "Don't you guys leave people on at night to hold the fort on cases until the mornings?"

"Usually. But I left word to be called."

"Why?"

"I don't trust you as far as I can throw you."

"How sweet!"

"I was right."

"Um."

"What were you doing there, Al?"

I didn't really know what to tell him. Whether to tell him. But on the other hand the general idea of the tape was to play it to the forces of law and order.

"I went to get a taped recording of Holroyd confessing."

"Why?"

"Maybe you would have gotten him eventually, and maybe you wouldn't. I had to think of my client. I needed something soon to convince people not to send him away."

"He could always have been got out again."

"It would have destroyed him," I said. It sounded good. "Once you've been in a place like that you can't just erase it by saying, OK, we've found some new evidence. Come on out. There's no way to take back that you've been punished for something you didn't do."

"But he did do it."

"But he wasn't responsible for it. I truly believe that."

I told him about the original plan. I even showed him my microphone. When a specialist puts a microphone underneath your lapel, it stays there.

"You couldn't use a tape like that as evidence," he said disgustedly.

"Not against Holroyd and Ephray, maybe. But in defense of Tomanek it would be OK."

"You'd be throwing away the whole case against Holroyd."

"Well, we figured that the prosecutor would make a deal. Let Tomanek off for the tape and his testimony."

Miller shrugged his shoulders. We were not far from home. Just crossing Thirty-sixth Street.

"Did you get Ephray?" I asked.

He turned sharply. "Was he there?"

"Yeah."

"All we got was Holroyd and the kid who apparently shot him."

"Maxwell," I said.

Miller radioed for a pickup on Ephray.

"He shouldn't have been able to get far," I said. "The air was supposed to be let out of the tires on both cars."

"There was only one car."

"Somewhere there's a gray sports car with sore rims."

"I think we maybe better go and see this friend of yours. Lubart."

"A lawyer," I said. "Not a friend. I don't know him that well."

We rode on in silence.

"Where does he live?" Miller asked.

"Who?"

"Lubart."

"I don't know. I've only been to his office."

"I think I'd better try to track him down tonight."

"You don't mind if I don't come along," I said. "I feel shitty. You'll know where I am if you need me."

He shrugged. "I'll be along tomorrow morning," he said.

"Not too early."
"Not before eight."
"Ho-ho."
He left me off in front of my building. Quiet place, my building, late at night.
I walked in the front door and found the damned "Out of Order" sign on the elevator. Still.
The perfect end to a perfect evening. At least there would be no trouble sleeping tonight. I would recommend to all insomniacs that they follow the regimen I was pioneering. I would write a book about the Samson Method. It would be a best seller and make me moderately wealthy and excessively lazy. I would become a professional sports spectator. The perfect life, a calling.
I nearly fell on the third flight of stairs. Pure carelessness.

55

I barged straight into my office. I found a visitor. Mr. Edward Ephray. Eddie to his friends. Pure carelessness.
"I been waiting for you," he said.
"I can't imagine why," I said. I was too tired to be surprised, shocked, scared, or even very interested.
He slowly withdrew his left hand from his overcoat pocket. It didn't come out empty. I became more interested. It seemed like I'd been looking down barrels all night. "To kill you."
"Oh yes?" I was at my desk. "Would you like a drink?"
"No."
"Do you mind if I have one?"
His lips curled at the extremities. I wouldn't have called it a smile, though. "No," he said, but stepped behind the desk so that he could see what was in the drawer as I opened it.
I let my hand hover over the drawer handle and then opened up in a burst and grabbed for the drawer's con-

tents. I nearly got him—that is, he nearly got me. But I came up with a bourbon bottle, and he just came up nervous. When I'm exhausted, my sense of humor gets a little peculiar. I took a very long slug from the bottle. It made me cough.

"Now, sir, you say you want to kill me. When did this desire first make itself known to you?"

"What the hell are you talking about?" I guess that I really had him upset. I was supposed to get all meek and girly as he waved his thing in my face.

"You purport to want to make me deceased. Wherefore? Why? Whence? Whither?"

He just shook his head. In fairness, he had had a hard night too. "You know too much," he said.

"Indeed!" I made a 360-degree swivel on my chair. "But I don't know anything at all. I know so little it embarrasses me."

"You know I was there tonight," he said.

"Aah. The dawn begins to dawn. The color is fawn, the dawn. You think that I'm going to tell the police that you were there tonight!"

"That's right."

"Well, don't worry, old man. Don't worry. They already know."

"What?"

"They know. What do you think I've been doing all this time? Playing dominoes? If you take my advice, you'll go home and wait for the police to come and get you, and then you'll tell them that you were having a pleasant chat with your good friend Holroyd when all of a sudden, wow! This guy walks in and lets Holroyd have it, and he was going to let you have it, too; only you ran and got away. They'll believe it, and you'll be home in time for breakfast. Now you be a good fellow and let me get some sleep. If you still want to kill me in the morning, I'll be here. I refuse to be killed tonight. I'm too tired."

I don't know what happened to him, but I got up and went into my back room. I lay down on the bed without even flossing my precious teeth. I have a vague memory of a door slamming before I went to sleep.

Ephray was no real gunman. Too infirm of purpose. You get spoiled when you get used to people doing your dirty work for you.

I awoke most rudely. I was being shaken. Most rudely. It irritated me, so I came up with a fist and hit my awakener sharply enough to knock him or her down. I groped for the light by the bed. While I did, the clock began to sing.

"Cuckoo. Cuckoo. Cuckoo. Cuckoo. Cuckoo," sang the clock. I was still tired unto death. I found the light. It was a him. It was Miller.

More stunned than stunning. While he sat there rubbing his right temple, I realized that my left knuckles hurt. One more entry in the catalogue of Samson debilities.

"So what did you want?" I asked.

He just sat and looked depressed. I guess everyone was having a long night.

"I wanted to know what kind of game you were playing."

"And what is that supposed to mean, or is there a full moon?"

"I mean your lawyer, Lubart, says that he didn't get anything on the tape at all; that's what I mean. He played me five minutes of scratches and then gave it to me. There's nothing on it."

If anything could have made me feel lower, that was it. "Well?"

"I don't believe it."

"What?"

"I don't believe that it was a blank."

"Well, what does it have to do with me?"

"I want you to find out. I want you to go over there now and tell him to cooperate."

"Go away. I'm tired."

"It serves me right," he said, "for trying to cooperate with a lazy fucking gumshoe."

"You missed a friend a little while ago," I said after I rested. "Ephray."

"He was here?"

"That's right. He wanted to kill me."

"Did you get him? You didn't just let him go, did you?"

I was hurt that he didn't ask whether Ephray had succeeded in his attempt. "I hit him on the head and tied him up and put him in the closet. You can pick him up on the way out."

I watched as Miller, poor trusting soul, drew his firearm and approached the door to my office carefully. He didn't leave it open enough for me to see his face when he opened the closet door. His face when he came back to me wasn't very funny.

"Very funny," he said.

"I'm tired. I'll catch him for you tomorrow. Or if you can't wait, you might try his house."

"I've got his house staked."

"Then you've probably already caught him and you didn't even know it. Good night," I said, turned out the light, and rolled over.

I definitely heard the door slam in the front this time.

But I didn't go to sleep. I just lay there. I saw gun barrels galore. I saw blood. I saw gore. I was swept away in a flood. And I saw a lot more.

At six cuckoos I lay shaking. Not from the cold.

At about six thirty, I got up and watered my ivies. They took, the six of them, more than nine coffee cupfuls of water. I sometimes wonder if they'd do better out on the fire escape, where nature could water them.

By seven the sun was coming up. My window is eastern. I relaxed in my dining-room chair and watched the sun rise. I guess it was what I had been waiting for. To be sure another day would come. By eight I must have been asleep in the chair because I don't remember the little bird.

I heard the phone ringing. It forced my first contact with consciousness. It pulled me up from a long, long way away.

My inquisitor was Sidney Lubart. "So you're there at last," he said.

"I've been here all night."

"Really?" He sounded dubious. "I tried there a couple of hours ago."

"I must have been asleep." Blessedly deep. Logs don't answer phones.

"I've got to see you," he said. "As soon as possible."

"All right."

I forgot to ask him what he wanted to talk about. I nearly went without coffee, but it wouldn't have been a saving of time. I would have got in the car in a daze and been as likely to crash into something as get lost as make it over to his office.

It wasn't even till after coffee and I was downstairs that I remembered that I didn't even have a car. That valuable treasure of the fifties had gone the way of Alexander, not Samson.

The walk did me good.

It stimulated enough blood into my head for me to begin to get a grasp on current events. Lubart was in his office when I pounded on the door.

At least someone said, "Who's there?" when I pounded on the door. Then the same person said, "Are you alone?"

I indicated that I was alone in more words than were technically sufficient.

He let me in. Then locked the door behind me.

"Why the razzmatazz?" I asked innocently.

"I've got the tape, and I don't want the police getting it," he said bluntly.

"I thought that it came up blank."

"Don't be stupid. You use a technician to keep things like that from happening. How did you get away, anyway?"

"Foot and ambulance. Alexander made it all right?"

"Yes. I was afraid you'd come to grief, but there wasn't much that I could have done about it."

"Holroyd must be dead by now, and they've undoubtedly got Ephray sewed up, too."

"Doesn't help us much," he said somberly.

"Why not?"

"Have a listen."

He played the tape. I listened. It was a nightmare revisited. I had to discipline myself to think of it just as a tape. And I also had to keep in mind what had been so elusive in my general range of activities: that I was working on behalf of Ralph Tomanek, stop. Lubart had no difficulty remembering that. It was of little interest how the others fared as long as the tape helped Tomanek.

The problem was that it didn't. Holroyd and Ephray's general responsibility for what happened was fine. It was the words spoken specific to Tomanek:

> "He's happiest under care, and he knew it," said Holroyd.
> "What do you mean, he knew it?" said Samson.
> "He knew what was going to happen to him."

"The problem," said Sidney Lubart, "is that Holroyd seems to suggest that Tomanek was in conscious complicity, and that is of no use at all."

"You can't just use part of the tape?"

"Not safely. Even if we can edit it plausibly, as soon as Ephray and Holroyd, if he lives, hear about it, they'll make sure Tomanek sinks with them. They would do that anyway. What we hoped for was a portion of the tape which would clearly exonerate Tomanek before there was any reason for them to lie about it one way or the other."

We listened to it again. "It doesn't necessarily damn Tomanek," I said.

"But it doesn't clear him. It doesn't mean that we can't go to court for him, but it would have helped."

Which was why we'd set the whole thing up in the first place.

We listened to the tape again. It didn't wear well. There was no reason for Holroyd to admit that Ralph had been an unwitting tool while he was talking to me, but what he had said could conceivably step Ralph's charge up from manslaughter to first-degree murder.

So the story was that the tape didn't exist, as far as Ralph was concerned. Lubart assured me that soon after I left his office it wouldn't exist. Any evidence it contained against Ephray could be supplied by my memory as confirmed by Alexander's testimony of what he heard as he monitored the supposed tape recording.

It should be sufficient.

* * *

Considering the strain and shock and deprivation which my body had experienced in its last twelve hours, I felt pretty good. A splitting headache was the only strong complaint. I got dizzy with it in the bright sunlight.

I wasn't ready to rest, but I did sit for a while in the car. I repossessed my car keys before I left. Lubart had picked up my car from Alexander. He explained where it was parked. Thinking and thumbing through my notebook. The radio news confirmed that Ephray had been arrested, but still described Holroyd's condition as "critical." There'd been more life in him than expected.

After a while I started the car. I drove out to the west side of town. Past General Hospital. Past Bush Field. Turn right.

There was a man working in Mrs. Jerome's front yard. The swing on the porch had been fixed. The man was raking the dirt between the grass clumps.

"Nice morning," the man said to me, as I walked up to the porch.

I didn't answer.

I knocked hard on the door. No one came in ten seconds, so I knocked again, harder. Longer.

I was about to turn to ask the man in the yard whether they were out when Mrs. Jerome opened the door, at last.

"Mr. Samson," she said. "I wondered if we might see you today."

I walked in.

"I heard on the radio that Mr. Holroyd got shot," she said. "Isn't it awful? Isn't it bad luck? I don't know what it's going to do to Ralph's case. Mr. Holroyd was always so helpful. He was very good to Ralph. How this could happen I just don't know."

"I know," I said. "I want to talk to you."

Maybe the bandages on my face made me look threatening or something, but she just sat down on her couch to listen. I sat at the other end.

"Now, Mr. Samson, what's this all about? Not some more bad news, I hope."

"I see you are beginning to have the house and yard fixed up."

"Oh, yes. I think that it's good to set things in order in the spring, don't you? It's a fresh time of year, time to make new starts, get things in order. They'd got out of hand for so long, I just decided 'Martha,' I said, 'it's time to do it.' So I am." She beamed.

"Where did you get the money?" I asked.

"The money?"

"And where did you get the money you gave me when you tried to get me to stop working on the case?"

"Stop you? I just thought that—"

"You gave me four hundred dollars for no special reason. You didn't ask for a receipt, or any accounting, or any change. Where did you get the money?"

She didn't answer in the first available instant.

"The money, Mrs. Jerome. Whose name will we see on the check you deposited? Or did he give it to you in cash? Small unmarked bills, perhaps?"

She puffed up like a swollen ankle. "You seem to know everything," she said. But she wasn't sufficiently hostile. I began to believe she actually felt a little guilt.

"I don't know *everything*. I don't know exactly how much you got for your son-in-law, and I don't know exactly what you had to say to get him to take that job. I don't know exactly how much you got for making Ralph feel so small, so guilty, so worthless that he took a job he knew would get him in trouble. And I don't know the words you used, day after day, to justify to yourself having sent your daughter's husband off to murder. No, Mrs. Jerome. I don't know everything."

"All he said was he'd do it if he had to! That's all he ever had to say!" she shouted at me. But she was crying, too. "Mr. Holroyd said he knew about men like Ralph. That Ralph would be better off in a hospital. He said that he'd give him a chance, but that if he had to kill someone in the line of duty, he'd just have to do it. Ralph knew he might have to do it. Ralph knew. I didn't do anything. Not really."

"Nothing but taunt him into taking a job that would destroy him. Nothing but negotiate the price that Holroyd would pay if Ralph did as he was supposed to."

"Mr. Holroyd said if something bad happened, Rosetta would get insurance, so she wouldn't want."

"Money paid to you?"

"But I'm spending it for Rosetta, I really am. It's really best that she keeps working. It helps take her mind off things, and she meets people. It will help her start a new life, find new people. Ralph's no good for Rosetta. He never was."

She cried and cried. The flood, after forty years without rain. She fell toward me on the couch. I held her and tried, after all that, to comfort her. What can you do to explain to a lady that her daughter's life is her own?

Especially when you have to explain to the daughter as well.

Mrs. Jerome quieted after a considerable time. Grief of ages.

"What shall I do?" she said at last.

"Give her up," I said. "Give her the money; then you sell your house. Go away. Get a job yourself. *You* meet people."

That was what I had done, when my life, my marriage, had given me up.

"But what will Rosetta do?"

"She'll visit Ralph in the hospital or whatever else she wants. That's her business."

Mrs. Jerome picked up a handkerchief from the coffee table. "Part of the money comes as insurance after Ralph goes into a hospital. The rest was two thousand dollars."

Cheap at the price.

I got up.

"Where are you going?" she said, half-harshly, half-desperately.

"I'm going to Speedway to talk to Rosetta," I said.

She wept again. It was once too often. "Mrs. Jerome, I'm going to see that you don't profit out of this." I was as menacing as I knew how.

When I left, the gardener was still at work. Things were really coming along. He had moved some dirt from around back to bring the level of the gaps up so that the yard was even. With a little grass seed, a little water, a little protection, and a little time it would look peachy. As I passed, I said, "Nice afternoon."

At the Green Stamp center I was insistent. Rosetta finally came out with me. We walked around and around the shopping center. I wished I could do for her what was being done in her mother's front yard. After an hour and a half I took her back to the world of trading stamps.

And left her for the last time. I had no idea how I'd done. There aren't many things about a life that talking to someone can really alter.

I got in the car and drove back to town along Sixteenth Street. I thought about taking another sentimental lap around Victory Field. Instead I just pulled over and sat in the car for a while. In the shadow of the left center field wall. Outside Ted Beard's old shagging grounds. Out where balls pitched by Herb Score didn't end.

I thought for a while. Tried to. What had been clear when I stomped up to Mrs. Jerome's porch nearly three hours before had long since grown fuzzy. My head still hurt. I was tired. I was depressed. I didn't know whether I had decided to send Rosetta both the money she'd given me and the four hundred dollars her mother had contributed or just the four hundred dollars.

I settled for the four hundred dollars. I'd worked for the other, even if Ralph Tomanek was headed for exactly the same future that he'd been heading for when I'd first been hired. I don't undertake to make life conform to your fondest dreams when I work for you. Do I?

I made another decision while I sat there. I decided to sell my car. You can't run on relics of the past forever. It was good while it lasted, but maybe it was time for a change. And this way I wouldn't have to bother to have the flat tire fixed.

I've always fancied having a little panel truck. One just big enough that I could sleep in it if I wanted to. Or had to. Or that I could carry bulky things in. They're more flexible than cars. I could even paint my name and address on the side. It would be some advertising.

That's what I'd do. Buy a little van. Advertise. "Albert Samson. Money taken. Questions asked."

THE PERENNIAL LIBRARY MYSTERY SERIES

Delano Ames

CORPSE DIPLOMATIQUE P 637, $2.84
"Sprightly and intelligent."
—New York Herald Tribune Book Review

FOR OLD CRIME'S SAKE P 629, $2.84

MURDER, MAESTRO, PLEASE P 630, $2.84
"If there is a more engaging couple in modern fiction than Jane and Dagobert Brown, we have not met them." *—Scotsman*

SHE SHALL HAVE MURDER P 638, $2.84
"Combines the merit of both the English and American schools in the new mystery. It's as breezy as the best of the American ones, and has the sophistication and wit of any top-notch Britisher."
—New York Herald Tribune Book Review

E. C. Bentley

TRENT'S LAST CASE P 440, $2.50
"One of the three best detective stories ever written."
—Agatha Christie

TRENT'S OWN CASE P 516, $2.25
"I won't waste time saying that the plot is sound and the detection satisfying. Trent has not altered a scrap and reappears with all his old humor and charm." —Dorothy L. Sayers

Gavin Black

A DRAGON FOR CHRISTMAS P 473, $1.95
"Potent excitement!" *—New York Herald Tribune*

THE EYES AROUND ME P 485, $1.95
"I stayed up until all hours last night reading *The Eyes Around Me,* which is something I do not do very often, but I was so intrigued by the ingeniousness of Mr. Black's plotting and the witty way in which he spins his mystery. I can only say that I enjoyed the book enormously."
—F. van Wyck Mason

YOU WANT TO DIE, JOHNNY? P 472, $1.95
"Gavin Black doesn't just develop a pressure plot in suspense, he adds uninfected wit, character, charm, and sharp knowledge of the Far East to make rereading as keen as the first race-through." *—Book Week*

Nicholas Blake

THE CORPSE IN THE SNOWMAN P 427, $1.95
"If there is a distinction between the novel and the detective story (which we do not admit), then this book deserves a high place in both categories." —*New York Times*

THE DREADFUL HOLLOW P 493, $1.95
'Pace unhurried, characters excellent, reasoning solid."
—*San Francisco Chronicle*

END OF CHAPTER P 397, $1.95
". . . admirably solid . . . an adroit formal detective puzzle backed up by firm characterization and a knowing picture of London publishing."
—*The New York Times*

HEAD OF A TRAVELER P 398, $2.25
"Another grade A detective story of the right old jigsaw persuasion."
—*New York Herald Tribune Book Review*

MINUTE FOR MURDER P 419, $1.95
"An outstanding mystery novel. Mr. Blake's writing is a delight in itself." —*The New York Times*

THE MORNING AFTER DEATH P 520, $1.95
"One of Blake's best." —Rex Warner

A PENKNIFE IN MY HEART P 521, $2.25
"Style brilliant . . . and suspenseful." —*San Francisco Chronicle*

THE PRIVATE WOUND P 531, $2.25
[Blake's] best novel in a dozen years . . . . An intensely penetrating study of sexual passion. . . . A powerful story of murder and its aftermath."
—Anthony Boucher, *The New York Times*

A QUESTION OF PROOF P 494, $1.95
"The characters in this story are unusually well drawn, and the suspense is well sustained." —*The New York Times*

THE SAD VARIETY P 495, $2.25
"It is a stunner. I read it instead of eating, instead of sleeping."
—Dorothy Salisbury Davis

THERE'S TROUBLE BREWING P 569, $3.37
"Nigel Strangeways is a puzzling mixture of simplicity and penetration, but all the more real for that." —*The Times Literary Supplement*

Nicholas Blake (cont'd)

THOU SHELL OF DEATH P 428, $1.95

"It has all the virtues of culture, intelligence and sensibility that the most exacting connoisseur could ask of detective fiction."

—*The Times* [London] *Literary Supplement*

THE WIDOW'S CRUISE P 399, $2.25

"A stirring suspense. . . . The thrilling tale leaves nothing to be desired."

—*Springfield Republican*

THE WORM OF DEATH P 400, $2.25

"It [The Worm of Death] is one of Blake's very best—and his best is better than almost anyone's." —Louis Untermeyer

John & Emery Bonett

A BANNER FOR PEGASUS P 554, $2.40

"A gem! Beautifully plotted and set. . . . Not only is the murder adroit and deserved, and the detection competent, but the love story is charming." —Jacques Barzun and Wendell Hertig Taylor

DEAD LION P 563, $2.40

"A clever plot, authentic background and interesting characters highly recommended this one." —*New Republic*

Christianna Brand

GREEN FOR DANGER P 551, $2.50

"You have to reach for the greatest of Great Names (Christie, Carr, Queen . . .) to find Brand's rivals in the devious subtleties of the trade."

—Anthony Boucher

TOUR DE FORCE P 572, $2.40

"Complete with traps for the over-ingenious, a double-reverse surprise ending and a key clue planted so fairly and obviously that you completely overlook it. If that's your idea of perfect entertainment, then seize at once upon *Tour de Force.*" —Anthony Boucher, *The New York Times*

James Byrom

OR BE HE DEAD P 585, $2.84

"A very original tale . . . Well written and steadily entertaining."

—Jacques Barzun & Wendell Hertig Taylor, *A Catalogue of Crime*

Henry Calvin

IT'S DIFFERENT ABROAD P 640, $2.84

"What is remarkable and delightful, Mr. Calvin imparts a flavor of satire to what he renovates and compels us to take straight."

—Jacques Barzun

Marjorie Carleton

VANISHED P 559, $2.40

"Exceptional . . . a minor triumph."

—Jacques Barzun and Wendell Hertig Taylor, *A Catalogue of Crime*

George Harmon Coxe

MURDER WITH PICTURES P 527, $2.25

"[Coxe] has hit the bull's-eye with his first shot."

—*The New York Times*

Edmund Crispin

BURIED FOR PLEASURE P 506, $2.50

"Absolute and unalloyed delight."

—Anthony Boucher, *The New York Times*

Lionel Davidson

THE MENORAH MEN P 592, $2.84

"Of his fellow thriller writers, only John Le Carré shows the same instinct for the viscera." —*Chicago Tribune*

NIGHT OF WENCESLAS P 595, $2.84

"A most ingenious thriller, so enriched with style, wit, and a sense of serious comedy that it all but transcends its kind."

—*The New Yorker*

THE ROSE OF TIBET P 593, $2.84

"I hadn't realized how much I missed the genuine Adventure story . . . until I read *The Rose of Tibet*." —Graham Greene

D. M. Devine

MY BROTHER'S KILLER P 558, $2.40

"A most enjoyable crime story which I enjoyed reading down to the last moment." —Agatha Christie

Kenneth Fearing

THE BIG CLOCK P 500, $1.95

"It will be some time before chill-hungry clients meet again so rare a compound of irony, satire, and icy-fingered narrative. *The Big Clock* is . . . a psychothriller you won't put down." —*Weekly Book Review*

Andrew Garve

THE ASHES OF LODA P 430, $1.50

"Garve . . . embellishes a fine fast adventure story with a more credible picture of the U.S.S.R. than is offered in most thrillers."
—*The New York Times Book Review*

THE CUCKOO LINE AFFAIR P 451, $1.95

". . . an agreeable and ingenious piece of work." —*The New Yorker*

A HERO FOR LEANDA P 429, $1.50

"One can trust Mr. Garve to put a fresh twist to any situation, and the ending is really a lovely surprise." —*The Manchester Guardian*

MURDER THROUGH THE LOOKING GLASS P 449, $1.95

". . . refreshingly out-of-the-way and enjoyable . . . highly recommended to all comers." —*Saturday Review*

NO TEARS FOR HILDA P 441, $1.95

"It starts fine and finishes finer. I got behind on breathing watching Max get not only his man but his woman, too." —Rex Stout

THE RIDDLE OF SAMSON P 450, $1.95

"The story is an excellent one, the people are quite likable, and the writing is superior." —*Springfield Republican*

Michael Gilbert

BLOOD AND JUDGMENT P 446, $1.95

"Gilbert readers need scarcely be told that the characters all come alive at first sight, and that his surpassing talent for narration enhances any plot. . . . Don't miss." —*San Francisco Chronicle*

THE BODY OF A GIRL P 459, $1.95

"Does what a good mystery should do: open up into all kinds of ramifications, with untold menace behind the action. At the end, there is a bang-up climax, and it is a pleasure to see how skilfully Gilbert wraps everything up." —*The New York Times Book Review*

Michael Gilbert (cont'd)

THE DANGER WITHIN P 448, $1.95

"Michael Gilbert has nicely combined some elements of the straight detective story with plenty of action, suspense, and adventure, to produce a superior thriller." —*Saturday Review*

FEAR TO TREAD P 458, $1.95

"Merits serious consideration as a work of art." —*The New York Times*

Joe Gores

HAMMETT P 631, $2.84

"Joe Gores at his very best. Terse, powerful writing—with the master, Dashiell Hammett, as the protagonist in a novel I think he would have been proud to call his own." —Robert Ludlum

C. W. Grafton

BEYOND A REASONABLE DOUBT P 519, $1.95

"A very ingenious tale of murder . . . a brilliant and gripping narrative." —Jacques Barzun and Wendell Hertig Taylor

THE RAT BEGAN TO GNAW THE ROPE P 639, $2.84

"Fast, humorous story with flashes of brilliance." —*The New Yorker*

Edward Grierson

THE SECOND MAN P 528, $2.25

"One of the best trial-testimony books to have come along in quite a while." —*The New Yorker*

Bruce Hamilton

TOO MUCH OF WATER P 635, $2.84

"A superb sea mystery. . . . The prose is excellent." —Jacques Barzun and Wendell Hertig Taylor, *A Catalogue of Crime*

Cyril Hare

DEATH IS NO SPORTSMAN P 555, $2.40

"You will be thrilled because it succeeds in placing an ingenious story in a new and refreshing setting. . . . The identity of the murderer is really a surprise." —*Daily Mirror*

Cyril Hare (cont'd)

DEATH WALKS THE WOODS P 556, $2.40

"Here is a fine formal detective story, with a technically brilliant solution demanding the attention of all connoisseurs of construction."

—Anthony Boucher, *The New York Times Book Review*

AN ENGLISH MURDER P 455, $2.50

"By a long shot, the best crime story I have read for a long time. Everything is traditional, but originality does not suffer. The setting is perfect. Full marks to Mr. Hare." —*Irish Press*

SUICIDE EXCEPTED P 636, $2.84

"Adroit in its manipulation . . . and distinguished by a plot-twister which I'll wager Christie wishes she'd thought of."

—*The New York Times*

TENANT FOR DEATH P 570, $2.84

"The way in which an air of probability is combined both with clear, terse narrative and with a good deal of subtle suburban atmosphere, proves the extreme skill of the writer." —*The Spectator*

TRAGEDY AT LAW P 522, $2.25

"An extremely urbane and well-written detective story."

—*The New York Times*

UNTIMELY DEATH P 514, $2.25

"The English detective story at its quiet best, meticulously underplayed, rich in perceivings of the droll human animal and ready at the last with a neat surprise which has been there all the while had we but wits to see it." —*New York Herald Tribune Book Review*

THE WIND BLOWS DEATH P 589, $2.84

"A plot compounded of musical knowledge, a Dickens allusion, and a subtle point in law is related with delightfully unobtrusive wit, warmth, and style." —*The New York Times*

WITH A BARE BODKIN P 523, $2.25

"One of the best detective stories published for a long time."

—*The Spectator*

Robert Harling

THE ENORMOUS SHADOW P 545, $2.50

"In some ways the best spy story of the modern period. . . . The writing is terse and vivid . . . the ending full of action . . . altogether first-rate."

—Jacques Barzun and Wendell Hertig Taylor, *A Catalogue of Crime*

Matthew Head

THE CABINDA AFFAIR P 541, $2.25
"An absorbing whodunit and a distinguished novel of atmosphere."
—Anthony Boucher, *The New York Times*

THE CONGO VENUS P 597, $2.84
"Terrific. The dialogue is just plain wonderful."
—*The Boston Globe*

MURDER AT THE FLEA CLUB P 542, $2.50
"The true delight is in Head's style, its limpid ease combined with humor and an awesome precision of phrase." —*San Francisco Chronicle*

M. V. Heberden

ENGAGED TO MURDER P 533, $2.25
"Smooth plotting." —*The New York Times*

James Hilton

WAS IT MURDER? P 501, $1.95
"The story is well planned and well written."
—*The New York Times*

P. M. Hubbard

HIGH TIDE P 571, $2.40
"A smooth elaboration of mounting horror and danger."
—*Library Journal*

Elspeth Huxley

THE AFRICAN POISON MURDERS P 540, $2.25
"Obscure venom, manical mutilations, deadly bush fire, thrilling climax compose major opus.... Top-flight."
—*Saturday Review of Literature*

MURDER ON SAFARI P 587, $2.84
"Right now we'd call Mrs. Huxley a dangerous rival to Agatha Christie." —*Books*

Francis Iles

BEFORE THE FACT P 517, $2.50

"Not many 'serious' novelists have produced character studies to compare with Iles's internally terrifying portrait of the murderer in *Before the Fact,* his masterpiece and a work truly deserving the appellation of unique and beyond price." —Howard Haycraft

MALICE AFORETHOUGHT P 532, $1.95

"It is a long time since I have read anything so good as *Malice Aforethought,* with its cynical humour, acute criminology, plausible detail and rapid movement. It makes you hug yourself with pleasure."

—H. C. Harwood, *Saturday Review*

Michael Innes

THE CASE OF THE JOURNEYING BOY P 632, $3.12

"I could see no faults in it. There is no one to compare with him."

—*Illustrated London News*

DEATH BY WATER P 574, $2.40

"The amount of ironic social criticism and deft characterization of scenes and people would serve another author for six books."

—Jacques Barzun and Wendell Hertig Taylor

HARE SITTING UP P 590, $2.84

"There is hardly anyone (in mysteries or mainstream) more exquisitely literate, allusive and Jamesian—and hardly anyone with a firmer sense of melodramatic plot or a more vigorous gift of storytelling."

—Anthony Boucher, *The New York Times*

THE LONG FAREWELL P 575, $2.40

"A model of the deft, classic detective story, told in the most wittily diverting prose." —*The New York Times*

THE MAN FROM THE SEA P 591, $2.84

"The pace is brisk, the adventures exciting and excitingly told, and above all he keeps to the very end the interesting ambiguity of the man from the sea." —*New Statesman*

THE SECRET VANGUARD P 584, $2.84

"Innes . . . has mastered the art of swift, exciting and well-organized narrative." —*The New York Times*

THE WEIGHT OF THE EVIDENCE P 633, $2.84

"First-class puzzle, deftly solved. University background interesting and amusing." —*Saturday Review of Literature*

Mary Kelly

THE SPOILT KILL P 565, $2.40

"Mary Kelly is a new Dorothy Sayers. . . . [An] exciting new novel."
—*Evening News*

Lange Lewis

THE BIRTHDAY MURDER P 518, $1.95

"Almost perfect in its playlike purity and delightful prose."
—Jacques Barzun and Wendell Hertig Taylor

Allan MacKinnon

HOUSE OF DARKNESS P 582, $2.84

"His best . . . a perfect compendium."
—Jacques Barzun & Wendell Hertig Taylor, *A Catalogue of Crime*

Arthur Maling

LUCKY DEVIL P 482, $1.95

"The plot unravels at a fast clip, the writing is breezy and Maling's approach is as fresh as today's stockmarket quotes."
—*Louisville Courier Journal*

RIPOFF P 483, $1.95

"A swiftly paced story of today's big business is larded with intrigue as a Ralph Nader-type investigates an insurance scandal and is soon on the run from a hired gun and his brother. . . . Engrossing and credible."
—*Booklist*

SCHROEDER'S GAME P 484, $1.95

"As the title indicates, this Schroeder is up to something, and the unravelling of his game is a diverting and sufficiently blood-soaked entertainment." —*The New Yorker*

Austin Ripley

MINUTE MYSTERIES P 387, $2.50

More than one hundred of the world's shortest detective stories. Only one possible solution to each case!

Thomas Sterling

THE EVIL OF THE DAY P 529, $2.50

"Prose as witty and subtle as it is sharp and clear. . .characters unconventionally conceived and richly bodied forth . . . . In short, a novel to be treasured." —Anthony Boucher, *The New York Times*

Julian Symons

THE BELTING INHERITANCE P 468, $1.95

"A superb whodunit in the best tradition of the detective story."
—August Derleth, *Madison Capital Times*

BLAND BEGINNING P 469, $1.95

"Mr. Symons displays a deft storytelling skill, a quiet and literate wit, a nice feeling for character, and detectival ingenuity of a high order."
—Anthony Boucher, *The New York Times*

BOGUE'S FORTUNE P 481, $1.95

"There's a touch of the old sardonic humour, and more than a touch of style." —*The Spectator*

THE BROKEN PENNY P 480, $1.95

"The most exciting, astonishing and believable spy story to appear in years. —Anthony Boucher, *The New York Times Book Review*

THE COLOR OF MURDER P 461, $1.95

"A singularly unostentatious and memorably brilliant detective story."
—*New York Herald Tribune Book Review*

Dorothy Stockbridge Tillet
(John Stephen Strange)

THE MAN WHO KILLED FORTESCUE P 536, $2.25

"Better than average." —*Saturday Review of Literature*

Simon Troy

THE ROAD TO RHUINE P 583, $2.84

"Unusual and agreeably told." —*San Francisco Chronicle*

SWIFT TO ITS CLOSE P 546, $2.40

"A nicely literate British mystery . . . the atmosphere and the plot are exceptionally well wrought, the dialogue excellent." —*Best Sellers*

Henry Wade

THE DUKE OF YORK'S STEPS P 588, $2.84

"A classic of the golden age."
—Jacques Barzun & Wendell Hertig Taylor, *A Catalogue of Crime*

A DYING FALL P 543, $2.50

"One of those expert British suspense jobs . . . it crackles with undercurrents of blackmail, violent passion and murder. Topnotch in its class."
—*Time*

THE HANGING CAPTAIN P 548, $2.50
"This is a detective story for connoisseurs, for those who value clear thinking and good writing above mere ingenuity and easy thrills."
—*Times Literary Supplement*

Hillary Waugh

LAST SEEN WEARING . . . P 552, $2.40
"A brilliant tour de force." —Julian Symons

THE MISSING MAN P 553, $2.40
"The quiet detailed police work of Chief Fred C. Fellows, Stockford, Conn., is at its best in *The Missing Man* . . . one of the Chief's toughest cases and one of the best handled."
—Anthony Boucher, *The New York Times Book Review*

Henry Kitchell Webster

WHO IS THE NEXT? P 539, $2.25
"A double murder, private-plane piloting, a neat impersonation, and a delicate courtship are adroitly combined by a writer who knows how to use the language." —Jacques Barzun and Wendell Hertig Taylor

Anna Mary Wells

MURDERER'S CHOICE P 534, $2.50
"Good writing, ample action, and excellent character work."
—*Saturday Review of Literature*

A TALENT FOR MURDER P 535, $2.25
"The discovery of the villain is a decided shock." —*Books*

Edward Young

THE FIFTH PASSENGER P 544, $2.25
"Clever and adroit . . . excellent thriller . . ." —*Library Journal*